ECHO

PAST

Jenny Cheshire was born in Leeds, Yorkshire in 1963. By the age of ten she had written a series of adventures for young children and during her teens she developed this interest further. Having excelled in English at school, Jenny chose a career in International Television Distribution. During this time, she travelled extensively selling programmes to foreign TV stations, specialising in the Caribbean area.

Her first published novel, FIRE AND PASSION was written when Jenny was expecting her son, Sebastian and was leaving the television arena to concentrate on writing and motherhood. She followed this up with a series of three children's illustrated books called SECRET KITCHEN TALES, and another called BIRTHDAY SECRETS which won the David Thomas Charitable Trust Award in the children's category in 1999.

Having established herself as an award-winning author, Jenny went on to write her second novel, ECHOES OF THE PAST. She currently lives in rural Worcestershire with her husband Sam and their two children.

This book is dedicated to the memory of my grandmother, Lysbeth – 23.2.02 – 1.1.00 whom I greatly miss.

ECHOES OF THE PAST

Jenny Cheshire

Gala Books

Published by: Gala Books

ISBN: 0 9538452 0 6

British Library Cataloguing in Publication Data.
A catalogue record for this book is available from the British Library.

First published 2000
Gala Books, PO Box 20, Bromsgrove, B60 1RE

Printed and bound in Great Britain

ACKNOWLEDGEMENTS

There are a number of people I would like to mention and thank because without their support and advice, this book would never have achieved publication.

I must include my husband Sam and my children Sebastian and Rebecca who fill my life with such purpose. My wonderful parents, David and Mary, my brother Richard and my sister Caroline who have always been there for me and continue to be a tower of strength and support. The book's invaluable production team, Liz, Jackie, Astrid and Jo.

I would also like to thank a group of my oldest friends who through our years of holidaying together have contributed to the ideas for this book! Lastly, my thanks go to one anonymous person for inspiring me so powerfully to write this story …

J.C.

THE DESERTED HOUSE
By Mary Coleridge

There's no smoke in the chimney,
And the rain beats on the floor;
There's no glass in the window,
There's no wood in the door;
The heather grows behind the house
And the sand lies before.

No hand hath trained the ivy,
The walls are grey and bare;
The boats upon the sea sail by,
Nor ever tarry there.
No beast of the field comes nigh,
Nor any bird of the air.

GUIDE TO FAMILIES/BOATS/DOGS AND NANNIES!

BOATS	ADULTS	CHILDREN + DOGS	
JUST IN Sea Ray	Justin – *super-sporty insurance broker* Amelia – *domineering hairdresser* Rosa – *Au Pair (Italian)*	Amber - Violet - Indigo - Golden Labrador Jack Russell	aged 12 aged 12 aged 7
OCTOPUSSY Sea Ray	Jack – *City financier*	Black Labrador – Buster	
DR NO Fletcher	Brad – *film director* Ruth – *Nanny (English)*	Luke - Annie -	aged 6 aged 4
MONEY-PENNY Sun-seeker	Sandy – *super-social estate agent* Camilla – *housewife and mother* Roxanne - *Au Pair (Danish)*	John - Joe - James - Junior -	aged 7 aged 4 aged 2 baby
JAWS Bayliner	Jamie - *prep school house master* Savannah – *housewife and mother* Kelly – *Nanny (English)*	Charlie - Carly -	aged 4 baby
OVER HUNG Jetstar	Kristian – *mobile 'phone salesman and younger brother to Justin* Juliet - *journalist – not married*	Two huge Alsatians	
HIGH DIVE Fletcher	Marcus – *retired boating expert* Sophie – *unflappable primary school teacher*	Grown-up children	
LOVEY Sun-seeker	Toby – *hen-pecked manager of family brewery* Tanya – *pregnant dentist's receptionist*	First child on the way!	

Prologue

Saturday, July 19th

'Push, Fenella, push!'

'I *am* flaming well pushing ... and by the way ... it's Nelle ...' hissed Nelle through firmly gritted teeth, as the sweat began to show through her hospital-issue nightie.

She glared at the midwife who had begun to remind her alarmingly of the headmistress at her boarding school. Just then she felt an equal loathing for both women, and indeed the entire human race, as that pain, which no-one had had the decency to warn her about, crashed through her body again.

'You're doing very well, Fenella. I can almost see the head now,' came the voice which appeared to be buried between Nelle's rigid thighs.

Nelle bit frantically on the mouthpiece of the entenox tube they had given her to relieve the pain and furiously wondered why she didn't have the immediate feeling of wooziness they had promised. Instead, it made her feel sick.

'Get ready to push again, Fenella, the head is coming.' The headmistress's comrade-in-arms came to hold her hand in the noticeable absence of Nelle's 'partner'.

Suddenly Nelle panicked. A vision clouded her mind. She found herself hanging over the edge of a cliff, desperately searching for a baby in the water below. But she couldn't see it. Thoughts raced through her head. She was the only woman alive. She had to look after a newborn baby and she had no idea how to do it. Worse still, she couldn't *find* the baby. Perhaps the entenox was working after all? But no-one had told her it would make her hallucinate.

'Count with me, Fenella ... and push,' a voice echoed in her head.

Nelle felt trapped in a strangely familiar tunnel from which she couldn't escape.

More voices. There seemed to be a man in the room now. Lights flashed in her face. Alarm bells rang but she had no idea whether they were in the room or in her head. But that pain ... oh, that pain ...

'It's coming, Fenella! Push one more time, love.'

But Nelle's body would not obey her mind. Or was it her mind which would not obey her body? She felt as if her insides were being torn from her. Then, more noises. But try as she might, she couldn't find the one noise she most wanted to hear. Why not? Where was it? Babies were supposed to cry when they were born.

She was vaguely aware of more people in the room. Machines working. She clung to the need for that one sound, but it never came, and she felt herself slipping over the cliff, down ... into that icy water far below.

Something must be terribly wrong ...

Chapter One

Sunday, July 19th – one year on

The telephone rang. Nelle crawled under her pillow to block out the sound which threatened her comfortable drowsy state. But the persistent noise permeated the feathers of her pillow and flatly refused to leave her alone.

She fumbled for the receiver and pulled it under her duvet.

'Hello ...?'

'Nelle, darling, have I woken you?' screeched a voice that she instantly recognised as Henrietta's. Why did people always ask you that when they could tell perfectly well from your feeble voice that they had?

'Yes, Hen. What time is it?'

'It's eight thirty, darling, and I want you to get out of bed and come down to Hampshire for lunch.'

Henrietta had obviously not consumed the amount of alcohol that Nelle had the night before, or there was no way she would be calling anyone at eight thirty that Sunday morning.

'I can't,' replied Nelle.

'What, get out of bed or come to lunch?' asked Henrietta.

'Both.' All Nelle wanted to do was to stay in bed and skip the date to the 20th July.

'I had a feeling you might say that, sweetie. I know what day it is and I think it's frightfully important you don't spend it shut away on your own.'

'But Hen, I feel lousy. My head's throbbing and I've got my period. I wouldn't be the greatest company.'

'Take some pills then. Look, you shouldn't be on your own today, and Mummy and Daddy would love to see you again. Edward and Sarah Clarkson are coming and I've got the most delicious member of the male species to introduce you to, called Jack Hornby.'

'But I've got a volcano threatening to erupt on my chin ...' protested Nelle weakly. She hated it when Henrietta tried to thrust her together with one of her endless supply of 'delicious' males. She especially hated it today.

'If that's the best excuse you can come up with, then we'll expect you around twelve. And darling, you only have to *meet* the chap. Besides, you must get out more.'

Henrietta was probably right. Annoyingly, she often was. Nelle had spent much of the last year in sorrowful isolation, interspersed with heavy boozing sessions, which usually sent her back into isolation by reason of necessity.

There was possibly no harm in getting out of London for the day. It was a date she was trying hard to forget, so perhaps this would help to send it on its way for another year.

'Alright, Hen, I'll come. But on a serious note, please

don't mention the baby today, OK?'

'Credit me with some tact, sweetheart. Drive safely and we'll see you later ...' and with that Henrietta hung up abruptly before Nelle had time to change her mind.

If she really was going to make the effort to go to Hampshire for lunch and meet this Jack ... she'd already forgotten his other name, she'd better haul herself into the shower and take drastic action to reduce the throbbing in her head, while her ageing Golf would definitely need filling up with petrol.

After getting lost twice and vowing that she would not accept any more last minute Sunday lunch invitations in the country, she drove through the rather imposing (but also rather rusty) gates which led to Henrietta's impressive Georgian family pile.

As she tried to hide her Golf at the end of a line of expensive-looking cars and avoid hitting the black labrador who had come to greet her like a long lost friend, she couldn't help wondering to herself which car belonged to the 'Jack' character. She just had time to conclude that if the labrador was his, then it must be the Range Rover with the private number plate, but if not, then it was definitely the BMW convertible, when Henrietta burst through the French windows like a tornado, with an enthusiastic: 'Nelle, darling, you made it! Well done!' as if at the very least, she'd just won the Grand National.

Nelle immediately felt underdressed in her skimpy skirt and Polo shirt when she saw the little Chanel number (or rather large one, in her case) that Henrietta had on. Never mind, it was too late to change.

Henrietta scooped her up into a breath-threatening embrace which Nelle felt ought to be reserved for the opposite sex, and said: ‘Oh, *do* come in, everyone is simply *dying* to see you!’

Nelle, who was busy trying to prevent the now obviously male labrador from implanting itself in her crotch, started making her way towards the French windows.

The scene must have been witnessed from inside the house because before they got there, a tall dark figure, declaring 'I love Gucci' from every angle, appeared on the terrace and called: ‘Buster, that's no way to greet a lady.’

Nelle made one last-ditch attempt to side-step the dog and followed the voice back to the face.

‘Nelle, I'd like you to meet Jack Hornby,’ smiled Henrietta in her most matchmaking way.

As the Stilton (which she always thought smelt of rancid socks) was being passed round after the gourmet lunch, during which she was sandwiched between Henrietta's father and Edward Clarkson, Nelle tried to work out what was behind Henrietta's table plan.

Henrietta had made it plain, in fact embarrassingly plain, that Jack and Nelle would make a perfect couple, from the moment she'd introduced Nelle to Jack as 'single and in need of cheering up' - for which Nelle could have hit her.

While the champagne had flowed from fluted glasses before lunch, Nelle had wrongly predicted that she would be seated next to Jack at the table and would be subjected to a public cross-examination of why she needed cheering up. However that was not to be, thankfully. But by putting the potential couple opposite each other, Henrietta had given them both a chance to weigh each other up from a distance. So maybe that was her tactic?

Either way, Nelle had inadvertently found herself admiring the dark layered hair, the deep brown eyes and the flashing white teeth. She also found herself being charmed by the conversation, possibly because he was the one making most of it. In fact, the whole package sent her fluttering in a way that, after everything which had happened to her last year, she'd sworn she would not allow again.

Warning bells rang. Time to offer to help with the washing up.

•

'Don't you think he's utterly gorgeous?' Henrietta cornered her in the kitchen, and when Henrietta did that, it was virtually impossible to escape.

'He seems very nice,' she managed and then rather regretted it because it sounded a bit feeble.

'Nice!' Henrietta pouted her lips indignantly. 'He'd be perfect for you, darling. *And* he's got pots of dosh!'

Somewhere along the line, even though they'd been friends for years, Henrietta had clearly misunderstood just what would be 'perfect' for Nelle. 'Pots of dosh' came a good way down the list. Well-meaning though Henrietta undoubtedly was, she could be a bit overpowering if you were on the receiving end of her blatant desire to pair off everyone she knew.

'Do you mind, Hen, if I slip out into the garden for a bit of fresh air? There isn't much of it in London.' Nelle needed some time to think.

'I'll put the kettle on. Come back for coffee when you're ready.' Nelle reasoned that Henrietta must have had an ulterior motive for permitting her exit so unquestioningly and it didn't take too long for this to become obvious.

Nelle stepped gratefully down the lawn towards the brook which gurgled and splashed its way through the bottom of the attractive gardens. She found a rock which must have been the shrine for countless previous contemplations because it was worn quite smooth and was somehow rounded at the edges.

As she leant back on her hands, the warm sun folding softly around her slim bare legs, she jumped when something hurled itself onto her lap and covered her face in sloppy, wet kisses.

The sun blinded her for a moment and she put up a hand to shield her eyes, deciding that this was too forward even for Henrietta's taste and that it must be Buster, rather than his master, who had disturbed her.

'Hey, I really am desperately sorry, Nelle,' and actually, the flustered-looking Jack who arrived on the scene at that moment, in hot pursuit of his amorous dog, did look most apologetic.

Nelle was highly embarrassed and shot up, causing Buster's front paws to slide reluctantly off her lap.

'Don't worry, I don't mind. I always seem to have this

effect on dogs.'

'Actually, Hen suggested I came out to find you, only Buster got here first. She said you needed cheering up earlier and, as her father is now snoring in his chair, I thought I'd see if there was anything I could do to help.'

Nelle wasn't sure if he was deliberately flirting with her or showing genuine concern. Both made her feel uneasy because here was a man she'd only just met, who might just trespass on the forbidden ground she found hard to discuss with anyone. For twelve months now, it had been far easier to bury her head in the sand and repress her need to seek sympathy and understanding.

'Let's just say, it's been a bad year. One I'm trying to forget.' That would hopefully give him the hint.

However it didn't seem to deter him from his planned leap into the unknown: 'Oh, I think I could handle it and I am a good listener.'

'Yes, but the trouble is, *I* can't handle it ...' Damn those tears which threatened to betray her.

For all his failings, of which he could recognise a few, Jack knew when he needed to play the hero in shining armour and he was pretty good at it. After all, he'd had rather more practice than he cared to admit.

'Let me guess ... you've been let down, two-timed and trampled on emotionally by some unworthy man who failed to recognise your obvious charm and beauty, and you're off men for ever?' He thought the best way to tackle it was to try and bring her out of herself without venturing too deep.

Nelle was taken aback by his direct approach and

wasn't sure whether to be insulted or flattered by what he'd said. She found it hard to respond, particularly when she looked up into those dark, seductive eyes.

'Not exactly.'

'What, worse than that?' He was standing squarely before her.

'Yup.' Nelle felt tongue-tied.

'Is there anything worse than that?' In Jack's experience, the problems of emotionally-charged women could usually be traced back to men behaving badly. The fact that he'd left a string of broken hearts in his own wake often conveniently escaped him.

Nelle lowered her gaze. Suddenly she felt the urge to puncture his arrogance. 'Losing a child,' she said quietly. 'Nothing is worse than that.' Her voice broke. 'I should know. It happened to me.'

For some reason, Nelle suddenly found herself telling him and gambled that he would understand. Then out of the blue, for the first time since the baby died, she considered for a fleeting second whether part of her might just be ready to move on, but definitely not too fast.

'Miscarriage?'

'No, full term. It was a boy and he was born dead.'

This was definitely a first for Jack.

'Right ...' He breathed in sharply, not quite sure how to go on, whether to question her further or to make some meaningless remark which would change the subject. So instead, he opted for the most natural thing he could think of in a crisis and reached out and gave her a hug, touching her with a tenderness long missing from her life. With a sob, she leant against him and felt the strength of his arms around her.

'Forgive me,' he murmured, stroking her head. 'I didn't know.'

It was the first time she'd been held by any man since Roger-the-rat, as she liked to think of him. Actually, she didn't really like to think of him at all, remembering only too clearly how hastily he'd managed to disappear from her life once she'd told him she was pregnant.

Nelle was surprised to find just how much she liked this unexpected security, however temporary it might be.

Jack pulled away after a moment or two but took her by the hand and led her back to her rock, where he sat her down, perching on his heels in front of her.

'So you have been hiding away ever since?'

'Pretty much.' She nodded.

'What a waste,' he said, pushing her long, dark hair behind her shoulder and brushing her chin as he did so. 'Well, we can't let you do that any more. I think it's time you were re-launched on to the market.'

'You make me sound like a commodity.' She laughed.

'Sorry. Maybe that comes from working in the City for too long. By the way, it's good to hear you laugh. I could get used to that.'

'There hasn't been much to laugh about for a while.'

'How about we try and change all that?' Jack was never short of confidence.

'You sound like Henrietta. She's been on my case for months.'

‘Funny you should say that, she's been on mine for years! So, how about it?’

‘How about what?’ Was all this moving too fast?

‘How about I take you out for dinner in London and we work on that laugh of yours together?’

‘You're very direct, Jack.’ She felt torn. On the one hand she wanted to accept his invitation and felt flattered that this obviously attractive man was seemingly interested in her, but she was very wary of raking up all the hurt of the past year.

‘Does Wednesday sound OK? There are some real 'commodities' I have to deal with for a couple of days first.’

It was true, he did make her laugh and his smile made her feel good, and one dinner wouldn't actually mean that she'd fallen for him ... and wouldn't it just make Henrietta's day!

‘Alright, Wednesday it is. I'd like that ... and thank you, Jack.’

He smiled warmly and squeezed her hand which he'd never stopped holding. ‘I can't wait ...’

Chapter Two

Wednesday, July 22nd

Nelle had guessed right. Jack's car had been the Range Rover which she now watched draw up outside her flat, thirty-five minutes later than it should have done.

Being on time would have been horribly keen, she had to admit. Ten to fifteen minutes late was cool. Twenty to thirty minutes was verging on the 'is he coming or isn't he?' But thirty five minutes was heading for the 'I'm not bloody well going out with him now, even if he does show up.' Whatever had she been thinking of anyway, accepting a dinner invitation from this man she hardly knew?

Trying hard to put the latter thoughts to the back of her mind, Nelle decided that on this occasion she really had nothing to lose by answering the persistent ringing on her intercom.

'Hello?'

'Before you say anything, I know I'm indecently late. I had to go to Paris today and the 'plane was delayed coming back. So, please come down and put a smile on that pretty face of yours so that I can make it up to you.'

He was cute. She had to give him that. She really

felt she had very little alternative but to reply: 'Hello, Jack, I'm on my way,' and concentrate on the smile he'd requested.

When she opened the door, all six feet two of dark city suit grabbed her, gave her a whopping great kiss on each cheek and led her to the car as if her life depended on it.

'The table was booked for eight thirty,' he told her as he buckled his seat-belt, 'and by the way, before I forget, you look fantastic tonight!'

Jack promptly whisked her off at great speed to Mayfair, where it wasn't long before she found herself sipping pink champagne at the elegant bar of Partridges, acting as if she did it every night of her life.

He seemed to be well-known at the restaurant, judging by the familiar way he'd been greeted, and she couldn't help wondering how many others before her had been swept off their feet and deposited in Partridges by Jack.

'So what were you doing in Paris?' During the main course Nelle decided to move the subject on from family histories, after discovering that hers paled into complete insignificance compared to his somewhat impressive one.

'Oh, there have been problems in the Paris office for some time. Nothing that can be sorted out overnight but we're working on it,' he replied vaguely. 'But I'm much more interested in what you have been doing since I saw you on Sunday.' He put his knife and fork together and gave her his full attention.

'Nothing as exciting as going to Paris, I'm afraid.' She laughed, glancing rather shyly up at him. 'At work, I've been compiling a piece about cosmetic surgery for next month's issue of the magazine.'

'I do hope you're not planning on having any.'

'Cosmetic surgery? Not for a bit, but who knows, I might need a nip or a tuck some day.'

'The only kind of tucking up I would consider would have nothing to do with surgery!' Jack smiled before continuing: 'And besides your busy executive life as a feature writer, what have you been up to in the evenings?'

They were interrupted by Jack's mobile 'phone, which at that moment started to make its presence in his jacket pocket very apparent by playing a tune.

'Excuse me a sec.'

She had very little choice, as Jack mumbled hurriedly into the 'phone, acting ostensibly as if he was really quite annoyed at being called in a restaurant, but she suspected he secretly liked the idea of seeming so important that he had to be interrupted during dinner.

'That was New York,' he said in a rather loud voice when he'd finished the call, as if 'New York' was someone she knew well. 'Care for a pud?'

Trying to act suitably impressed by the New York bit, Nelle replied: 'Gosh, was it? ... No pud for me, but do have one if you like. I think I'm just going to pop to the loo.'

The security of the ladies gave her a chance to assess the evening so far. This was the first real 'date' she'd been on for well over a year. He was good-looking, charming, considerate - perhaps even chivalrous, and contrary to her previous encounters with several City financiers, he didn't talk incessantly about himself. He seemed genuinely interested in her. She came to the conclusion, encouraged by several glasses of extremely good red wine, that she could afford to drop her guard just a little and see where the evening took her.

It actually took her to Knightsbridge, or more specifically, to the basement flat, number ten Walton Street, which was where Jack lived.

Throwing all caution to the wind, Nelle decided that his offer of coffee, or something stronger if she preferred, did sound appealing, and by this stage she was quite curious to see inside his flat.

Predictably, it turned out to be a further example of his expensive taste. Nelle tried hard not to ask herself who had influenced the style or whether he'd commissioned the services of some posh interior designer to create an environment suited to his personality. There was more than just a hint of a woman's touch around the place.

'Will it be coffee or alcohol?' he asked, after he'd taken her coat and hung it on a hook in the hall, where it blended perfectly and rapidly began to look at home.

'Coffee please, Jack,' she replied. 'I do have to get up for work tomorrow.'

'Come this way and please excuse my aversion to washing up.'

He led her to the kitchen, throwing her an impish grin which made her laugh, about ten seconds before she was hurled flat against a wall by a large black cannonball who wanted to vet his master's latest lady friend. Finding to his delight that he recognised her, Buster wiggled wildly across the room, thumping his tail round the cupboard doors in search of his chewed red rubber bone to offer by way of a welcome present.

'Love me, love my dog,' apologised Jack, shrugging his shoulders and smiling again in a way Nelle decided she now definitely approved of.

It took Jack a minute or two to locate two clean mugs among the confusion of dirty ones, and watching him make the coffee, Nelle doubted that Jack spent much time in his kitchen, from the way he hunted around for the things he needed.

They took their mugs through to the sitting room and Jack began to flick through some CD boxes, none of which appeared to contain the CD it was supposed to.

'I'm not very organised at home. All my self-discipline gets used up at work.' He yanked off his tie and sat down beside her on the sofa-made-for-three - Nelle, Buster and now Jack.

'You've got a very nice flat.' Nelle tried her coffee which was far too strong but would no doubt help to sober her up.

'Thanks. It's home, although I don't plan to stay in London for ever. Look, I'm sorry about Buster. I hope you don't mind him sprawling all over you?'

The more comfortable Buster became, the more he stretched across Nelle, forcing her to move closer to Jack.

'No, it's OK. He's a lovely dog.'

'He's supposed to be a working dog and I do shoot with him in the winter, but he's rather got a mind of his own the rest of the time.'

'I'd like a dog but it's not that easy living in London.'

Jack's arm flopped casually along the back of the sofa.

'I guess I'm lucky. I have this little old lady called Mrs Pie (at the mention of which, Buster's ears pricked) who calls for him and takes him to Hyde Park every day. There are about four other dogs that she takes too, all of which are bitches. From what she tells me, Buster thinks he's died and gone to heaven with so much female company! I keep wondering about having him ... you know ... done ... but I can't bear the thought of depriving him of his dog-hood, so to speak.'

Nelle giggled. Parallels between dog and owner began to present themselves.

'Why are you laughing?' His eyes sparkled at her.

'I'm just picturing Buster, surrounded by other dogs in the park, trying to sniff all their bottoms.'

'I'm afraid it gets worse than that when he's in the mood ... and talking of 'in the mood', I think we're working quite well on that laugh of yours tonight. What do you think?'

'I think I'm having a good time, Jack. Thanks for asking me out this evening.'

He moved his arm so that it now rested on her shoulders.

'I'm really glad, sweetheart, because no-one should be allowed to look the way you did on Sunday.'

'Was it that obvious?'

‘It was obvious to me that something was badly wrong. You looked all distant and defensive, and intuition told me you could use some understanding company.’

‘I'm glad you came out after lunch. I've probably spent too much time brooding lately.’

‘I'm sure it's not healthy for you.’

‘Probably not. But after something like what I've been through, you arrive at a situation where your head - and the likes of Henrietta - tell you to open up and talk about it and to get out there and meet new people, but your heart says it's too soon and you're not ready.’

‘Thank heavens for your head and Henrietta, is all I can say,’ flirted Jack.

‘You're really sweet, Jack, but I can't help wondering whether I've got what it takes to 'give' again.’

‘Isn't it worth a try?’ asked Jack, taking the coffee gently out of her cupped hands and leaning a little nearer to her. ‘If you don't try, you might never find out.’

Nelle's heart began to pound. It was so strong that she felt certain Jack could hear it too. She knew where this conversation was leading and surprisingly, she didn't immediately feel like slamming on the brakes the way she might have predicted. But nevertheless, she felt wary.

Jack put his fingers under her chin and lifted her face slowly towards his own. She was paralysed for a moment, not wanting to resist, not really able to resist, but plagued by the thought that she ought to. She couldn't meet his eyes.

'Relax, Nelle, it'll be OK,' he reassured her, as he brushed his lips against hers, moving across her cheek and settling back on her mouth, where his tongue met hers.

Why hadn't anyone like Jack been there for her a year ago, in that hospital delivery room? The thought of it made her hold back.

'I'm sorry, Jack. It's just ...'

'I know.' He kissed her words away.

Strength quickly gave way to weakness and Nelle felt herself sucked under the weight of her own desire. Desire which was matched beat for beat by Jack's own.

What followed would not have been out of place in a Hollywood movie. They left behind a trail of hastily discarded clothing which began in the corridor and ended at the foot of the bed.

The urgency with which they shed their clothes surprised them both. Neither could stop kissing the other as they struggled with shoes, belts and shirt buttons.

They reached the bed without pausing to switch on the light. Suddenly Jack pulled away and she was worried that she'd done something wrong.

'Wait a sec,' he told her. 'I need to know this is really what you want.'

She forced herself to look into his eyes.

'I need this,' she replied steadily, convincing herself at the same time.

'In that case, I think this where I come in,' he told her, unhooking the clasp on her bra before lifting her on to the bed.

He lay down beside her and began to explore her with his tongue. She started to pant rhythmically and all thoughts of the past, and indeed of anything except the indulgence of Jack at that moment, were despatched swiftly from her mind.

When he finally entered her she soared to the stars and dived back down into the deepest ocean before she became aware of anything around her that was real. And then she dissolved into tears.

'I'm really sorry, Jack. It's not you, it's me,' she sobbed, overcome with emotion.

'Hey, it's OK to cry you know,' he replied softly, wiping away her tears as he propped himself up on his elbow and looked down at her.

'I could use a drink.' She glanced up sheepishly, her mascara streaming out of control.

'You and me too. Don't go away.' He stepped out of the bed and walked into the hall without bothering to put anything on.

She didn't exactly feel like going anywhere just then. If she could have pictured this moment last week, she would never have believed it. Half of her still wondered when she would wake up out of this dream that seemed to be lingering.

Jack came back with two glasses of ice-cold champagne, a lighted cigarette held securely between his teeth, and Buster, who had finally been let out of the sitting room to take up his regular spot on the end of Jack's bed.

'You don't mind this do you?' He took the cigarette out of his mouth. 'Only the first one after sex is something else.'

'Actually, I've been trying to give up but if you don't mind I'll share it with you.'

'That's something else we've got in common,' he replied as if he'd been calculating, and then, almost as if it were an afterthought, he said: 'Where have you been all my life?'

'I bet you say that to all the girls,' Nelle answered, swiping at a tissue on his bedside table and attempting to soak up the rivers which flowed from her eyes.

'No ... I don't think I said it to the last one. At least I don't remember it if I did,' he grinned at her.

She sipped her champagne, snuggling cosily up to him and trying hard to shift the 'where do we go from here' thought from her mind.

Suddenly he stubbed out the cigarette which they'd both thoroughly enjoyed (and which had erected huge barriers in the way of their respective give-up-smoking campaigns) sat up straight and said: 'I've got it' - as if he'd just remembered the answer to a nagging crossword clue.

'Got what?' She was startled.

'What are you doing for ten days from August the first?'

'Working ... why?' she replied, even more startled.

'Not any more you're not. You're coming on holiday to Wales.' Speechless would now describe her better.

'Pardon?'

'Listen, we go every summer to this great place called Rhoslown. There's a team of us who take our speed-boats up there and we spend the days boating, beaching and boozing. You'd love it and what's more, it'd be perfect schooling for that laugh of yours. I'm sure that a good holiday is just what the doctor ordered right now for you.'

'Rhoslown? I've never even heard of it.' She was definitely going to wake up soon. This was all getting decidedly weird.

'Not many people have, which is its main attraction, because it's not heaving at this time of year, the way the south coast is. It's near Holyhead. Being brutally honest, it's not exactly a picture postcard to look at, but it's got great beaches and we really take our own entertainment with us, if you know what I mean.'

'Talk about impulsive, Jack. I've only known you for four days. Are you sure you want me to come, really?' She was playing for time, trying to take in just what he was suggesting.

'Never been more sure!' He kissed her right in the middle of her tummy which made her squirm.

She found herself speaking her thoughts aloud: 'I suppose I could get the time off. In fact I haven't taken any holiday yet this year.'

'Well there you are, what's stopping you then?'

She didn't know what to say. He'd taken her so much by surprise that she couldn't really tell what she thought. The only thing she knew for sure was that the reassurance of intimacy with Jack had done her the power of good. She wasn't certain that he was definitely her type - whatever that vague word meant, or indeed if she was even looking for a relationship at all, but there was something about him that you just couldn't help but like.

Then her secret loomed on to the horizon, dark and menacing, but she fought it bravely. He was only inviting her on holiday after all. He was offering her a chance to start to live again. Perhaps there was something in what he said about the holiday helping to restore her faith in life. Perhaps not, but whatever the outcome, she couldn't think of one plausible reason she could give for turning his offer down, and so, quite out of character, she shocked herself by accepting there and then.

'OK, maybe it would be nice to get away and I suppose nothing's really stopping me at all.'

'That's settled then. Further details to follow.'

'That sounded like another business deal, Jack,' she teased.

'Did it? It wasn't meant to,' he laughed. 'You hear that, old boy?' Jack called to Buster. 'You're going to have to be on your best behaviour in Rhoslown. We'll have company.'

Buster raised his head momentarily and gave the loudest yawn Nelle had ever heard from any dog in her entire life, before flopping back down on to the sheet with a sort of 'this is way past our bedtime' sigh.

A few moments later, from somewhere in the room, Nelle heard Jack's 'phone playing the same tune she'd heard in Partridges.

'Oh, to hell with the 'phone. It won't be important,' mumbled Jack, whose entire day had just caught up with him. 'Come here ...'

Nelle responded willingly to his outstretched arms,

but could not stop herself wondering at the same time who on earth could be 'phoning him at quarter to one in the morning? But she didn't feel she could pursue it at that moment.

Chapter Three

Saturday, August 1st

'Be ready by four,' Jack had told her on the 'phone the previous evening.

'Four o'clock ... in the morning? Isn't that a bit early?' Nelle seriously doubted she could remember the last time she'd seen the world at that time in the morning.

'I want to get as far as we can before the traffic builds up,' had been his response.

Nelle had hardly felt it her place to remind him that on a Saturday most of the traffic enjoyed a lie-in, and promised she would do her best.

It had taken her hours to pack. Apparently there was a very strict dress code in Rhoslown. One was expected to wear shorts by day at all times, regardless of the weather. Since she hardly ever wore shorts in London, she had had to do some serious shopping in Oxford Street during the week leading up to Saturday.

Jack had also informed her that fleeces were the other uniform which one could simply not be seen without. Luckily, she'd bought a couple of those for a skiing trip once, and managed to dig them out, albeit rather crumpled, from under her bed. Her lift pass was still attached to one!

Having made a conscious decision to savour ten extra minutes in bed rather than spending them in the shower and then under the hair dryer, Nelle dressed and tried to stuff the last minute things into her bag. It looked pathetically up at her as if to say: 'If you think you're going to do up my zip over all that lot, then forget it.' She would just have to hope nothing fell out if she left it open.

She drew back her curtains just in time to see Jack's Range Rover snake slowly down her street, towing all twenty three feet of Sea Ray speed-boat, and avoiding the double-parked cars by centimetres only.

Help! What had she let herself in for? She'd better grab her bag and run so they could get away before Jack hit any cars and caused a hell of a row with the neighbours.

'What ever time did you get up?' she asked him on their way to the A40.

'I didn't.' He slurped a bottle of Lucozade noisily, sending the bubbles dancing down to the bottom.

'You mean you didn't even go to bed?'

'No, I didn't. Don't look so worried! It isn't the first time I've been up all night. Actually, I didn't leave the office till after eight last night. I rather lost track of time with everything I had to do, which included going over the river and fetching the boat so I wouldn't be late for you, sweetheart.'

'Can you drive on no sleep?'

'Sure. Anyway, there'll be plenty of time to catch up on sleep over the next ten days.'

She could sense his excitement. He had talked of not much else on the three occasions they'd seen each other since he'd first invited her to Wales.

Nelle hadn't seen him in shorts before, even if he was still wearing the familiar Guccis on his feet. She suddenly feared that she'd made her first social blunder of the week by starting out in jeans. She'd failed to realise that the holiday actually began on her doorstep and not when she got there. Perhaps he wouldn't notice? Besides, he'd told her twice now how good her long legs looked in jeans.

They had just reached the North Circular and it wasn't even four thirty, when his 'phone went. All she could hear from it was a long, strange sound, which Jack must have recognised because he immediately laughed and said to the mystery noise: 'Hi! Where are you?'

Silence.

'We're almost on the M40.'

Silence.

'She's looking good!' Nelle wondered for a moment if he was talking about her, but then he added: 'And Nelle's not looking bad either,' winking at her. He must have been referring to the boat previously.

Silence.

'You'll meet her soon enough. We should make the Little Chef around nine, but we'll keep in touch. 'Bye for now.'

Jack turned to Nelle again. 'That was Justin. They're coming up from Surrey and they've just reached the M25.'

Rather like a jigsaw forming before her eyes, pieces of information about the holiday started to fit together throughout the five hours it took them to reach the Little Chef on Anglesey Island.

On average, either Jack's 'phone went or he rang someone about every twenty minutes. The people on the other end seemed to vary. Sometimes they were male, in which case they, too, were towing a boat. Sometimes they were female, in which case they were passengers and trying to prevent those towing from causing road rage as the August holiday traffic poured on to the motorways.

The language spoken on the mobiles convinced Nelle that they were talking in code and it appeared to be a universal code they all understood. Heaven help her when she got to Rhoslown.

Meanwhile, Buster, who was stretched out luxuriously along the back seat, seemed to take it all in his stride - or would have, had he been striding. He appeared determined not to suffer a broken night's sleep.

After meticulous and repetitive 'phone planning of his exact ETA at the Little Chef with super-sporty Justin (an insurance broker), super-social Sandy (an estate agent from Yorkshire), jovial Jamie (a prep school housemaster from Hampshire) and their respective entourages, they eventually arrived. Fortunately, the car park had ample provision for the invasion.

They were not the first to get there. Nelle immediately realised that Justin had beaten them to it when she saw another Range Rover, hitched to an equally huge boat, which happened to be called 'just In'. As she watched, three sleepy-looking children, a foreign au pair, a golden labrador, a very yappy Jack Russell, an immaculately-dressed woman with a Princess Diana hairdo and a grinning man spilled from the car. All appeared to go in different directions and the already-hassled au pair started to run round the car park shouting 'Mamma mia' to anyone who was prepared to listen - which no-one was.

From there, matters became even more complicated. One more Range Rover and one Land Cruiser, each towing boats and bursting at the seams with excitable children, dogs and vast amounts of luggage, arrived within a quarter of an hour.

Jack did his best to introduce her to everyone, but he didn't appear to have a clue what half the children were called because several disagreed with his choice of name for them. He was, however, so caught up in the euphoria of re-uniting with his friends who seemed equally thrilled to see him, that she immediately felt insecure and went to see if Buster was still safely in the car park.

The Little Chef was obviously used by many as a way of breaking their journey and relieving their dogs. Nelle had to watch extremely carefully where she stepped. Buster, who from an early age had learnt to take care of himself, was fondly greeting the golden labrador bitch and certainly did not seem inclined to come when Nelle called him.

Matters did not improve significantly once they were inside the restaurant. Excessive amounts of greasy fried breakfast were ordered by everyone except Nelle, and as the men promptly sat together at a table for four, Nelle had little choice but to join the wives. Jack had the grace to look a little uncomfortable about this and threw Nelle an apologetic look, to which she smiled dutifully, thinking 'beam me up, Scotty.'

Nelle felt conspicuous as the only one not in the regulation shorts and Docksiders. The wives were most interested in her.

'It's always nice to meet friends of Jack's,' said a painfully thin Camilla (wife of Sandy) as she beckoned to Nelle to sit on the bench beside her.

'He brought up a lovely girl two years ago called ... now what was she called, Savannah?' asked Amelia (wife of Justin), examining her perfectly painted nails.

'I can't remember,' replied flame-haired Savannah (wife of Jamie), feeling they possibly ought to be careful what they said to Nelle about her predecessors. 'Where did you meet Jack, Nelle?' she asked moving swiftly on.

'At Henrietta Bingham-Blade's house in Hampshire,' she replied truthfully.

'Oh, I was at school with Hen,' interrupted Camilla. 'As a matter of fact, she introduced Sandy and me some years ago.'

That figures, thought Nelle to herself, as the waitress appeared with their fresh orange juice and herbal teas.

'OK over here?' Nelle felt her shoulders squeezed tightly from behind and she jumped. Turning round, she found Jack looking incredibly sexy with his hair ruffled and a shadow of stubble forming on his face.

She tried to feel a bit more forgiving towards him for throwing her in at the social deep end.

She put her hand on his, which did not go unnoticed by the present company.

'Fine, thanks. How about you? Breakfast here yet?'

'Just around the corner. I'm off for a paper to check the market prices while we're waiting.'

'Jack, you're on holiday, for God's sake!' protested Amelia. 'And it's Saturday. Can't you leave the City behind for a few days? I insist that Justin forgets all about insurance when we come away. Why can't you do it too?'

'Possibly because I haven't got anyone like you in my life, darling, and besides, I need my fix of share prices in the mornings,' he replied, looking more desirable by the minute.

'Sandy needs his fix of me in the mornings!' remarked Camilla, which the others all found highly amusing. Camilla looked rather like a beanpole which threatened to snap in two if treated with anything but extreme care.

Just then, the noise level of the two children's tables, which were being supervised by three rather desperate-looking nannies and au pairs (Nelle wasn't sure what the difference was) rose to fever pitch. This caused both Justin and Jamie to get up from their table and bark at their rebellious offspring, two of whom immediately rushed to their mother's table for reassurances of love and affection.

Unfortunately, Savannah's little Charlie, who looked about four, was so keen to get to his mother that he pushed past Nelle and sent her orange juice cascading over her jeans.

Commotion ensued and the poor unfortunate Charlie was forcibly removed by a deeply apologetic Jamie, at which point Nelle felt great sympathy for the child and said: 'Please don't worry. I was going to put my shorts on as soon as I got to Rhoslown anyway.'

The last part of the journey to Rhoslown took less than half an hour. The nearer they got to the sea, the stormier the weather became. Menacing grey clouds gathered over the coastline and they could feel the wind tugging at the trailer behind them.

The first glimpse of the wild sea, blowing up to at least a force five, sent an unexpected cold shiver down Nelle's spine. She told herself that surely they wouldn't put out to sea in weather like this. Jack must have read her thoughts.

'What a vile day to introduce you to Rhoslown. I promise it's not always like this. We're almost there now.'

'Is everyone who comes down here married with children?' she enquired, not sure whether to be relieved at the lack of responsibility or to feel like the odd one out before she even got there.

'Almost, but hey, don't let it bother you. Think of the morning sleep you'll get over the others.'

'And why aren't you married with children then, Jack?' She couldn't help herself.

'I'm in training for the first bit, and the second, well I'd prefer that to be put on hold until I've made a success of the first. By the way, I'm sorry in advance if you get a bit of an interrogation from the others, but for some reason I can't put my finger on, the subject of my love life has always been of great interest here.'

Having already caught a few vibes of the way the other girls were around Jack, Nelle thought she could see why. Besides, she too found him attractive, in a way she couldn't quite define.

'It must be your amazingly good looks and charm,' she teased, unprepared for his reaction which was to lean over and kiss her, causing the car and boat to swerve violently.

'I hope you don't mind us staying at my great-aunt's house.' He changed the subject once he'd straightened up the car.

'No, of course, it's fine. I'm looking forward to meeting her.'

'I wouldn't go that far,' he grinned. 'She's eighty eight, looks like this ... (he made a horrible face which made her laugh) cackles like this ... and keeps you talking for hours at a time.'

'I bet that's absolute rubbish!' she replied.

'See for yourself. Well, perhaps I am exaggerating a bit. She's OK really, and we're all making sure we keep on the right side of her. She won't be there for ever.'

'I think I know what you're implying, Jack, and it's awful!' Nelle acted shocked.

'I know, but at least I'm honest about it.'

'Does she know that's why you come down?'

'It's not the only reason.'

As they arrived at Rhoslown and drove down the

grey, misty main street with a few forlorn-looking shops doing their best to attract trade on such a miserable day, Nelle tried to ignore a nagging doubt as to whether she'd really done the right thing in coming at all.

Jack's aunt's house stood tall and proud at the far end of the village. They drove in through a gateway which had lost its gate over the years. Already lined up in the small field behind the house were three other boats and two rusty tractors which had certainly seen better days.

'Most of our lot keep their boats here,' explained Jack. 'It's more secure than on the beach.'

'Doesn't your aunt mind?'

'No. Several generations of friends have always done it. It's just an accepted thing.'

'What are the tractors for?' Nelle couldn't see a farm or an animal in sight.

'Launching the boats. It saves us having to drive the cars right into the sea.'

'Of course,' said Nelle, wondering how she could have asked anything so stupid.

At that moment, Buster came to life. He suddenly realised where he was, and remembered all at once the lovely romping he'd done there last Easter. He clawed his way into the front, and using Nelle's lap as a springboard, hurled himself out of the car the second she opened the door.

Nelle watched him promptly disappear across the field, in the direction of the sea, and Jack said: 'He does his own thing down here. He'll be back,' leaving Nelle to assume it was normal behaviour.

There followed a good hour of what Nelle quickly learnt was fondly recognised by all the regulars as 'faffing time'. This generally meant that everyone became frightfully busy doing nothing at all in particular.

People filed on to the field from all corners. Boat covers were ripped off and luggage transferred to cars. Wilful children, with faithful au pairs in tow, clambered across all the boats. Dogs bowled each other over and stooped to squat in the very spot where someone was about to walk. Wives appeared, already moaning about the fact that their husbands had gone AWOL. General chaos ensued from which Nelle gathered several useful things which would equip her well for her stay in Rhoslown:

1 - It was important always to greet everyone, even the children, with a kiss on both cheeks.

2 - Most of the men were referred to by the name of their respective boat - she'd better learn those fast.

3 - A healthy liking of alcohol would stand her in good stead, as she watched case after case of booze emerge from cars and boats.

4 - Most mobile 'phones were affected by poor signals in the town and so the essential accessory became the ship-to-shore radio.

5 - Everyone had a dog, most of which looked the same, and no-one seemed to know, or care, about their whereabouts for long.

and,

6 - Almost without exception, everyone she met appeared to be checking her out as if she was Jack's

latest achievement, and she was beginning to feel rather uneasy about it.

The rain came down in buckets and looking across the field to the blustery beach and the sea beyond, Nelle wondered if she'd ever been anywhere so bleak.

'Let's get the kit inside,' yelled Jack from the cockpit of his boat, which Nelle had noticed was called Octopussy.

'Right,' agreed Nelle, wishing she'd thought to buy a waterproof jacket.

Jack unhitched Octopussy and drove the car nearer to the back door of the house. Nelle had just the one bag, which had so far managed to keep all her belongings contained, despite the open zip. Compared to the luggage she'd seen in the other cars, she noted just how much lighter Jack travelled.

'Hi, Aunt Flora!' Jack greeted the elderly lady they found making a cup of tea in the kitchen.

Of course, she wasn't at all how Jack had described her. She was small and immaculately dressed, with her silvery hair swept neatly into a bun on the back of her head. She smiled warmly at Nelle as she offered her cheek to Jack.

'How are you, dear? And who is this nice young girl?'

'This is Nelle, Aunt Flora.' Jack began to shed his jacket which was dripping all over her polished tile floor.

If Aunt Flora had previously played host to a steady stream of potential suitors for Jack, she didn't show it in the friendly way in which she greeted Nelle.

‘A pleasure to meet you, dear. I'm sorry you've arrived on such a wet day. Still, it's forecast to change tomorrow. Have you been here before?’

‘No, never even been to Wales,’ replied Nelle truthfully.

‘Then I hope you'll have a very nice holiday here. Treat this like home and anything you need, you've only to ask.’

‘That's very kind of you ... er ...’ What should she call her?

‘Call her Flora, Nelle, everyone does. You know, like the margarine?’ Jack helped her.

Nelle didn't know where to look after that and hoped that Flora was used to Jack - which she was.

‘Don't mind my nephew. Now, Jack, instead of soaking my kitchen floor, why don't you show Nelle upstairs to your rooms? You know where they are.’

Jack threw Nelle a look which she didn't understand at first and replied: ‘Of course, Aunt Flora. Off for your nap now then?’

Again, Nelle wasn't sure how Flora would react, but she answered: ‘You know me too well, Jack. Is Buster with you?’

‘Yup. I suspect he's getting his leg over on the beach.’

Nelle already saw an ally in Flora, who seemed to have the measure of her nephew and simply winked at Nelle.

‘You're not very nice to your aunt, Jack,’ said Nelle as he trotted up the stairs in front of her.

‘I do love her really.’

'You have a funny way of showing it.'

'Did you gather from what she said that she's made up separate bedrooms for us?' He'd stopped on the landing.

'Not exactly.'

'... but take no notice. Just dump your stuff in yours and you can come and sleep in mine, if you're good. She sleeps downstairs anyway.'

'Thanks. I'll try hard to behave,' promised Nelle.

'I don't think sex before marriage was on the menu when she was young. Yours is in here ...'

Jack showed her into a small but cosy single room, with a basin in the corner. He put her bag down on the bed and allowed her a five-second glance out of the rain-streaked window, before pulling her across the corridor into his own room.

'This ... on the other hand, is where it all happens.'

It was a larger room, with a double bed and long windows through which, on a better day, there was a great view of the beach and the sea. Today the visibility was hampered by a blanket of sea mist.

Jack threw the few belongings that he'd brought up on to a chair, and collapsed heavily on the bed.

'Now, as the weather outside is so bloody awful, the pub will have closed for the afternoon and Aunt Flora will be occupied for a couple of hours, how about us catching up on a bit of sleep ourselves?' He patted the duvet, suggesting she join him.

Nelle remembered only too well her early start and thought it sounded like a great idea.

She crawled across the bed and snuggled up to him,

laughing as she did so.

'What's funny?' he asked, stroking the damp hair from her face.

'You. All of this. Me, if you like ...' she was lost for words and couldn't explain herself.

'Which, I do happen to do, by the way ...'

'I can't quite believe that two weeks ago, I had never met you or knew any of this existed.'

'Let me help you out of those sticky jeans, sweetheart.' Jack had something else on his mind.

Before she could answer, Jack rolled on to his front and began to kiss her expertly. Tired though she was, Jack managed to rekindle in her a fire which had all but burnt out until recently. She put her hands on him, responding to his needs as he peeled off their clothes until they lay naked together.

Maybe she imagined it, but there seemed to be less foreplay than she remembered from the last time they had made love on Tuesday that week. He didn't hurt her, but he certainly didn't seem to be hanging around for any specific pleasure of hers. He must have been aware of it because when he had come and before they parted, he kissed her on the lips and said quietly: 'Sorry about that. It wasn't great for you, was it?'

Nelle nearly gave in to her annoying urge to cry and didn't trust her voice. Instead she buried her head in his chest. He pulled the duvet protectively around them and sighed.

Nelle had no idea how much time had passed when she looked over and realised the rain had stopped outside.

Hesitant patches of blue sky peeked through the dividing clouds.

'Jack,' she whispered to the sleeping form next to her.

He didn't stir, which was hardly surprising seeing as he'd been up for two days. She decided to pull on his fleece which she found lying on the floor and go in search of a bathroom, wondering to herself just what was in store for her over the next ten days - if only she knew ...

Chapter Four

Sunday, August 2nd

'Jack, Jack, wake up!' Nelle prodded his arm, causing Buster to prick up his ears at the end of the bed.

'Why, what's wrong?' He strained to open an eye.

'The sun's shining!'

'It is?' He raised himself on to one elbow so he could look out of the window. 'So it is, and guess what ... that engine we can hear is Justin skiing in the bay. He's always up and out early on a good day, doing some sport or other.' Then he grimaced and said: 'Just how much did we drink last night? My head's doing 360s,' before sinking back down on to the pillow.

'You and Sandy hit the whisky pretty hard after we left the pub,' replied Nelle, recalling a difficult first evening during which she felt that everyone knew everyone else and it was perfectly obvious that she didn't.

'Must've done. Still, days like this just can't be missed. So, pretty one, we'd better get ourselves up and dressed and find out which beach we're going to today.'

Nelle went back to her own room. There was something about it which made her feel safe, which was odd because the rest of the house was welcoming enough and she certainly didn't feel threatened there.

She had unpacked her things the previous night and now rifled through her drawers looking for suitable clothes to wear. Jack hadn't been much help on the subject when she'd asked him what to bring for the day. All he'd told her was to make sure she had a swimming costume and a warm top in case the weather blew up. Apparently, he had towels and sun cream already on board.

Part of a moral code instilled in her during her upbringing made her jump on the bed and then straighten the cover again, ensuring it looked different from before, just in case Flora came up to her room.

She was about to go in search of Jack, when she realised she hadn't opened her curtains. As she did so, her attention was drawn to a house clearly visible, right at the end of the bay. It was obviously deserted and in a poor state of repair. From what she could see, there wasn't any glass in the windows either upstairs or downstairs, and the windows of a turret, which faced out to sea, were boarded up. Strangely, it immediately intrigued her, with its dirty cream walls and crumbling shed. It seemed to occupy one of the best views of the bay, so why was it empty? What would prompt anyone to leave a large house like that to go to rack and ruin?

Jack's voice interrupted her thoughts from the bottom of the stairs.

'Nelle? Amelia's got breakfast on and she's asked us round. Are you ready?'

Jack delivered Nelle to Justin and Amelia's rented bungalow before disappearing almost straight away with Buster, Jamie and an older, grey-haired man, called Marcus, to fill up the boats with petrol. This involved towing them to a garage just out of the village.

Nelle felt it was sink or swim time and decided to swim. She went up to a woman she presumed was Marcus's wife as she also appeared to be a little older than the others and introduced herself.

'Hello, I'm Nelle.'

'Nice to meet you, Nelle. I'm Sophie. Are you down here with Jack?'

'Yes.'

'First time?'

'Yes, it is.'

'I know what that feels like. I remember the first time Marcus brought me down here some years ago. I knew no-one and everyone around me seemed to have known each other since they were in nappies together.'

At that moment, Amelia finished dictating the picnic shopping list to the Italian au pair, Rosa, and joined the conversation.

'That's the great thing about this place. We've all just grown up together like one big happy family. Coffee anyone?'

'I'd kill for one,' enthused Justin who walked through the door with one towel wrapped round his slim waist, rubbing his shaggy wet hair with another.

'Just In, Just In, this is Jaws ... over,' crackled the ship-to-shore radio on the table, making Nelle jump.

Justin pounced on it.

'Jaws, this is Just In, go ahead ... over.'

Nelle could just make out Jamie's voice on the other

end.

'Just In, Octopussy and I have just completed the fuel mission and are on our way back. We would like to know if you have all systems go at your end yet ... over.'

Justin smiled and everyone stood still and listened.

'Jaws, I can assure you that things are keeping nicely warm and awaiting your arrival ... over.'

'Just In, message from Octopussy to the chef. Could his delivery be sunny side up, please ... over.'

'Message received and understood. Standing by for your arrival. Out.' Justin put the radio back on the table.

'Are they supposed to chat on those radios?' Nelle asked Sophie, rather surprised by what she'd just heard.

'Not really. They're careful to avoid the emergency channels, but strictly speaking, they should only be using them for serious boating issues on the sea.'

Breakfast was an interesting meal with a number of different children and adults trooping in and out, helping themselves to cereals, bacon sarnies, toast, sausages and anything else that was on offer.

Meanwhile outside, the weather was becoming more and more glorious. However, Jack had prepared Nelle for a degree of faffing time before they would actually be on the water. He told her that for safety reasons, they usually went out in groups of boats and that as most of the others had children to organise, substantial picnics to pack and family groups to assemble, it would probably be nearer lunch time before they went anywhere. While Nelle could understand why that was so, she did feel it was rather a waste of a lovely day.

Jack's picnic consisted of a French stick, butter, a hunk of cheddar, two apples and a pack of six Kit-Kats, all of which he'd bought in two minutes at the supermarket. Back at the house, he filled a cool-box with enough bottles to satisfy a small drinks party, explaining to Nelle that it wasn't the done thing to be caught short.

'I think we'll take her down to the beach now,' he told Nelle once they'd stowed the food and drink in Octopussy's small cabin. Meanwhile, Buster had made himself quite at home on the driver's seat.

The boat was hitched to the larger of the two tractors, ready to be taken down on to the sand.

'You hop into the boat for now,' Jack instructed.

It was as she climbed aboard Octopussy via the ladder at the back, that Nelle felt a little apprehensive. She'd never spent much time around boats before and realised how clueless she would be if anything happened to Jack.

'Jack, have you got life jackets on board?' It suddenly seemed very important.

'Of course, don't worry. I won't let you drown,' he promised, making her feel paranoid for asking.

'Just checking,' she replied, trying to make light of it.

The boat lurched forward as it crossed the field.

'I'll come back with the tractor for yours in a minute,' she heard Jack call to Jamie, who'd just appeared on the scene.

Several holiday makers on foot, who weren't about to

brave the elements of the sea, watched as Jack drove a little way down the main street before veering to the left and bumping on to the sand.

'I'm going to launch her,' Jack yelled from the tractor, 'and then you can hold her in the water while I take the trailer back and fetch Jaws.'

'OK,' she shouted back, wondering what was about to be expected of her.

'Hold her by the nose and keep her straight with the engine out to sea,' Jack had instructed after he'd jerked the boat off the trailer. Luckily, the sea was flat calm. What he'd unfortunately neglected to tell her however, was that the current, even in the shallows, was quite strong and it had every intention of dragging the boat (and her) down the beach, pulling the engine round towards the sand as it did so.

The place he'd chosen to launch had horrible big stones underfoot, covered in green slimy seaweed. At first the water was up to her knees, but soon she found herself deeper, and every so often she would stub her foot hard against a stone and swear loudly.

The boat had a mind of its own. One minute she'd push the nose out because the tide was bringing it in. Then the engine would swing round so she'd have to roll up her shorts even further and wade out to heave it over again, invariably damaging her feet further in the process.

Around her, the beach was alive with activity. Other boats were being launched. Dogs were running around barking. Children were jumping up and down in life jackets that swamped them. Anxious au pairs held wriggling babies, while trying to pass kit bags, buckets and spades and several other things up into waiting boats. Husbands were cursing wives who were taking far too long to be ready, while wives were cursing husbands for doing nothing at all to help all morning.

Nelle wasn't the only one holding a boat in the water. As she waited for Jack to return, she noticed several others around her doing the same. She watched boating expert Marcus back his green Fletcher, High Dive, into the water with precision. In fact, she watched him for a moment too long because it was only when she heard a loud bang that she turned and saw, to her horror, that Octopussy had swung round again and exchanged sharp blows with Dr No!

'Help! I'm so sorry.' She put her hand to her mouth as she turned to face Dr No's owner.

'Don't look so worried, there's no harm done. I'll just fend you off at the back here,' replied a voice which made her stop dead in her tracks.

'It's ... not my boat.' She fumbled for words.

'I know. It's Jack's.' Her eyes met his large blue ones for the first time.

'You know Jack?' She knew she hadn't seen him before. It was a face you would not forget.

'Sure. We were at school together.' What a smile!

'You were? And I didn't think there could be anyone else to meet down here!' She tried to pretend she knew exactly what she was doing as she manoeuvred the boat across.

'Bit confusing, I know. Hello Jack.' He greeted the

figure which sprinted towards them through the water.

'Brad! When did you get down here? I see you've already met Nelle.' Jack shook him enthusiastically by the hand.

'Late last night and yes, we sort of bumped into one another,' beamed Brad, and Nelle felt herself go red in the face.

'The children with you?'

'They'll be here with Ruth in a minute.'

Nelle quietly took in Brad's bronzed figure, while the boys chatted and the breeze toyed with his sun-kissed hair.

Shortly after that, Nelle spotted an older-looking woman, leading two children of about four and six by the hand and heading directly for them.

Brad cut Jack off in mid-sentence and turned to listen to the woman on the shore, who, at that moment, looked both tired and rather unenthusiastic about the prospect of a day's boating.

'You'll have to bring the boat a bit nearer,' she told Brad. 'We can't get in unless you do.'

'Time to go,' said Jack under his breath, and motioned to Nelle to climb aboard.

That was a feat in itself. There was no way she could scramble on to the nose, it was just too far out of the water. The back of the boat could not be turned round for fear of damaging the prop in shallow water and so she had no alternative but to hoik her shorts up to her crotch and wade to the ladder.

'Who was that?' she inquired, drying herself, after Jack had fired up the engine and hauled an indignant

Buster off his seat.

'Brad?' He examined his Armani sun glasses for a moment, before squeezing the throttle enough to make the engine growl and the boat glide out through the speed-boat channel.

'No, the woman who got into his boat. It can't be his wife.'

'No, it's his nanny, Ruth.'

'Oh, I see ...' she pondered, checking for the tenth time that her life jacket felt secure.

As they left the bay, they drew level with the empty house which had attracted Nelle's attention earlier that morning. She stared at it with further interest. It seemed sad and very much alone. Just as she turned away, something caught her eye in an upstairs window. Was it a person? No, it couldn't have been, could it? No-one could possibly live there. It looked totally unsafe for one thing. It must have been a seagull. She tried to push it from her mind.

'Octopussy, Octopussy, this is High Dive ... over,' boomed Marcus's voice from the depths of the boat and Jack reached for his radio, which he'd put into a drinks holder.

'High Dive, this is Octopussy receiving you ... over.'

'Octopussy, is it only Just In we're waiting for? They seem to be having a little crew trouble ... over.'

'Yes, High Dive. I think Just In spent too long rigging his craft and not enough time assisting his crew this morning ... over,' agreed Jack, and to Nelle he explained: 'Apparently, after breakfast, Justin spent two hours servicing his engine and Amelia isn't speaking to him.'

'Octopussy, shall we motor on out and wait for him by Big Rock? By the way, are we headed for Pound or Shilling Beach? ... Over.'

'I think Shilling is better, High Dive. It's easier for dropping people off there ... over.'

'Righto. Standing by. High Dive out.'

As they slipped effortlessly through the water, Nelle told herself to relax. Jack was a very capable skipper. She regretted not tying up her hair, as it streamed out behind her. The knots would be a nightmare. The wind felt cold on her face despite the sun, and as she fished in her bag for her sun glasses, she noticed Dr No fly past them with Brad standing tall at the helm and his nanny in the back with the two children.

Eventually, six boats roared round the rocks of Shilling Cove at breakneck speed, each competing for the most impressive rooster tail of water. They slowed down as they approached the beach.

It was only then that Nelle dared prise her stiff, white fingers from around the pole she'd been gripping for dear life. As they entered the shallow water, all the boats were turned nose to sea to prevent the wash breaking over them as they were unloaded.

Everyone piled out. The small children were carried to the beach. Other than that, it was every man and his dog (of which there were several, including the yappy Jack Russell who was already grating on everyone's nerves) for himself.

Nelle thought the amount of luggage which rapidly

began to accumulate on the sand was enough to camp for a week. It all had to be shifted rather quickly because the tide was lapping hungrily towards it in no time at all.

Base camp was established a little way up the beach, against some protective rocks. There was little or no shade and only one of the party had brought a sun umbrella. This was duly erected by Sandy for his four boys, John, Joe, James and Junior, who were told to sit under it and not to move until their au pair, Roxanne, had coated them in sun cream.

Throughout the commotion, the most organised group stood out as the one with Brad's nanny, Ruth, in charge. She had placed their picnic rug a little apart from the others and had creamed and hatted the children before most of the other families had even begun to unpack their bags.

Nelle waited, rather unsure where she should settle herself, and subconsciously checked around for Brad.

The men were either anchoring their boats safely away from the shore or swimming back to join the party through an excited wall of squealing, naked children splashing about on the water's edge.

Savannah could see that Nelle was hovering and came to her rescue.

'Come and sit by us, Nelle,' she called, smiling as the numerous freckles on her face seemed to multiply before Nelle's very eyes. 'I'm just going to feed the baby and then we'll get some lunch out.'

Her baby, Carly, was gurgling happily and squeezing the contents of a sun cream tube all over her mother's tartan rug.

'Now, have you got a drink, Nelle?' asked Sandy, standing before her in a pair of fading Bermuda shorts over which his generous stomach hung comfortably. He held a tower of plastic glasses in one hand and a wine box in the other.

'No, I haven't.'

'The old boy not looking after you?' he teased, squirting some warm white wine into a glass for her. 'I say, you haven't got a fag, have you?' He pushed up the brim of his cap which was designed to prevent his balding head from burning.

'Sorry, I'm trying to give up.' She took a sip, which tasted like vinegar.

'Wait until after the holiday, I would,' advised Sandy.

'Wait for what?' asked Jack joining Nelle on the rug and dripping over her as he reached for a towel.

'To give up the fags, old boy. Fancy a drink?'

'Thanks,' replied Jack. 'Who's that girl you've got with you this year, Sandy?' He nodded towards Sandy's umbrella.

'What, Roxanne you mean? Hands off, mate, I saw her first!'

'She's a bit of alright, isn't she?' admired Jack, as he took in the dark sleek body clad in the briefest bikini she could have worn and still be called decent.

'Actually, she's Danish and doesn't speak a word of English. It's marvellous because I can say anything to her and she just looks at me with that delicious smile.'

'Did Camilla know she was going to be that good-looking before you hired her?'

'No. You should've seen her face when I brought her back from the station! It quite made up for a poor week in the housing market.'

'Moneypenny, Moneypenny this is Just In ... over.' They were suddenly interrupted once more.

'Just In, receiving you loud and clear ... over.' Sandy looked in Justin's direction, over the top of the rug parties.

'Moneypenny, we seem to have a bit of a dry old house over here. Would you have a corkscrew up at your end? ... Over.'

'No, sorry, Just In, we're slumming it with wine boxes today, but if you hang on, I've just spotted one which I'm sure you could borrow in High Dive's extensive drinks cabinet to my right ... over.'

'That's affirmative, Moneypenny. Help yourself ... over,' came Marcus's voice through the radio. Goodness knows where he was, because he didn't seem to be anywhere in sight.

'That's most kind, High Dive,' replied Justin's voice. He continued: 'Dr No has brought some interesting-looking things to cook on a fire and apparently we need to go on a hunt for wood ... over.'

Nelle could see Brad crouching down, unpacking various foil-wrapped objects from a bag, and she nearly died when he suddenly stood up and caught her watching him. She considered for a second whether he'd looked her way deliberately. But that was absurd.

'Tell the Doc that sounds like an excellent children-occupying pastime and we're unanimously in favour. We'll give him a hand ... over.' Sandy gulped the rest of his wine.

'Thank you, Moneypenny. This is Just In standing by for a firewood expedition. Out.'

'Come on, sweetie. Let's go and see what we can find up the beach.' Jack was up and off. 'We might catch some mackerel later and we can cook that too,' he added over his shoulder.

Nelle followed Jack straight away and it wasn't until she was half-way up the beach that she realised none of the other girls had moved. With the exception of Savannah, who was still trying to feed her baby, they had stripped off, stretched out, refilled their glasses and were deep in discussion about whether they had bought their new summer swimwear from Selfridges or Harvey Nicks.

'Daddy, Daddy, look what I've found!' shouted a good-looking, freckle-faced boy to Brad, who happened to be quite close to where Nelle was hunting for driftwood.

'Well done, Luke,' laughed Brad as he scooped the boy into his arms, careful to avoid the nails in the plank his son was brandishing. 'Take it over to Ruth, and mind the nails.'

Ruth was busy building a sandcastle with Brad's daughter, Annie.

'Are you alright there, Nelle?' he called to her.

She was touched by his unexpected concern.

'Fine, thanks.'

'It's good of you to help. You didn't need to, you know. It's really something to keep the children busy.'

She could see that several of the men had stopped to

chat at the top of the beach and not one of them appeared to be searching for wood.

'I don't mind.' She felt tongue-tied and was shocked at the effect he had on her.

'Have you known Jack long?' asked Brad, stopping in his tracks and looking at her, his eyes fixed on hers.

'No, only a couple of weeks.' She couldn't look away.

He ran his fingers through his hair and told her: 'That's Jack for you. Always impulsive!'

Nelle's emotions sent her confusing messages, but Brad continued. 'He's a great guy though, always life and soul ...'

Nelle sensed there was a 'but' coming. However, he must have thought better of it because instead, he added: 'Come on, let's go back and see if we've got enough wood to get the fire started.'

She strolled back to base camp with Brad, aware of one or two icy stares from the assembled company. Had she done something wrong already?

'Brad, darling,' called Amelia, flattening her stomach. 'What are you cooking us?'

'Come and have a look,' he smiled, glancing at her only fleetingly. 'The children and I raided the butcher's this morning.'

Amelia, who was desperately trying to forget her morning, replied: 'Give me a shout when it's ready and we'll gather the troops.'

'Will do.'

During the course of the afternoon, another boat, this time a rather elderly Jetstar called Over Hung, containing Justin's trendy, younger brother Kristian (who Nelle later discovered worked for a mobile 'phone company) his girlfriend, Juliet, and her two enormous Alsatians joined them.

The Alsatians wasted no time in causing havoc by rampaging through the picnics, shaking water over the sun-bathing wives and picking a fight with the Jack Russell, who, after biting one of the Alsatians on the nose, had to be restrained and tied to a rock for the rest of the day.

Jack and a thickly sun creamed Sandy took an expedition of children over six (which included Justin's daughters Amber, Violet and Indigo, as well as Sandy's eldest, John) on a fishing trip. Jack didn't ask Nelle if she would like to join them, presuming by now that she was well in with the wives who were busy romping through their second wine box.

'Well in' couldn't have been further from the truth! 'Completely out' was nearer to it. It wasn't as if they were unfriendly. Indeed, Savannah and Sophie did their best to include her. It was just that she had no idea who they were talking about most of the time and, although they didn't seem inclined to get too involved in their children's beach activities, they certainly discussed their offspring and their respective schools in tremendous detail.

Nelle tried to keep her feelings about Jack's behaviour in check. After all, what exactly had she expected? Did she honestly want him hanging on her every word, fussing round her like some mother hen? Definitely not! That would've been far too suffocating.

However, a little more attention might not have gone amiss. But it was only their first day and there was plenty of time ... and she forced herself to admit, room, for improvement.

Sleep had overcome both Marcus and Jamie. As Nelle also noticed that Justin and Kristian were locked in conversation about their various sporting achievements over a couple of cigars, she decided to take Buster for a walk down the beach to silence the whining he'd been doing ever since Jack had left him behind too. She could sense it was irritating the others.

A small group of au pairs wearing long sarongs over their costumes sat on rocks by the sea, supervising several of the children who had donned wetsuits and braved the icy water.

The next thing she knew, Buster had spotted Brad throwing a small white ball across the sand, and he barged through the little group who were happily playing Boules and bolted off down the beach with the ball in his mouth.

'BUSTER!' she yelled. 'Come back here!'

Buster totally ignored her and charged off towards the sea and Justin's golden labrador.

'I'm really sorry,' she apologised to Brad whose daughter, Annie, began to cry.

'We've got another one, Annie.' He wiped her tears with his finger and picked up a box. 'I know Buster of old,' he smiled to Nelle. 'Once he's got something, he won't let you have it. He's a nightmare when Jack takes him shooting.'

'He's been driving everyone mad since Jack went out

on the boat,' she told him.

'It's not your fault. Jack should've taken him.' Then he asked her: 'Do you want to join us?'

There was nothing else she would rather do at that precise moment.

'I haven't played before,' she warned him.

'Doesn't matter. It's just a bit of fun.' He handed her two red balls which was the first actual physical contact between them.

A while later, they heard Ruth's voice calling across the beach. It hadn't escaped Nelle that Ruth kept her distance from the other nannies. While her attention to Luke and Annie could not be faulted, she appeared rather disapproving and intolerant of the fun-loving younger generation around her. When she looked over, Nelle could see Ruth standing with her hands on her hips, still wearing the skirt and shirt she'd had on when Nelle had first noticed her on Rhoslown beach.

'Brad, it's time for the children's tea. Send them over, will you, please?' she shouted.

'I guess we'd better call it a day,' frowned Brad, gathering up the scattered balls. 'You did fine, you know.'

'I enjoyed playing,' she replied.

'You soon get the hang of it if you have an eye for a ball.' Which Brad obviously had.

Eventually, as the sun disappeared reluctantly over the headland and no-one could stand listening to Camilla's baby, Junior (which was the only name anyone seemed to call him) screaming any more, it was decided they should clear up and get back to Rhoslown in time to shower and go to Sandy and Camilla's for a steak supper. Everyone had been invited.

Jack was warm and affectionate but rather drunk when he returned from fishing, triumphantly carrying a bucketful of warm, dead mackerel which he deposited next to Nelle. Yuk!

'Having a great time?' He gave her a boozy kiss on the cheek as he threw some empty bottles into a bin liner.

'Yes, thanks,' she lied, prickling with irritation.

'Of course she's not having a great time, you huge plonker,' interrupted Amelia, rather the worse for wine. 'You sodded off for two hours and left her! Really, Jack, I'm amazed anyone wants to go out with you at all. I'd kill Justin if he did that.'

'Nelle was alright, weren't you?' asked Jack, suddenly sobering up and feeling marginally guilty.

Trying to appear unconcerned, Nelle looked up. 'Buster managed to disrupt a game of Boules by pinching the jack,' she informed him, folding the rug, 'and then Brad taught me how to play the game.'

'Brad's a gem, Jack. You should take a leaf out of his book,' said Amelia, getting unsteadily to her feet and checking her hair with her hands. 'I'd play Boules with him any day.'

'Have you got everything, darling?' asked Justin who had just arrived carrying the disgraced Jack Russell.

'If you put that damn dog down and help, it'd be a lot easier,' she snapped. 'Where's Rosa, anyway?'

By the time they got back to Rhoslown and Jack had delaunched Octopussy, leaving her stranded on the trailer with Nelle on board trying to prevent a soaking Buster from shaking over her for the fifth time, it was already half past seven.

Nelle was cold. She was tired and she was way behind everyone else's alcohol consumption, mostly because what had been offered at the beach tasted disgusting.

A warm bath and an early night would have suited her perfectly. Instead, Jack told her she had exactly seventeen minutes to shower, change and be ready to go round to Sandy and Camilla's, because the steaks would be cooked for eight.

Of course, when they got there, they found Camilla frantically trying to bath John, Joe, James and Junior all at the same time, a lobster red Sandy in his boxers uncorking more wine, and Roxanne smiling beautifully at everyone as they came through the door.

The steaks were in fact ready for half past nine. This had given Nelle time to feel more and more out of it and everyone else time to drink their way through seven more bottles. It had also given Nelle more than enough time to wonder why Brad had not turned up to the party. Where was he? And where was his wife? No-one had mentioned her all day. She promised herself she would find out when she got the chance.

Eventually, as she was helping herself to some marge to go with her underdone jacket potato, Jack came up and put his arm around her, studying her plate of steak and brownish, wrinkled lettuce.

‘That looks delicious!’ he slurred - which it didn't.

‘Aren't you having some?’ She tried to avoid his breath.

‘In a minute. Have I told you how sexy you look tonight?’

She'd been uncertain as to what to wear for the party. She had assumed, correctly, that the other women would dress casually but expensively, and so she'd opted for her leather trousers and a cashmere polo neck, hoping she would blend in.

‘No, you haven't.’ She sliced her potato in half.

‘Well, you do. In fact you look gorgeous! Come to think of it, you've looked gorgeous all day! Doesn't Nelle look gorgeous?’ he called to Sandy, adding to Nelle's horror.

‘Quite fantastic from where I'm standing,’ agreed Sandy.

A little more sensitive than some of the others, Savannah could tell that Nelle was embarrassed, and taking Jack by the elbow, she led him to the pile of steaks on the table.

‘Come on, Jack, you need food.’

Nelle later congratulated herself on how well she'd survived the evening. Jack had been little or no help as he became more and more inebriated. Savannah had been sweet and rescued her more than once. She had ended up by talking to Kristian's girlfriend, Juliet about work, once she discovered that Juliet wrote for a rival magazine. It crossed her mind more than once during the evening that she could well have the outline for an amusing feature on family holidaying in the UK developing right before her eyes. All that rather saved the evening.

One by one, people either left to nurse their sunburn, which they'd spent much of the evening comparing, or they fell asleep. Jack was one of the first to nod off.

'I think I'd better get him home,' Nelle told Camilla, who was visibly suffering under the weight of carrying Junior who'd flatly refused to go to bed.

'Yes, you're right. Still, it's been a brilliant day, hasn't it?' she enthused rather too brightly.

'Great fun,' replied Nelle, trying to sound as if she meant it.

'Sandy, give Nelle a hand with Jack,' called Camilla. 'You know what he's like for waking up.'

It took all the strength and determination of Sandy, Kristian, the smiling Roxanne and Nelle to rouse Jack and get him to his feet at the door.

'Take me home, country road ...' sang Jack, trying to make his legs work.

'This way.' Nelle guided him down the main street towards Flora's house. 'And will you stop making so much noise, for goodness sake?'

'Why?' He turned to her and laughed. 'You are funny when you're cross.'

'I'm tired, Jack, and you're heavy.' She struggled under the weight of his arm.

'Take me to the place ... where I belong ...' His singing was appalling.

'Yeah, OK. Watch the step ... and will you shut up or you'll wake your aunt.'

They had finally reached the back door.

'You're even more sexy when you're angry!'

'Well you're not sexy when you're drunk,' she hissed, dragging him up the stairs.

'Where's my dog?' he asked.

'In bed, where you're going to be in a minute.' They had arrived at his room and sure enough, Buster was curled up on the bed. He sighed deeply when Nelle sat Jack down, as if he knew there was no point in seeking any fuss.

She took off Jack's shirt and laid him flat, tugging his jeans down as best she could.

'You'd make a great nurse,' he grinned hopelessly at her.

'I can think of better patients,' she replied, going to her room to change.

When she came back, he'd pulled up the duvet and turned to face the window. All she could hear was the deep rhythm of his snoring and she knew at once there was no way she could sleep next to that. Instead, she patted Buster lightly on the head, and closing Jack's door behind her, stepped gratefully towards her own bed in the little room she now saw as her bolthole.

As sleep eluded her, she was disturbed for a long time by one nagging thought which just wouldn't go away. It was the fact that she had really minded that Brad had not come to the party, and just how much she minded, surprised her even more.

Chapter Five

Monday, August 3rd

'Jack?' Nelle put her head round his bedroom door.

'Come back tomorrow,' groaned Jack from under his duvet.

'Do you want some tea?' she tried again.

Buster began to beat the bed with his tail.

'Pack it in, Buster,' growled Jack. 'You're doing my head in.'

Buster whimpered and put his head between his front paws.

'Can I get you something for your head?' asked Nelle, giving it a last shot and wondering if she should just go downstairs and forget it.

'I don't know if I can move,' came the reply. 'What time is it?'

'Almost nine and I thought I'd go down for breakfast.'

'Whatever you do, please don't mention breakfast!' Jack's head appeared slowly, his hair plastered in all directions.

'Welcome to the world.' She laughed, feeling very little sympathy for him. He looked really ill.

'What the hell happened last night?' He began to come to.

'Can't you remember?'

'No. The last thing I remember is putting the cover on the boat after we came back to the field.'

'So you don't recall what you did to Roxanne then?' She decided to have a game with him, partly because deep down, she hadn't been that impressed with his behaviour the previous day.

'Oh, please tell me I didn't do anything too awful ... and who's Roxanne, anyway?' he asked.

'Roxanne is Sandy and Camilla's au pair and you disgraced yourself badly.'

'Doing what?' He sat up sharply and then nursed his throbbing head. He looked so worried and sickly that she couldn't hold out the pretence any more.

'Only teasing. Actually, you fell asleep at the party and snored.'

'Well that's better than whatever I might have done with the au pair.' The relief showed in his face. 'Don't do that to me so early in the morning,' and then as an afterthought, 'but I guess it's about all I deserve. I'm sorry, Nelle.'

'And so you should be.' She relented and smiled.

'So where did you sleep last night?' He looked thoroughly sheepish.

'In my own room. After I put you to bed, you snored so loudly, it's a wonder your aunt didn't come up and tell you to shut up. There was no way I was sleeping next to that.'

'I swear, I'm never touching another drop,' moaned Jack, lying carefully down again.

'You can add that to the cigarettes you're giving up.'

‘Did I do that too?’

‘Yes, all evening.’

‘No wonder my throat feels like the bottom of a parrot's cage. You couldn't get me some water, could you?’

‘OK, but then I'm going down for breakfast.’

‘Excuse me if I pass on that, just for today. What's the weather doing, by the way?’

She drew back a curtain, making him squint as a shaft of light shot diagonally across his bed. ‘Sunny, but the sea looks rough. It sounds windy too.’

‘Thank God I don't have to get the boat out just yet.’

‘Maybe it's as well,’ she commented as she filled a glass for him. ‘There are probably several other hangovers around the village this morning.’

‘At least I'm in good company,’ he sighed, sipping the water. ‘Just be grateful you're not one of them.’

‘I might take Buster for a walk after breakfast and have a look round the village.’

Buster heard the magic 'W' word and was smart enough to realise that it wasn't going to be with Jack. He leapt off the bed and attached himself firmly to Nelle while the going sounded good.

‘Turn right out of the field and go to Shell Beach. That's where we surf. It's also a great beach for dog walking, less people than Rhoslown.’

‘Thanks, I will. Well, if I can't do anything more for you, then I'll see you in a bit.’

‘OK. Have a nice walk.’

As she headed for the stairs, Jack's mobile 'phone started to ring. She heard him say: ‘Oh, go away and leave me alone, whoever you are,' and smiled to herself. Jack really wasn't in a fit state to talk to anyone.

'Good morning, Nelle. Do come and have some breakfast.' Flora greeted her with a cheery smile.

'Thanks, Flora,' she replied, pulling up a chair at the kitchen table.

'Jack coming down too?'

'Uhm ... no. He's having a lie-in.' She helped herself to coffee.

'The way he snored last night, I would've thought he'd have had more than enough sleep already.' She passed the cereals to Nelle.

'Did he wake you?' Nelle was concerned.

'Not just me, but I expect most of the neighbourhood, dear.'

Nelle couldn't tell exactly what Flora was thinking, but she didn't seem unduly upset.

'Sorry about that. I did try to keep him quiet.' She reached for the milk.

'Not your fault, dear, and not the first time he's come home like that, either.'

Nelle was getting a few too many vibes about Jack's past for comfort. Flora continued: 'Of course, I blame his parents. He's an only child ... but I expect you knew that. Far too much money pushed his way and not enough discipline.'

Nelle suddenly remembered what Jack had said about keeping in with his aunt and realised that Flora was no fool.

‘I haven't known him long and you're the only one of his family that I've met so far.’

‘What he needs is a wife. A wife to look after him and get his feet firmly down on the ground.’

If Flora was hinting at anything where Nelle was concerned, it hit Nelle like a thunderbolt that she wasn't about to fit the bill.

‘I don't think he's ready to settle down, Flora.’

‘Nonsense, dear! He just needs to find the right girl. Now, tell me a bit more about yourself. What do you do for a living and whereabouts are your family?’

Jack had been partly right in his unflattering description of Flora. She'd kept Nelle talking for almost an hour over breakfast. But just when Buster had given up all hope of his walk and Nelle thought she'd go mad if she didn't get some fresh air soon, Flora's cleaner, Mrs Flash, knocked at the door.

Hastily clearing her place, Nelle grabbed Jack's Helly Hansen boating jacket from the hall and slipped out with her four-legged shadow.

To hell with the fact she hadn't put shorts on that morning, she thought to herself. It was a lot colder than yesterday and besides, was it really necessary to conform?

As she wandered down the road, several paces behind Buster, she began to consider, not exactly for the first time since she'd left London, whether she'd made a huge mistake in coming to Rhoslown.

Jack was a nice guy. He was good-looking, more understanding than most men she'd dated, which wasn't saying a lot, and although she'd never been materialistic, his comfortable lifestyle was appealing. But ... and there were several big 'buts', he was ... she struggled to think of the best way to sum him up ... he was ... hopeless. He was also unreliable, and that was one thing she couldn't stand in a man. She had been let down several times too often and she'd learnt to be self-protective.

She also felt different from his other friends, most of who brimmed with confidence. Yesterday, it had been as if her confidence had been zapped in their company, except perhaps with Brad. She saw herself a bit like a square peg trying to fit into a round hole.

Was she just being paranoid? After all, the events of the past year gave her plenty of excuses for that. Maybe she should just stick around and make the best of her time in Wales, seeing it as a break from work and routine in London? Jack didn't look as if he was about to put any pressure on her, so why put it on herself? Just try to relax and enjoy the holiday, without further expectation on either side. She liked Jack, but already she felt something had died. Perhaps they could view the past two weeks as a fling and leave it at that?

Once she'd made the admission to herself that the relationship would never have the future Flora might have hoped for, she felt better.

Buster led her down a narrow track which opened out on to a long, broad beach. The waves charged fiercely up the sand and she could see why people went there to surf. Indeed she could see a small group doing just that, a little way from where she was standing.

It soon became obvious too, why they called it Shell Beach. When last night's tide had receded, it had literally left behind a carpet - a shell hunter's paradise. Nelle recognised razor shells, black mussels, winkles and several others she didn't know by name.

She could see a beach-comber with a large red bucket, bending over as he scoured the sand, stooping to examine something every once in a while. The wind flapped at his clothes and Nelle zipped up her jacket as she set off down the beach towards the rocks at the far end.

Buster tried to play a game with her without teaching her the rules. Time after time he dropped a piece of sodden wood on her feet, but snatched at it again just as she went to pick it up.

'I can't throw it for you if you won't let me have it, you stupid dog,' she told him, wagging her finger and laughing.

It didn't make a blind bit of difference. He didn't let up until they were almost at the end of the beach and even then, it was only because he spotted a striking Dalmatian which warranted serious investigation.

Not far ahead, Nelle noticed a tall, blond figure on the edge of the water, wearing a thick navy fleece zipped to his chin and a pair of faded jeans rolled up below his knees. He hadn't seen her and for a second, when she recognised who it was, her instinct told her to run. Too late. Buster had just jumped all over him.

Brad turned as soon as he recognised Buster and strode purposefully out of the water towards Nelle.

'Hello again,' he greeted her, screwing up his eyes in the wind.

She wasn't sure whether he would kiss her on the cheeks like everyone else did, but something made her hang back and say: 'Hello, Brad,' wondering straight afterwards if it was really the best she could manage.

'Am I glad to see you. That water's freezing!' he continued.

'What are you doing in it then?' That came out wrong too. She needed to take a hold of herself.

'We've been looking for sand crabs, haven't we, Luke?'

Luke and Annie trotted over, curious to see who their Daddy was talking to. Ruth was not far behind.

'Daddy, is that the lady who played Boules with us on the beach yesterday?' asked Luke.

'Yes, it's Nelle.' He rolled his jeans back down.

'Would you like to see what we've found?' Annie asked Nelle in a tiny voice.

'Yes please, will you show me?' Nelle dropped to her knees to look into the little girl's bucket. 'Hey, Annie, that's a huge crab, isn't it?' Nelle admired the creature who was about the length of her finger and who was frantically trying to climb the sides of the bucket.

'Daddy found that one. Daddy's really brave.' Annie's sincerity was touching.

'He must be.' Nelle could feel Brad watching her.

'Ruth,' said Luke, 'will you come with us into the rock pools? We've got our nets.'

When Nelle looked up again, Ruth was towering over her. She was a stout, matronly woman who gave everyone the impression that she was a complete professional at her job.

'Did you meet Ruth yesterday, Nelle?' asked Brad, sensing that Nelle felt a bit overpowered.

'No, not properly. Hello Ruth.' She put out her hand.

'How do you do?' Ruth smiled briefly and shook Nelle's hand firmly, before turning back to Luke.

'Of course, Luke love, bring your net and we'll have a look over there.'

Brad sat down on a nearby rock to lace up his shoes.

'Where's Jack this morning?' he asked Nelle.

'Still in bed, nursing a hangover.'

'Hope you don't mind me pointing this out, but I don't think he's exactly playing the dutiful host to you down here, from what I can see.'

Nelle looked away for a second.

'Sorry, did I put my foot in it?' asked Brad, looking up concerned.

'No, it's OK. You wouldn't exactly call it a marriage made in heaven, you're right.'

She sat down near to him on the rock.

'I probably shouldn't say this either, but I wouldn't want to see you get hurt. I reckon it'll take a lot to pin Jack down to marriage. I've known him for a long time and I wouldn't say he looks any more ready to settle down now, than he did ten years ago.'

'I'd much rather people be honest with me. To tell you the truth, I think I've got my eyes wide open where Jack's concerned. Besides, I'm not sure I'm ready to settle down either.'

'It's a big step.' He gave nothing away about his own

circumstances.

There was a short silence.

'Brad, you seem to know everyone well down here, do you mind if I ask you something?' She plunged straight in.

'Fire away. I'll help if I can.'

'Do you think people are laughing at me, knowing what Jack's like? Should I just pack my bags and go home or would that only be acting spoilt and letting pride get in the way?' She surprised herself that she could spill her innermost fears to Brad, but she was already beginning to sense an easiness between them.

'I wouldn't think for a minute that anyone's laughing at you. Probably the reverse. If anyone has noticed anything at all, which I doubt, they're more likely to be feeling sorry for you that Jack's not being more sensitive.'

'I don't think I want anyone to feel sorry for me.' It was part of her new determination to get on with her life. She did have Jack to thank for some of that.

'Everyone comes here for a good time, so I shouldn't let it worry you. You may have gathered that you're not the first girl he's brought down and so I should think it might arouse curiosity rather than anything else. Most people here are married so there's a limit to the new relationships they can talk about.'

'Maybe you're right. I'm probably reading too much into it.'

'As for packing your bags, unless you've got something special to get back for, you might as well stay and enjoy yourself. I just hope Jack lays off the booze a bit for you.'

'Does he usually drink this much?'

'Everyone drinks too much up here. There's no real reason to drive except to fill the boats up first thing, and often people meet up for breakfast, lunch and dinner, so it's drinks all day.'

'Do you include yourself in that, Brad?' It was the first time she'd dared to ask him anything about himself.

'Sometimes. Depends on what and where.' She could feel his eyes on her face and she turned towards him.

'So what did you get up to last night?' She needed to know and perhaps the questions didn't have to be quite so safe now. 'We went to Sandy and Camilla's.'

'I suppose that's where Jack drank so much.' He didn't answer her question.

'Yes. Well actually, I think it was a gradual thing through the day and evening.

'I had intended to go, but I fell asleep after we got in and woke up several hours later.' He picked up a stick and began drawing patterns in the sand.

'Lucky you. I could have done that quite happily.'

'A day on the beach takes it out of you. Hey, look at that!' He turned the sand over carefully with his stick.

'What is it?' She watched him pick something up.

'It's a cowrie shell. There used to be quite a lot of them around here, but they're hard to find now.'

He brushed the sand off it and put it into the palm of her hand.

'Keep it for good luck, Nelle.' She felt his eyes

exploring her deeper and deeper.

They were interrupted by Luke.

'Hey, Daddy, we've got some fish now!'

'Well done. But mind the crabs don't eat them,' he warned, winking at Nelle. 'Do you both want to stay a bit longer?'

'Yeah!' came the chorus from both Luke and Annie. Ruth said nothing but her eyes were focused on Brad and Nelle.

'That OK with you, Ruth?' Brad called above the wind.

'Give them about ten more minutes, Brad.'

The waves continued to crash over the rocks not far from where they sat. High above them, seagulls circled, screeched and then swooped down on to the water.

'There's something I meant to ask Jack but I haven't had much chance since yesterday.'

'What's that?' He gave her his full attention.

'Why are some of the boats named after characters in James Bond films?'

He laughed. 'I guess we're all just big kids really. We've grown up with Bond films and if I think about it, we've certainly copied the speed-boat chases over the years. Now we're bringing our children up on them too.'

'I think my upbringing was seriously lacking!' she admitted.

'There's always time to make up for it.'

'There's quite a unique set up here, isn't there?' observed Nelle.

‘Several of us have been friends for years. Considering we live a distance apart, it's great to get together each August. Of course the children are now starting to get to know each other too. It's been a generation thing. Some of them stay in family houses that have been passed down. The older people tend to sail more and leave the speed-boating to us, but when it comes to partying, they show us how to do it!’

‘Brad, I think I'd better get back and see if Jack's up.’ She checked her watch and stood up reluctantly because her heart told her to stay, but her head told her otherwise.

‘OK ...’

She put her hand lightly on his arm.

‘Thanks for the chat, and the advice.’

‘Anytime. It's important not to bottle things up ...’ Did she see a flash of pain cross his face? Was he talking from experience? Were there things in his past that he'd bottled up?

Out of the corner of her eye, Nelle could see Ruth helping the children down from the rocks and walking with them towards Brad and Nelle.

Brad thought better of anything else he might have said at that moment.

‘Oh help,’ exclaimed Nelle, suddenly remembering Buster. ‘I'd forgotten the dog. Can you see him anywhere?’

They looked in both directions but although there were a few dogs roaming the beach, there wasn't a black labrador in sight.

‘Damn! What'll I tell Jack? This isn't going to

improve his day, is it?'

'Don't worry so much. Buster knows every blade of grass in Rhoslown. He's probably gone home without you.'

'Do you think so?' she gasped.

'Go back and see. I'll catch you later.' She froze his face in her mind as he bent to kiss her lightly on the cheek.

She turned her back slowly and called: ''Bye Brad.'

Nelle didn't look round as she walked along the beach. If she had, she would have met Brad's gaze which followed her closely, as he helped his children with their shoes.

Nelle was thoroughly confused. She felt drawn by a strange magnetism to Brad. But it was ridiculous and she knew it. She was staying in Rhoslown with Jack, although she did feel clearer and clearer about where she stood on that one. But Brad was married with two children, so the whole thing was a non-starter. She ought to think about behaving herself. But there had still been no mention of his wife. Perhaps she was away? Nelle needed to find out, but she didn't want to discuss it with Jack for fear of sounding too interested.

The wind sent the pounding of the sea drumming through her head. As she reached the road, she noticed the old house that she could see from her bedroom. It looked almost ghost-like and the sight of it close up sent an unexpected icy shiver down her spine.

There was something about Brad which was different from the others she had met in Rhoslown. She couldn't see exactly where he fitted in. He was obviously very comfortable in their company but there was something else. Something she couldn't put her finger on and it intrigued her. Mixed up with this was an attraction towards him which she knew she ought to fight, but in her heart of hearts, she didn't want to.

She simply had to find out more. She would draw on all her experience of investigative journalism to do it without arousing suspicion about the way she was feeling. Right or wrong, something had already begun and she wasn't sure if she could stop it.

As she turned into the field, Buster crawled towards her on his tummy across the grass. His ears were bent back in a bizarre fashion and his whole body seemed to be saying sorry for running off.

'Hey, boy.' She bent down to stroke him. 'I'm sorry I stopped walking. I guess you got bored. I can't really blame you. Where's that master of yours, eh? Shall we go and see?'

She approached the door and shoved one hand into her pocket, where her fingers rested on something small. When she pulled it out to see what it was, she found the little cowrie shell that Brad had given her for good luck.

Chapter Six

Tuesday, August 4th

Nelle was subdued as she listened to Jack's seemingly endless advice for Flora as to which shares were tipped to go up and which to go down, while they sat across from one another at the breakfast table. He spoke as if her best financial interests were dearest to his heart. In truth, that's just about where they were.

If Flora sensed any kind of atmosphere between Nelle and Jack, she didn't show it. Indeed, it wasn't exactly an atmosphere that existed - more a lack of the intimacy that had been there a couple of days before.

Jack, who had spent much of the previous day horizontal, while his body recovered from its alcohol abuse, had positively bounced back by late afternoon. He had explained to Nelle with great gusto that they were to go to Kristian and Juliet's barbecue that evening and his spirits didn't appear to have been dampened much when Nelle had asked if he'd mind terribly if she skipped that one and stayed at home.

To give him his due, he'd been very understanding and hadn't given her the third degree as to why. Nor had he seemed to find it a problem that she'd put herself to bed in her own room several hours before he returned home.

He had amazed her by being up early that morning and waking her with a welcoming cup of tea and a peck on the cheek.

She had heard the wind still howling outside, which she'd learnt meant no boating due to rough seas, and so good weather couldn't account for his brightness. Perhaps he'd stuck to his promise to quit drinking? But somehow she had doubted that would last very long.

Still, without being aware of it, he was making it easier for Nelle to find a way through the confusion in her mind. Perhaps he was having second thoughts about their relationship, too? Perhaps she just wasn't the type to blend in with his other friends in Rhoslown and this was his way of letting her down gently? Perhaps he was giving her space and being incredibly sympathetic after all she'd been through? Perhaps he felt guilty for not looking after her very well so far? But then she also felt guilty because of the way she was feeling about Brad. Or was Jack just an emotionally thick-skinned guy, out for a good time? Whichever, it was all rather a mess for the time being.

'You're quiet, dear.' Flora was getting tired of listening to figures. Financial talk bored her rigid.

'Sorry, Flora, I was miles away.' Nelle pulled her thoughts together.

'Do you play the stock market?' asked Flora.

'I have had the odd flutter in the past. But I've usually had my fingers burnt.' Nelle was disillusioned by her experiences with shares.

'That's because you haven't had the right advice, sweetie,' said Jack. Was that just a touch patronising?

'Maybe. That, and the fact that I've never had much spare cash to invest.'

Just then they were interrupted by Marcus's voice on Jack's ship-to-shore which was never far away from him.

'Octopussy, Octopussy, this is High Dive. Are you receiving? ... Over.'

'Yes, High Dive, good morning. What's cooking at your end? ... Over.'

'Well, Octopussy, apart from eggs, bacon and sausages, I thought that as we've got such a big sea yet again today - by the way, the forecast is good for tomorrow - I thought I'd try to round up a team to swing a few clubs this morning. Would you be on for that? ... Over.'

Without hesitation or consultation with Nelle, Jack replied: 'Sounds like a great idea, High Dive. Who else is coming? ... Over.'

Flora pushed her chair back noisily from the table, as if she didn't approve of this abuse of the airwaves. Nelle wasn't that sure that she did either.

'Well, there's us,' continued Marcus's voice for all to hear who happened to be tuned into that channel, 'and Dr No can join us, and I thought of calling up Just In ... over.'

Nelle felt herself blush unexpectedly at the mention of Dr No and the thought of Brad, and got up quickly to stack the plates into the dishwasher in case Jack noticed.

'Well done, High Dive. Dr No has been let out, then? That's good news ... over.'

What did Jack mean by that? Why would Brad have to be let out?

'Yes, Octopussy, he must have earned some Brownie points yesterday ... over.'

Did they mean Ruth? Was his wife there now?

'Thanks for the invitation, High Dive,' came Justin's voice through the radio. 'What time shall we tee off? ... Over.'

'How nice to hear from you, Just In,' replied Marcus. 'Delighted you will be joining our expedition. How about making our ETD around eleven? ... Over.'

'Sounds good, High Dive. I'll collect everyone in my vessel ... over.'

'Thank you for the transport, Just In. I'll make sure Octopussy and Dr No are informed. By the way, Octopussy, I have a message for Nelle from my wife ... over.'

The constant child-like enthusiasm for talking on the ship-to-shores reminded Nelle of the games she used to play on walkie-talkies with her brother when they were little. She couldn't help thinking that some men never grew up and often the only difference between men and boys is the price of their toys. It amused her and took her mind off the fact that Jack was planning further activity without her.

'Nelle? Do you want to go with Sophie or not?' Help! Jack was talking to her and she hadn't heard a word.

'Sorry, Jack. Go where?' She blushed again.

'Riding.'

'Horse riding?' Is that what he'd meant?

'Yes, horse riding,' he replied, a touch of agitation in his voice because Marcus was waiting for an answer.

'But I don't really ride.' She panicked.

'Don't worry about it. There's a great riding school here. You go down the beach. It's a good laugh. Everyone does it.' It would also make Jack feel less guilty about spending several hours at the golf course if he'd arranged for Nelle to do something else.

What could she say? If she said no, she'd feel like a wimp and she couldn't think fast enough of a reason not to go.

'OK, I'll go.' What had she agreed to now? But perhaps she ought be grateful to Sophie for including her, because what else would she have done for the day? She could hardly go looking for Brad. Anyway, he was going to play golf with Jack.

'That's affirmative, High Dive. Nelle can't wait ...'

That was a slight exaggeration, thought Nelle.

'... I'll send her over shortly. See you at eleven. Out.'

'You'll have a great time,' Jack assured her as he left the kitchen in search of his golf clubs.

'What am I supposed to wear?' she called after him, finding him burrowing into the cupboard under the stairs.

'What ...?' came his muffled voice, and she also heard: 'I'm sure I left them in here last month. Better check with Flora ...'

'Clothes, Jack. I don't have any riding clothes.'

He popped his head out of the cupboard: 'Go as you

are. You look fine.'

'But I thought you weren't supposed to ride in jeans?'

'Why not?' Jack was puzzled.

'Because they work their way up and, you know ... pinch.'

'Do they?' He smiled with interest.

'Have *you* ever ridden in jeans?' she asked him.

'Horse riding's not really my thing.' He grinned at her.

'But you said everyone does it.'

'Everyone except me. Actually, I meant every one of the girls, really,' he admitted.

'Fine.' She put her hands on her hips and tried to be cross with him, but she found it difficult. That was the thing about Jack, he was hard to be mad at. He never actually did anything really nasty. He just didn't think sometimes and that was part of his make-up. That, and a sizeable dose of male chauvinism.

Nelle turned on her heels and went upstairs to dig out the only pair of leggings she'd brought in the hope that they would do.

'I'm glad you decided to come, Nelle,' said Sophie as they drove out of the village towards the riding school, her grey curls bouncing in the wind which gushed in through the open windows of the car. 'Amelia and I usually ride a lot here, but Rosa's gone down with a tummy thing and Amelia can't leave the children with her this morning.'

'To be honest, I'm quite nervous. I haven't ridden for a long time.'

'Doesn't matter. The horses are used to all standards and I've booked for us to take ours out on a hack so we can go at our own pace. You'll be fine,' she smiled, her eyes shining warm and friendly.

Nelle tried to feel reassured but all that vanished in an instant when an enormous bay called Nash was led out of his stable and she was told to 'hop up on this one, love.'

'He's big, isn't he?' she gulped, thinking her heart would burst right through her ribs at any second.

'A big pussycat, this one, aren't you, boy?' The man tweaked the horse's ears fondly. 'Can you manage or shall we go to the mounting block, love?'

'I'll have a go,' replied Nelle sounding braver than she felt.

Just as she was about to try to bridge the vast gap between the ground and the stirrup, the man continued: 'Won at York, he did.'

The colour visibly drained from Nelle's face.

'You mean, York races?' She made no further attempt to lift her leg.

'Aye. Right good runner, till he got himself injured, that is. Come from those parts myself, you know.'

'I thought I recognised the accent,' she tried to smile.

What to do now? Run - was a possibility. But then she'd lose total face. Ask for another horse? But what reason could she give? After all, the man had described him as a pussycat. Fake a sudden illness? That was grossly feeble. She'd just have to say a quick word to Him up there and get on with it.

'Tell you what, I'll go round and hold t'other stirrup,

love. Stop the saddle slipping, like.'

Nelle took up the reins and did such a case of the splits to even reach the stirrup, that she wondered if she would ever be the same again. She hopped several times, during which the horse refused to keep still, and she was so frightened it would trample on her foot that she hauled herself up into the saddle.

She sat stiffly for a second, feeling just as if she was perched on top of a mountain, with a sheer drop on either side.

'Let's get those stirrups altered for you, love, and I'll just check your girth.'

At least she'd remembered how to hold the reins.

'OK, Nelle?' called Sophie, who sat neatly astride her chestnut, looking every bit the part.

Nelle would be OK if she wasn't on Nash.

'Fine, thanks. Won't be a minute.' She tried to sound convincing.

'There you are, nice and tight. Have a good ride, ladies. He patted Nash's hind-quarters which made him leap forward alarmingly and made Nelle cling on for dear life.

As soon as they left the stable yard, they took a bridle path which Sophie told her led down to the beach.

'There's nothing like cantering through the water,' she beamed at Nelle.

'I'm sure,' replied Nelle, concentrating on staying alive.

'When did you last ride?' asked Sophie as they walked side by side down the track.

'Far too long ago.' She didn't take her eyes off Nash's

head.

'You'll soon get used to it again. Rather like riding a bike, really.'

But you're not so high up and at least you have control over a bike, thought Nelle to herself, as Nash stopped to rub his nose on his leg, almost sending her over his ears.

'Mind you, you'll probably be a bit stiff tomorrow,' continued Sophie.

'I doubt if I'll be able to walk,' joked Nelle, telling herself to breathe deeply and try to calm down.

They soon reached the beach and it was as if the horses sensed it was their signal to speed up, as their hooves alighted on the wide open expanse of sand. They began to prick their ears and pull on their bits, dancing sideways at the same time.

'We don't have to canter yet if you'd rather take it steady.' Sophie was concerned that Nelle was tense.

'Do you mind if I just get used to it all again before we do?' replied Nelle gratefully.

'No problem. Relax and take a look at that lot out there.' Sophie pointed to a number of windsurfers who zig-zagged at great speed through the turbulent sea.

They weaved past wetsuited figures standing on the sand, looking like drowned rats clutching thermos cups of steaming liquid, still attached by leads to their precious boards.

'Have you ever tried windsurfing?' Sophie asked her.

'No. I'm afraid I'm a bit of a city girl. I've never had much to do around boats before,' replied Nelle. 'I bet it's harder than it looks.'

'Marcus and I had a go when we were in the Caribbean last year. I think I spent more time in the water than on the board, but it was fun. Marcus, of course, took to it like a natural.'

They headed down the beach and soon began to pass the houses of the village which had gardens leading down to the sand. Flora's was towards the far end.

'Is the weather always so changeable here?' asked Nelle, slowly getting used to Nash's stride.

'Put it this way, out of fourteen days here last August, we only managed four out with the boats. That's about average. But every so often, we do have a freak year, and everyone's saying they can't take the pace of going out every day. It also costs a fortune in boat fuel.'

'I think my clothes packing was completely misguided,' admitted Nelle.

'It's not exactly your Costa del Sol temperatures and I bet Jack wasn't much help,' replied Sophie.

'You're right about that one,' Nelle agreed.

'Come on, let's try a canter as far as the old house and then we can go on to Shell Beach.'

Just as Nelle was beginning to calm down, Nash broke into a canter, following Sophie's chestnut.

The only thing that came close to the way she felt then was the time she'd been conned into thinking a red run was a green one when she'd been skiing. It was the same feeling she'd had when she'd been hurtling down a precipice with the ground vanishing beneath her. Nelle told herself that she had a strong instinct for survival, and stay on she would. Did all race horses canter like that?

Sophie slowed down as they approached the ruined house at the end of the bay. Luckily, Nash did the same because Nelle was no longer in charge.

'Hope you didn't mind the gallop? This one's a bit hard to hold when he gets going,' laughed Sophie.

'Loved it!' pretended Nelle. 'It took me right back.' (It nearly took her right off as well).

'Spooky-looking place that house, don't you think?' Sophie had halted her mount just in front of the jagged rocks which led up to one side of the house.

'I think it looks sad, actually,' panted Nelle, catching her breath.

'They say it's haunted. I know I wouldn't want to go much nearer than this.' Sophie shuddered. 'Shall we go on?'

They steered their horses down the narrow alley which ran along the side of the house to the road. Nelle felt an urge to find out more about the house.

'Why don't they pull it down? The ruined house, I mean?'

'I don't know. I don't even know who owns it. All I do know is that everyone's warned not to go in because it's in a dangerous condition. The funny thing is that even the yobs you might expect to go into an old house like that seem to keep away,' Sophie told her.

'Maybe that's got something to do with the rumour about it being haunted. Do you know the history? What's supposed to have happened there?'

'I only know bits and pieces and how much is fact and how much is local embroidering of the story, I'm not sure.'

'Go on ...' Nelle was intrigued and for the first time, she allowed herself to sit back and relax on Nash.

'Well, I did hear that apparently, years ago there was a terrible storm one night. A ship was floundering on the rocks just out of the bay - it's a famous coastline for shipwrecks here, you know. Well anyway, the story goes that a father and his daughter, who lived in the house, put out to sea to help rescue the sailors from the ship. Local people say they never came back. They must've been lost in the storm.'

'How tragic!' Nelle was shocked.

'They say there's a curse on the house now and that the girl's soul never rested in peace. Sounds frightfully dramatic, doesn't it? Come to think of it, it's the kind of story my children at school would enjoy. They're quite a blood-thirsty lot!' They were walking together across Shell Beach.

'I think it would be really interesting to know more about it,' pondered Nelle, part of her unwilling to leave the subject alone.

'I'm pretty sure I'm right in saying that the family who used to live there, were very distant relatives of Brad's wife, Jane.'

That was the first mention by anyone of Brad's wife, and Nelle immediately felt uncomfortable.

'Were they?' she managed.

'Yes. Of course they moved on eventually. Well, they must have done, mustn't they, because the house doesn't look like it's been lived in for years.'

'I haven't met Jane yet,' said Nelle.

Sophie stopped her horse suddenly and stared at

Nelle, making her wonder what on earth she'd said.

'Gosh, hasn't anyone told you?' She sounded surprised.

'Told me what?' Nelle had no idea what was coming.

'Jane's dead!'

'Is she?' Then she tried to cover up her confusion with some inane remark. '... don't I just feel like the fool!'

'I'm amazed Jack didn't tell you. I mean, I know no-one talks about her much any more, probably because Brad hardly ever mentions her, but I would've thought Jack might've said something to you.'

'No, he hasn't.'

'Perhaps he didn't think it was important for you to know. I suppose it isn't really. It happened about four years ago, just after Annie was born.'

'What happened?' She needed to hear about it.

'Actually, I don't really know the details. All we were told was that she died in some kind of mysterious road accident just after Christmas. We never used to see Brad and Jane much during the year, living so far apart from them. It's been more of a summer friendship up here.'

'Poor Brad. How awful to lose your wife, and with two small children too.'

'Yes, I agree. He's lucky to have Ruth, though,' pointed out Sophie.

'She comes across as a bit severe,' said Nelle.

'I think that's just her way. She's worked for the family for a long time. She used to be Brad's nanny when he was young.'

'I guess she must feel very protective of the children, not having a mother,' Nelle remarked.

'She's devoted to them from what I can see.'

'And what about Brad? He's not re-married or anything?' Nelle frantically hoped Sophie wouldn't think she was too interested.

'No. There's no doubt about him being attractive and he can be great fun, but he never seems to let people get that close to him emotionally. It's as if he doesn't want to get hurt and so he won't let anyone in. But maybe he's just not over losing Jane yet.'

'The little I've seen of him, he seems quite serious.' Nelle was subtly trying to fish.

'Yes and no. He's a brilliant father and acts like a big kid around his children. Sometimes he's the centre of attention at parties. Other times he's not. You can never quite tell how you're going to find Brad.'

'Sounds like he's got a lot to be serious about, bringing up two children on his own,' observed Nelle.

'I can say this to you because I'm a lot older than you and I've been around longer, but I've watched girls flirt with him and he responds to a degree, but there's a definite cut-off point somehow.'

'What a waste.' Nelle couldn't help herself. 'He seems so nice.'

'Oh, he is and I know he sets a few hearts fluttering around here, if you know what I mean.' She laughed.

Did she mean Nelle? Help! Was it that obvious? It was time to steer away from the subject. Besides, Nelle needed a chance to chew over what she'd just learnt. It was fascinating new information to digest. Talk about hearts fluttering, hers was racing and it had nothing to do with Nash.

'Looking at the time, perhaps we should think about turning round, if that's OK with you?' asked Sophie.

They had arrived at the far end of the beach where Nelle had met Brad and his children the previous day.

'Yes, that's fine,' she replied.

'We can come out again another day, if you like. I love riding and I'm always looking for a companion,' said Sophie.

Secretly, Nelle wasn't sure if she could face going through the riding ordeal again for a bit. But she didn't want to be rude and give that impression to Sophie.

'Yes, sure,' she smiled.

As they turned their horses back towards Rhoslown, Sophie elaborated further on her teaching role at the primary school in the village in which she lived and she asked Nelle about her work on the magazine. Nelle responded easily enough, but only half her mind was on what they were discussing. The rest of it was having a very hard time leaving behind the subject of Brad.

Chapter Seven

Wednesday, August 5th

Nelle wandered aimlessly up and down the aisles of the little supermarket in Rhoslown, desperately trying to think what to put in the basket she'd picked up at the door.

True to forecast, it had turned out to be a sunny day. Gone, temporarily, were the wind and the biting rain which had set in with a vengeance the previous afternoon. Instead, the promised high had floated over from Ireland and was due to last for at least a couple of days.

This had turned everyone into a frenzy of excitement! Rather like bunnies popping out of their warrens to play when the coast is clear, you couldn't move on the high street for boats and people. Children dragged nannies to the post office to buy buckets and spades, and the chemist was selling out of sun cream fast. Men could be seen buying copies of the Sun newspaper which they neatly tucked into folds of the Financial Times. Copies of Hello magazine were in hot demand and other suitable (or not) beach reading was being snapped up.

The ship-to-shores had been frantically active and a

rapid plan to take the boats to a small island off the coast and camp the night under the stars had been devised. Apparently this did not include children. After much consultation, it had been agreed to leave the children in the capable hands of their nannies and au pairs so the adults could have a night off to enjoy themselves uninhibited. Anyway, it was good for the parents to have a break. It was their holiday too, after all, and besides, what else did they pay the nannies for?

Jack had thrust a twenty-pound note into Nelle's hand from his tractor seat and told her to get something to stick on the barbecue and something that would do for breakfast. He was off to fuel the boat. So were Justin, Sandy and Jamie.

Bread. Or baps - that was a good place to start, she reasoned. When she eventually found the bread shelves, whether the supermarket had not followed the forecast or whether everyone was stocking up as if for war, she couldn't tell, but whatever the reason, the shelves were just about empty. A few bake-your-own rolls peered sadly up at her from the bottom shelf. Not a bap in sight! She would have to settle for a loaf of thickly-sliced white and hope Jack wasn't on a health kick. If he was, so far she hadn't noticed it.

'Bit low on bread, aren't they?' came a voice she recognised.

Nelle spun round, startled.

'Brad! You gave me a fright.' Her heart pounding, she took in the bronzed figure in the white t-shirt and navy Bermudas.

'Sorry.' He leaned forward and kissed her. 'How are

you today?'

'Great, thanks.' She prayed he hadn't noticed the state his presence had thrown her into. Why couldn't she act cool when she most needed to?

'Are you and Jack coming to Puffin Island today?' He pushed back his blond fringe in a way she immediately found sexy.

Must concentrate. 'Yes. Jack sent me to get some food while he's filling the boat.'

'I did the boat this morning. Ruth's taken the children to the Sea Life Centre for the afternoon, so I've only just had the chance to get down here.'

'Do you know what sort of things we need to take along? I've really got no idea.'

'Something like bread, ham and some bacon and eggs for breakfast should do it. We usually pool what we take and someone is bound to have anything you've forgotten,' he told her.

They went round the shelves together gathering various bits, and couldn't help laughing when they realised that they both shared a passion for chocolate.

'It's for energy,' he tried to assure her.

'Yes, so's mine,' she giggled, putting a large bar into her basket. 'I need it every day.'

'If you eat it every day, it certainly doesn't show,' he commented.

Nelle felt embarrassed because it was his first indirect reference to the way she looked. She suddenly worried that her skirt was too short, and her t-shirt too tight. Perhaps she should have opted for big and baggy. But the truth was, she had a great figure and was lucky that she looked good in almost everything she wore, however casual.

His remark threw her and she didn't know how to respond. Instead, she ran her hands through her hair and down her parting in a sort of nervous way.

They had arrived at the checkout and, although Brad paid first, he hung around and waited for her to finish.

'I need the butcher next. Want to come?' asked Brad.

'For the ham and bacon? I suppose so. Where is it? I haven't been there,' she said.

'I'll show you.'

'Thank goodness I ran into you or I'd probably just've come back with bread, cheese and chocolate!' she laughed.

Nelle followed Brad out of the shop. They had no sooner stepped on to the pavement than they heard a loud: 'Brad, darling,' hail from across the road which embarrassed them both.

'Hello, Tanya. How are you? Have you just arrived?'

An obviously pregnant Tanya, with bleached blonde hair scraped back to reveal black roots, wearing a skin-tight top and cycling shorts, through which you could clearly see her protruding tummy button, launched herself at Brad.

'Just got here, darling,' she replied in a manner which reminded Nelle greatly of her friend, Henrietta. 'Toby's met up with the boys and they're all boat-faffing like mad. Are you coming out with us today? I say, isn't this weather fantastic?'

'Yes it's great. We're just getting some food organised.'

‘And who've you got here?’ demanded Tanya bluntly, much to Nelle's horror. She thought that Tanya had put two and two together and got about six.

‘This is Nelle. She's a friend of Jack's.’ Nelle felt shy being introduced by Brad. At least he hadn't called her Jack's 'girlfriend' - because she didn't feel as if she was any more.

‘Hi, Nelle.’ Tanya stuck out her bejewelled hand. ‘Jack certainly picks them.’ She looked Nelle up and down. ‘You're desperately lucky to be so thin,’ she continued. ‘I feel positively like a beached whale at the moment!’

Memories of feeling like that flashed through Nelle’s mind but she said nothing.

Brad came to Nelle's rescue: ‘When's the baby due, Tanya?’

‘Another couple of months. To tell you the truth, I would give up the job at the dentist’s today and go and have that Caesarean right now if I could. Haven't a clue what I'm doing going camping tonight. Must be bonkers!’

‘We're heading for the butcher,’ said Brad as if he needed to get away.

‘Brought all ours up from London. By the way, you look great, Brad. Have you been away?’

‘Not recently,’ he replied.

‘Good old English tan, then. Marvellous! Well, we mustn't waste this weather, must we? Never quite sure when we'll see the sun again, so we should make the most of it. Better go and pack the jolly old sleeping-bags. See you later, darling.’ And as an afterthought,

'And you, too, Nelle. Can't wait to see Jack again!'

Brad and Nelle escaped thankfully.

'Sorry, she's a bit O.T.T when you first meet her,' apologised Brad a few moments later, as he held the door of the butcher's open for Nelle.

'That's OK. She reminds me tremendously of someone I know in London.'

'Do we know what we want?' They were about to be served.

'I'm in your hands, Brad. You tell me,' she replied, hoping she didn't sound too incapable.

The trip over to Puffin Island took about fifteen minutes of motoring at top speed. The flat-calm sea glistened in the sunlight and the seven boats which carved a straight line through it, did so effortlessly. There was the usual competition to see whose boat had that little extra speed at the top end, but one thing which Nelle had noticed was the importance of safety observed by all. Life jackets were a must and the drivers showed a great deal of respect for the reefs which they circumnavigated with precision.

Most of the boats contained two people. The only exceptions were Marcus and Sophie's, which appeared to have an extra female passenger, and Brad's. Something tugged at Nelle's heartstrings when she saw Brad all alone at the wheel of his boat, even though he was grinning broadly as he flew past.

'Jump up on the nose, will you, Nelle?' asked Jack after they had slowed right down.

'Whatever for?' asked Nelle as if she'd been told to fly

to the moon.

'Well, it's either that, or you steer the boat and I'll do it, because as you can see, it gets shallow here and I need you to guide me up the channel.'

They had come out of Rhoslown bay and turned sharply right. This had brought them along the coast a little way before they headed back towards land. They were just about to go up a small channel of water which took them to what Jack called the Inland Sea, in the middle of which was Puffin Island.

Jack opened the central panel of the windscreen to enable her to scramble out on to the front of the boat.

'Get back here, Buster.' Jack yanked Buster down into the boat when he tried to follow Nelle. 'He loves swimming,' grinned Jack.

Nelle crept to the nose of the boat on all fours, having no idea what was expected of her next.

'Best thing to do is to sit down and put your legs over the front. That way, you can hang over and look down into the water.'

Cursing her lack of boating experience, at the same time as thanking God for providing a railing for her to hold, Nelle did as Jack asked.

'That's great. Now we need to follow the channel up here to the Island. Yell if you see any rocks. I have got a water depth gauge on board, but it's very uneven here and the sandbanks change every year because of the tides.'

Nelle could see that she wasn't the only one balancing precariously. Most of the boats had the same arrangement and the other girls looked as if they did it for a living. Luckily, they were only going about three knots at the time.

They rounded a corner and Nelle soon appreciated the need to respect the reefs. There was an old wooden fishing boat which had obviously got it wrong because half of it lay sunken under the water and the other half listed at a sorry angle against a rock. She'd better pay attention.

It didn't take them long to reach Puffin Island. It was much smaller than Nelle had imagined. It probably wouldn't have taken more than three minutes to go round the perimeter by speed-boat. There were no houses, and rocks around most of the island prevented landing, so they had to go to the far end where there was a small beach suitable for offloading passengers, dogs and belongings - of which, as usual, there were plenty.

Nelle was summoned back into the boat so Jack could throw out the anchor. He then jumped off the side into about thigh-deep water so he could take ashore the things that Nelle passed to him. No longer restrained, Buster leapt in after his master, sending a shower of water up on to the back seat where it unfortunately landed right over the two sleeping-bags which Jack had brought for himself and Nelle, leaving them soaking wet and therefore completely useless to sleep in.

Folded tents, disposable barbecues, rolled up sleeping-bags, crates of booze, cool-boxes, rugs, dog bowls, deck chairs and one camp-bed littered the beach in less than no time.

'Anyone'd think we'd evacuated!' announced Justin, a

bag under each arm and another round his neck.

'I say, what's with the camp-bed, anyway?' asked Sandy.

'Do you mind? That's mine!' protested a voice that Nelle recognised as Tanya's. 'You don't think I'm going to sleep on the floor in my condition, do you, darling?' She pouted her full lips.

'It's perfectly good enough for me,' answered Justin, with a wink.

'Well, you're not seven months pregnant, are you?' she snapped.

'Calm down, my love. He's winding you up.' Nelle presumed that was Tanya's husband, who peered out through thick-rimmed glasses and stood a good six inches shorter than his wife. Nelle automatically felt sorry for him for having to put up with Tanya.

'I know, Toby darling, and I love Justin dearly, don't I, gorgeous?' She proceeded to throw herself at Justin, who was defenceless because of his bags.

'Where are we going to pitch these tents? Anyone got a preference?' asked Marcus, doing a good impersonation of a tall pack-horse.

'Last year, we went up on the top and over to that dip, if you remember? It was quite sheltered up there,' replied Savannah.

'Why do the women always want to camp miles away from where we beach?' asked Jamie and then, catching the look his wife shot him, he added hastily laughing, 'Only kidding, Savannah. Lead the way, dearest.'

'Have you all brought tents this year then?' asked Jack, holding up three wine boxes.

'Yes, we have,' came several voices.

'Well, we haven't,' replied Jack, 'and now that Buster's managed to soak our sleeping-bags, Nelle and I will be well and truly on the scrounge later ... talking of being on the scrounge, has anyone got a fag? I've given up, but I could really do with one right now.'

'Given up buying them more like, old boy,' laughed Sandy. 'It's time you got your equipment organised like the rest of us. I'm sure you could find a camping shop in London somewhere.'

'Would ... you ... like ... one ... of ... mine?' came a thickly-accented voice to Jack's left.

'What are you offering, darling?' Jack turned in surprise to find Marcus and Sophie's teenage passenger clutching a packet of French cigarettes.

'Oh, sorry everyone. This is Annette. She's the daughter of friends of ours and she's over from France for a few days,' announced Marcus quickly.

'Did you say ... A-nnette?' said Justin with a grin as if her name amused him for some reason.

'Yes ... that's ... right,' smiled Annette sweetly, blissfully unaware of any joke.

'Surely not ... *the* A-nnette?' continued Justin, by which time Nelle felt for the poor girl, who still smiled.

'Oh, shut up, Justin. For God's sake, grow up,' snapped Amelia, and to Annette, she said: 'Don't mind my husband. A few of the boys have this thing about a character in a film who has the same name as yours. Take no notice. It's nice to meet you.'

Annette didn't really understand what Amelia said, so she just stood there holding the cigarette packet, looking concerned.

'You've got to take one now, old boy,' Sandy told Jack, 'and you'd better make her feel a bit more welcome than Justin just did.'

'I'd love one, Annette, thanks.' Jack gave her such a special look that she immediately blushed right to the roots of her very long, dark hair.

'When you lot have quite finished, can we move this stuff to wherever it is you all want to sleep tonight? I'm gasping for a drink,' said Toby, who had picked up the camp bed and was marching round the beach with it.

Everyone collected something and began making their way up the dunes to a large dip, which was indeed quite well protected by high dunes on all sides.

'Looks like someone else has had the same idea recently,' remarked Kristian, poking the ashes from a fire with his foot.

'Hope they don't come back,' said Tanya, carrying only her Louis Vuitton handbag, 'because it could get a bit over-crowded up here.' To Toby, who was now visibly staggering under the weight of the camp-bed, she said: 'Over here will do, my precious. Now, go and get the bags, will you?'

Rugs went down and tents started to go up, while for others, uncorking bottles was a higher priority.

'Just how the hell do you get this tent up anyway?' asked Jamie. 'Why on earth did you buy a new one, Savannah? The old one was fine.' He was surrounded by canvas, ropes and pegs.

'It was too small,' she told him.

'We're not exactly throwing a dinner party in it, are

we?'

'Don't make a scene, Jamie. Read the instructions. After all, you're the teacher around here.'

'My school duties do not include pitching tents and you know I'm allergic to instruction manuals unless they have something to do with boats,' he muttered under his breath.

'Oh, come here and give that to me.' Savannah snatched the sheet from his hand.

'Good to see you two getting on so well,' Justin remarked with faint sarcasm.

'Justin, is our tent up yet?' asked Amelia, knowing full well it wasn't.

'Oh, sod tents. I'm off for a ski. Anyone coming?' replied Justin.

'What a good idea. Shall we use my boat?' suggested Brad.

'Yes, OK,' said Justin. 'It'll pop us out better than mine up here. Fancy a ski, Jack?'

'Sure. I've got my drysuit somewhere. I think I left it on the boat.'

'Drysuit? You great girl's blouse!' teased Justin. 'You don't need a drysuit on a hot day like this.'

'Yeah, yeah. Come on. Some of us haven't brought too many pairs of dry shorts with us,' answered Jack defensively.

'There's always some excuse!'

Nelle wasn't sure what she was supposed to do next. Everyone else seemed busy doing something. As Jack had no tent, their wet sleeping bags were still on the boat, and she had already spread out his one rug, she felt a bit redundant and somewhat annoyed with Jack for yet again being so utterly hopeless.

'Coming Nelle?' called Brad, surprising her as Jack and Justin had already gone down to the beach.

She hesitated for a moment. 'Yes OK, why not?'

She followed him over the dunes, wondering how he stepped so easily across the spiky grass in bare feet.

'Thanks for rescuing me back there,' she said when they were out of earshot of the others.

'There'll be plenty of time for drinking and eating when we get back,' came his reply.

'You know, I haven't skied before,' she confessed.

'Doesn't matter, you can just come in the boat with us. Sometimes it's useful to have an extra rope handler.'

Just what did that involve? She didn't want to show her ignorance.

'Hi, Nelle!' called Jack as she and Brad approached, almost as if he'd forgotten he'd brought her along.

'Hope you don't mind, only Brad suggested I came.' She almost felt the need to apologise for intruding on a boy's trip.

'No problem at all. Great to have you along. Come to think of it, I should've suggested it myself. Thanks, Brad,' said Jack. 'I'll get your life jacket out of Octopussy. Hold on there a minute.'

Jack looked like an astronaut, just about to be launched into orbit, in his drysuit. Nelle climbed up into Dr No, which was a black and white, eighteen foot Fletcher with two fierce-looking outboard engines on the back. Justin was already coiling rope ready to throw out to Jack.

Jack had one foot in the binding of his mono-ski, which he rested on top of the ankle-deep water. He grabbed the ski-bar attached to the rope which Justin hurled at him and started hopping up and down in the water, ready for blast off.

Not sure where to sit, Nelle tried to be as unobtrusive as possible. She reasoned that as the action was going to take place mostly at the back of the boat, the best place for her was the front, so she sat down on the passenger seat beside Brad.

Brad fired up Dr No, which roared a bit like Concorde, sending choking smoke billowing out of the back.

One hand on the throttle and the other on the wheel, Brad turned to look at Jack and yelled: 'Ready?'

'Go!' was all they heard, and go, they did.

Brad floored the throttle and Jack held tightly to the ski-bar, digging his ski into the water before tucking his other leg into the back binding.

He was off! Out on to the wake, which he jumped before swinging right across the back of the boat to the opposite side, grinning broadly and flicking his dark hair back with his hand.

'He's really good!' Nelle was impressed.

'Don't tell him that or you'll make him even more big-headed,' laughed Brad.

'Wait until you see me, darling!' Justin was lounging casually across the back seat, wearing only a pair of Bermudas.

Brad alternated between watching where they were going and turning to check on Jack's position. Every time he turned round, the wind flattened his hair against his face and then flung it back as he looked ahead again.

Nelle felt an irresistible desire to touch him. The deep blue eyes, the smooth skin, the ruffled hair, the rippling muscles as he gripped the steering wheel, the sadness in his past, the caring attitude he'd already shown towards her, all added up to a package she wanted to know more about.

As if aware of her eyes on him, the next time he turned it was not to look at Jack but at Nelle. In that bumpy speed-boat, with the wind whipping through them, their eyes met and locked. Neither wanted to be the first to look away. Justin said something and they both missed it.

'Say again,' called Brad.

'He wants to do a fly past the shore at speed for the benefit of the audience,' repeated Justin. 'Typical! Always has to show off.'

As they passed the beach for the third time, Nelle could see a little group of spectators on the top of the dunes.

'Better give him what he's asking for then,' said Brad, raising his eyebrows and lifting his arm to indicate to Jack that he was about to turn the boat.

Jack came in off the wake as they turned and then flew out again sending a plume of water high in the air, right in front of the beach. The land party clapped and cheered.

'He's going to be impossible after that,' moaned Justin as Jack let go of the rope and skimmed across the water, right to the edge of the beach where a barking Buster almost flattened him.

'Text-book stuff,' Jack called as Brad brought the boat sharply round to the beach again.

'Nice one, Jack,' shouted Justin, gathering the rope in again.

'You go next, Brad. I'll drive you after we pick up Jack,' suggested Justin. 'How about you, Nelle? You having a go?'

'Not today. I think I'll need a few lessons first,' she answered, watching Brad rip his t-shirt over his head and put on his buoyancy-vest.

First Brad and then Justin showed off their expertise on a water-ski. Nelle would have found it hard to choose the best out of the three of them. If pushed, she thought Brad was just that bit more stylish, but then by now she was probably biased.

The sun was gently lowering its skirts over the scene when the skiers finally succumbed to exhaustion and the need for food and drink.

Jack and Justin anchored the boat and Brad helped Nelle down the back ladder. It was the first time she'd held his hand and she realised very quickly that she could get quite used to it, given the chance.

'Oh, give me a beer,' said Jack, struggling out of his dry suit.

'I thought you were off the booze, Jack,' grinned Brad, pulling on his fleece.

'Whatever gave you that idea?' Jack pretended to be horrified.

'You did, yesterday, on the golf course.'

'And the day before, after Sandy and Camilla's party,' added Nelle.

'Everything in moderation, sweetheart. But you are right, I did feel awful on Monday. Still, today's Wednesday and we're here to party!'

'Smell those barbecues!' exclaimed Justin, going up over the top of the dunes. 'Is my supper ready yet, Amelia?'

'It will be when you've cooked it,' answered his wife, who had her nose in a fashion magazine. 'It's taken me the last hour to put up the tent.'

'And a great job you've made of it too. Now, who's coming to share it with me?' And then addressing no-one in particular, he asked: 'Where's A-nnette?'

Luckily, Annette was out of earshot.

'Will you stop calling her that?' Sophie swiped Justin playfully on the arm.

'Why, that's her name, isn't it? Pity we haven't got a video here. We could've shown her the film.'

'What have you brought for us then, Nelle?' asked Jack, fishing in his cold box. 'Who put all this chocolate in here?'

'Shh, Jack, you're not supposed to announce it to everyone,' hissed Nelle.

'It's my fault, Jack. We shopped together.' Brad was standing not far away.

A couple of eyebrows shot up around the camp and Nelle wanted the earth to open and swallow her up, but Jack seemed to think nothing of it and said cheerfully: 'You know what they say about two heads ... personally, I loathe shopping, especially for food.'

‘Why don't we pool all our meat together and barbecue it? I've brought a few big salads that'll do for everyone,’ announced Sophie.

‘And I've got heaps of fresh bread from Fortnums,’ added Tanya, who had been uncharacteristically quiet since arranging her 'bedroom' in her tent.

‘That's what I love about you women,’ said Jack, putting his arm around Tanya. ‘You're always so efficient.’ All at once, Nelle felt totally inefficient.

‘What you need, Jack, is a wife,’ declared Tanya with the tact of a weighted stone.

‘So you tell me every year, sweetie. Trouble is, you're not available any more.’ Jack wasn't ruffled, but Nelle still felt uncomfortable, and even more so when she caught Brad's look of sympathy, aimed only in her direction.

‘You never asked me when I was available, Jack.’ By now the whole party was listening. It was hard to hear anything else above Tanya's voice. ‘You always had all those women hanging off your arm, there wasn't any room for me.’

‘Tanya, my love,’ interrupted Toby, looking worried and desperate to change the subject, ‘where did you actually *put* all that bread?’

‘It's still in the Fortnums carrier,’ she informed him.

‘Oh ...’ There was a long silence. ‘I think that might be the one I left behind in the pantry.’

‘Oh Toby, how could you? Well, looks like we'll be on the scrounge too, just like Jack and Nelle. Could be fun!’ She giggled annoyingly.

Kristian had brought his portable tape deck and soon the party was alive with the sounds of the 60s and 70s. Corks flew, charcoaled meat was eaten off paper plates, and cigarettes were smoked in large quantities, mostly by people who promised to give up at the end of the holiday.

No-one stayed close to their partners as they did the rounds of the rugs, offering food and drink wherever anybody wanted it.

Nelle's glass was never empty for long and she soon lost count of just what she'd had. She was beginning to get a feeling of being more at home with Jack's friends. They all seemed keen to include her and she'd never been hugged and kissed and generally handled by so many different men in one evening in her life! She felt far more welcome than she had previously.

Jack was around but they hardly spoke, because he was more often than not the centre of other people's attention. She tried not to wonder what they all thought about her relationship with Jack, although she did now have it straight in her own mind. What's more, she surprised herself by not really caring what the others thought. She and Jack were perfectly friendly towards one another, after all. Besides, her mind was pre-occupied in an entirely different direction.

Brad appeared to be letting his hair down more than she'd seen before, and he, too, was continually surrounded - mostly by women, she noticed.

As more and more empties began to pile up in one corner, Nelle trotted off to find a secluded spot because she was dying for the loo.

When she returned, she thought Brad must have noticed she wasn't there, because as soon as he caught sight of her, he beckoned her over and patted his knee, signalling her to sit down.

'Hey, Nelle, come and join us,' he called.

He was perched on someone's cool-box chatting to Justin, who still wore the same Bermudas that he'd skied in earlier. Jack had apparently vanished – surprise, surprise.

The music thundered forth from Kristian's machine and the volume was so high that the sound was completely distorted. But no-one seemed to mind as they bopped away on the rugs.

Through the open flap of Marcus and Sophie's tent, Nelle could see a card game in progress in the candlelight. It was hard to see who was in there, but she could make out several different figures.

'Have you got a drink?' shouted Brad above the din of the music.

'I had, but I think I've lost it.' She prayed he wouldn't think her too heavy and tried to keep some of her weight firmly on the ground.

'Here, share mine.' He thrust a plastic cup full of red wine into her hand.

'Thanks.' She liked the way he smelt.

Brad put one arm around Nelle's back, which she pretended not to notice, as he leant forward to talk to Justin, who sat cross-legged on the floor.

'I think we're lucky to get out here tonight. There's a low coming in after tomorrow,' said Brad.

'Is there? I say, your boat's running well this year.

Having a bit of trouble with mine,' Justin told him.

'Are you?'

'Yes, I think it's something to do with intermittent fuel starvation. I need a day to take it all apart.'

'That'll make you popular with the Management.'

'I know. Amelia'll love it - not.' Changing the subject, he enthused: 'Hey, I love this track ... come on, let's have a bop. Where's that A-nnette gone anyway?'

'Do you want to dance too?' Brad asked Nelle, almost deafening her at the same time.

'OK.' She covered her ears and stood up.

'Come on then.' He took her by the hand and led her over to where several others were wildly flinging themselves around. It was a song they'd all grown up with and they knew every word.

Nelle was self-conscious at first, but Brad had rhythm to spare and she soon found herself falling in with him, as he twisted and twirled her around.

Neither of them was in a hurry to stop dancing until finally, when they were well and truly out of breath, Brad suggested a drink.

This time, he took her to his own cool-box which he opened and asked: 'What would you like?'

'A beer'd be great, if you've got one. Thanks.'

He yanked the tops off two bottles and handed one to her, before stretching out on his rug. For a moment she hesitated. Everyone around them seemed pre-occupied. Jack was still missing and was clearly unconcerned about her welfare at that moment. She could either stay and talk to Brad, which was what she wanted to do, or she could go somewhere else. But where and to do what? So she decided to stay where she was.

She put the bottle to her lips and threw back the beer.

'Why is this called Puffin Island? Surely there can't be any puffins here?' she asked, sitting down beside him.

'Haven't seen any ... no, seriously, the island is owned, believe it or not, by a family called Puffin.'

'Do they mind people like us invading it?'

'Justin and Kristian know the family quite well and as long as we take all our rubbish away with us, there doesn't seem to be a problem. There's not much harm we can do here. There are no houses in earshot.'

'Do you always stay the night when you come up here?'

'No, we only do this occasionally, when the weather's good and everyone's up for it. Mostly we come up here for day picnics. You have to get the tides right, though. You can only come up here at high tide. Right now, as the tide is out, we couldn't leave by boat even if we wanted to. But by morning, the tide'll be in again and we'll all be desperate to get home for hot showers.'

'So you're saying we're trapped here?'

'Absolutely imprisoned!' He laughed at her serious face and put a finger under her chin briefly. 'Don't worry, you're in safe hands.'

She sighed and smiled, starting to feel a bit shaky. Better get back to the beer.

'Do the children like it up here?' she asked.

'It's a good place to teach them to ski because the sea is nearly always flat.'

'You're a very good skier, Brad. Where did you

learn?'

'Here, as a matter of fact. We've skied here for years. I also travel for work and so I get to ski a bit abroad.'

'You've never told me what you do when you're not holidaying in Rhoslown,' she told him.

'I'm a film director. Mostly documentaries and serious programmes ...' He pulled a face which made her laugh.

'Where do you travel to?'

'Oh, all over. Africa, Asia, the States - anywhere I'm sent, but I do try to limit the travel where I can because of Luke and Annie.' Nelle was just imagining Luke and Annie's life with their mother dead and their father travelling, when he changed the subject, almost as if he didn't want to pursue that one. 'But I'm much more interested in you.'

'Really?' She jumped at his words. She hadn't expected him to say that.

'Yes. Let me try and guess ...'

Nelle wasn't sure what was coming next.

'You're a journalist?' he said.

'How did you know?' She was amazed.

'I can spot them a mile off.'

'Is it that obvious?'

'Now don't get defensive.' He fingered the top of his beer bottle. 'Because there's more. I think you're quite a deep person so you're definitely not a door-stepping journalist. You're more of a researcher.'

'Are you psychic or something?' She was baffled.

'No, let's just say I'm perceptive when I want to be.'

'Actually, you're right. I write for a magazine and

most of it is features, and yes, they usually do require a good deal of research.'

'Bet you could write a great story about this lot.' Brad waved his arm casually in the direction of the other tents, which now seemed just like silhouettes in the darkness.

'It had crossed my mind,' she agreed.

When she looked around, she presumed people must have begun to retire into their tents because she could make out fewer figures than before. A group chatted around the glowing barbecues, and Kristian had changed the tempo, and the volume, of the music considerably. She could still see no sign of Jack.

The stars twinkled from their lofty perches in the velvet night sky and the air had chilled right down from the daytime temperature. There was almost certain to be a dew in the morning.

'Are you cold?' Brad had noticed her shiver and he glanced up.

'A bit,' she admitted, tucking her hands inside her fleece.

'Poor old you. No tent and no sleeping-bag.' He smiled, putting his hand casually on her knee. 'Come on, we can't leave you outside all night. I think we can just about squeeze two in here, if you don't mind sharing.'

He pulled back the flap of his small tent.

'Are you sure that's OK with you?' Nelle wasn't certain she should accept for a number of reasons.

'What do you think?' He began to shove his bags out of the tent to make room for them both.

She wasn't quite clear what he meant and decided she oughtn't to dwell on it too long either.

'Here, put this on to start with.' He handed her a large cream sweater which drowned her, reaching practically down to her knees.

'And I thought I was tall!' she laughed. 'But shouldn't you have it?'

'I've been here before, don't forget, so I've come prepared. Anyway, I've got a jacket as well.'

'Shame Jack didn't come prepared,' she commented, crawling on to Brad's blue groundsheet.

'Jack never does. He relies on everyone else. He's probably gone to kip on his boat,' he replied, zipping up the tent-flap.

'Do you think I should go and look for him?' she pondered briefly.

'Personally, no, but that's really up to you.'

'Do you know, you're absolutely right! I don't suppose he'll be worried about me, so why should I be concerned about him? I guess he'll assume I've scrounged my way into someone's tent. Besides, I don't exactly feel like sloshing around on the water all night.'

'I don't blame you. Here, put this over you.'

Brad had unwrapped a double duvet from a waterproof bag and he threw it over both of them, even though they were still fully-clothed. '... and have another beer.'

She accepted the beer and asked: 'Why do you bring a duvet all the way out here?'

'Because I hate sleeping-bags and a few creature comforts never go amiss.' And then he laughed.

'What's funny?'

'I just sounded like Tanya, didn't I?'

'Well you certainly don't look like her!'

They both took a swig of beer.

'Brad, can I comment on something that I've really picked up on since I've been here?'

'Sure, what is it?'

'It's only that I've noticed what a great father you are to your children.' Then she felt awkward so she followed it up by gabbling. 'I don't mean to blow your trumpet or anything, but it's just that most people up here appear to leave their children to the nannies a lot of the time, and you, well, seem to be around yours more. I know I shouldn't criticise anyone, and really, I don't mean to. After all, it's got nothing to do with me and it's everybody's holiday to enjoy. It's more of an observation ... what I'm really trying to say is that I've watched you making time for yours ...'

'Hey, slow down!' The lamplight flickered in his blue eyes which at that moment seemed huge, as they concentrated on Nelle. 'Don't forget, we're a bit different from the other families down here. I have to be both mother and father to Luke and Annie. That, and also the fact that I do travel during the year, makes it all the more important to share some quality time with them on holiday.'

She waited to see if he would mention Jane, but he didn't. He must have just assumed that Nelle knew Jane wasn't alive.

'That's how all our family holidays used to be as kids,' she told him. 'But then, we tended to go away more as one family and not with other people.'

'What you're saying is nice but don't make me out to be too good. There are loads of times when I'm sure I don't get it right.'

'I think everyone feels guilty sometimes. I'm not a parent but I know from friends that you can spend a lot of time feeling guilty about your children, for all sorts of reasons.'

'It's true. Look at tonight, for instance. Part of me says I should be at home with them now and not here.'

'But surely, wouldn't they be in bed now?'

'Yes, right now they would be,' he agreed.

'And Ruth seems very capable,' she pointed out.

'She is. They've known her all their lives and they're very fond of her. She has to look after them full-time when I'm away.'

'I'm sure, knowing what I know of you, you'll make up for it tomorrow.'

'I've promised to take them fishing. Luke loves catching mackerel.'

'There you go then, that proves my original point,' she smiled triumphantly.

'The bottom line is that they're great kids and I'm all they've got now, so it's important that I feature around them.'

Nelle was dying to ask about Jane. There was so much she wanted to find out. She was desperate to know about Jane's family and the history of the ruined house. But somehow, she just couldn't bring the subject up. The fact that Brad offered precisely nothing about his wife put the lid firmly on that subject and she didn't feel she could open it unless he did. She also didn't want to risk upsetting him or jeopardising their friendship which had become very important to her in a short time.

He was talking again. His eyes never left her face.

'What about you, Nelle? You seem very natural around children. Do you see yourself having them one day?'

He had unintentionally stepped on a nerve which was still raw, despite a slow healing of time. She wasn't prepared for his question and felt tears well up in her eyes, which irritated her.

She looked away. When Jack had pried into her life not even three weeks earlier, the direct approach by someone she'd never met before hadn't given her time to think. When it came to the crunch, she'd found it easier than she'd anticipated, to be matter-of-fact about losing the baby. But that was only part of the story. And it was different with Brad. Brad was altogether different from Jack. There was already more emotional water under the bridge. She almost felt that if she started, everything would come out and she wouldn't be able to stop. And would that be fair to Brad so early on in their friendship?

'What is it?' he asked softly, reading the pain in her expression. He took her free hand and gently bringing her face round with his other hand, continued: 'Have I said the wrong thing?'

'I'm not very good at talking about this.' She wiped a stray tear.

'You don't have to if you don't want to, but remember

what I said about bottling things up? I can tell you from experience that it does help to talk about some things.'

'I know now that you are right but I don't want to spoil a nice evening with emotional baggage.'

'Not much you could say right now would spoil my evening.'

'Do you mean that?' She looked into his face again.

He nodded. 'Yes, I do.'

She took a deep breath.

'Here goes ... I was pregnant last year ...' She looked up to check his reaction. He hadn't moved.

'Go on ...'

'I carried the baby to full term. I went into labour in the normal way ... if there is a normal way, that is. Anyhow, everything seemed to be going OK, but somewhere along the line it didn't, because when the baby came out, he was dead.' She swallowed hard, her mouth was dry.

Brad took both her hands and squeezed them as the tears ran freely down her cheeks. He waited for her to continue.

'No-one seemed to know exactly what went wrong. I just don't think he wanted to live.'

'And the father?' asked Brad quietly.

'... was no-where in sight. The whole thing was a mistake and should never have happened. Roger was his name ... he blamed me for not getting my dates right. He was definitely not ready to be a father. To be honest, I'm not sure I was ready to be a mother either, but the alternative was just too awful to consider.'

'So he left?'

'As soon as he found out about the baby. He did such a good disappearing act that I haven't seen or heard from him since.'

'And does he know about the baby dying?'

'If he does, he's never been in touch and said so. I'm sure the news must have filtered through eventually though, because we have a few mutual friends.'

'The bastard!' exclaimed Brad.

'It was probably as much my fault for allowing myself to get pregnant in the first place. You just never think it'll happen to you.'

Nelle wiped her nose on the tissue Brad found for her. He moved closer and put both his arms around her, kissing her lightly on the top of her head.

'You must have had a really rough ride after that.'

'It wasn't great. There were so many people to tell, all of whom had been expecting good news rather than that.'

'What about your family?'

'My parents aren't alive any more.'

'So you had to face it on your own?'

'Don't feel too sorry for me.' She tried to smile. 'I'm lucky to have some very good friends, but there's a limit to how much you feel you can burden other people with and mostly, I've found it easier to keep it all inside.'

'And you have got plenty of time for more babies.'

She closed her eyes and entwined her fingers in his, almost without realising.

'Jack was the first one after ...' Her voice tailed off.

'I guessed.'

'Thanks for listening and being so understanding, what with me supposedly being up here with Jack and all that.'

She looked up in the soft light.

'There are skeletons in every cupboard somewhere,' he said.

'I think I've really messed up recently. But I do have Jack to thank for bringing me out of what was proving to be a lengthy depression. Maybe post-natal blues, or whatever they call it. Only I don't have a baby to show for it.'

'And I have him to thank or I wouldn't have met you.'

'I suppose it was brave of him to take on such a vulnerable, emotional wreck of a person.' She smiled.

'Give him credit but I'm sure he asked you out with his eyes wide open.'

'You're going to have to believe me that I'm not usually the kind of girl who sleeps with someone and then disappears off into a tent with a friend of his shortly afterwards!'

'I told you before, I'm perceptive.' He began to nibble her fingers.

'Jack and I haven't discussed our relationship at all but I'm sure we both know there's no future in it. Cards on the table, we haven't slept together since the first night we arrived here.'

'I've watched the way he is with you. I probably shouldn't tell you this and please don't lose any sleep over it, but Jack comes up here with a different girl every year. It's almost a standing joke amongst the others to see who it is. It's like he needs to be seen with someone new. Perhaps you could call it insecurity.'

'But Jack always seems so confident.'

'People who come across as very confident, often have an incredibly insecure interior. Pierce their shell and they're all over the place.'

'I guess I haven't exactly been very happy about the way he's treated me up here, but I can't help liking him - only as a friend now, I hasten to add.'

'He's been a friend of mine for years. I just don't always think the way he treats his women is all that great.'

'You know, you were right the other day when you told me to stay here and enjoy myself. I am having a good time. Maybe you'd say it was therapy?' She giggled.

'At this point, can I admit to a slightly selfish motivation behind my advice?' He moved his mouth from her fingers to her earlobes and she could feel herself weakening fast.

'Oh Brad.' She squirmed down beneath the duvet. 'This therapy could become complicated.'

'Shh.' He cradled her head and looked down at her, his hair falling across his eyes as he bent to kiss her full on the lips. 'I know.'

Chapter Eight

Thursday, August 6th

Nelle opened her eyes and blinked. What the hell was she doing? She was tucked cosily into the folds of Brad's fleece, his arm protectively around her as he slept on, his head facing away from hers. In the sobering light of day, she wondered if she'd really done the right thing.

She could tell it was day by the chinks of light which forced their way through tiny gaps in the tent. But she had no idea what time it was and couldn't remember for the life of her, where she'd left her watch.

Very carefully, so as not to disturb Brad, she slipped under his arm and crawled out of the duvet, stopping to make sure he was still covered.

Holding her breath, she unzipped the tent-flap, the noise of which sounded like firecrackers in the stillness of the morning. Fortunately, Brad did not stir.

When she stood up outside the tent, she realised three things almost at once. One, she was still wearing Brad's enormous sweater which almost hid her shorts entirely. Two, her shoes, which had stayed outside all night, were horribly slimy with dew, and three, her head rattled like a freight train. Just how many of those beers had they consumed?

'Hiya, Nelle!' Oh shit, who was that?

Nelle squinted in the sunlight, struggling desperately to focus on the owner of the voice. As she became accustomed to the brightness, it was easier because there was only one other person up. Tanya - who else?

'Couldn't sleep, darling! God, I hate camp-beds, don't you?' Tanya was combing her hair with one hand and holding a large square mirror in the other.

'What?' Nelle hadn't really heard her.

'Camp-beds. Oh, never mind, I guess all these sleepless nights are preparing me for getting up to the baby when it's born. Still, that's where Toby comes in. Let him do his share, is what I say. After all, we lug the thing around for nine months before they even get to lift a finger, don't you agree?'

Nelle wished she would shut up. She had 'lugged' her baby around for nine months, only she never got the chance to find out what it would have been like to get up in the night to him and besides, she was still trying to deal with the idea that Tanya had seen her coming out of Brad's tent.

'Did you sleep OK, Nelle? Not ... cold or anything?' Fishing, or what?

'Yes, fine thanks.' Best to avoid the issue until she'd had time to think. 'I just wish I'd gone a bit easier on the beers last night,' she replied, holding her head between her palms.

'Well, that's one thing about being pregnant. No booze for nine months. Well, not much anyway. Must admit though, I can't wait to get absolutely sloshed again soon.'

The thought of Tanya being absolutely sloshed was not a pleasant one to entertain just then. Nelle slipped her feet into her shoes - yuk!

'Anyone'd think we'd had a raid last night, darling,' continued Tanya. 'Just look at the mess!'

Nelle tried to take in the scene. Spent barbecues, empty bottles, cups upturned, plates licked clean by the three dogs who had come on the expedition, scrunched up rugs and bits of clothing lay scattered in no particular order.

'I think I'm going to walk down to the beach,' said Nelle, needing space.

'OK. I do hope the others get up soon. I'm dying for some brekkie. Toby brought extra barbecues so we can have a jolly good fry-up this morning.'

The thought of a jolly good fry-up disturbed the contents of Nelle's fragile stomach considerably.

'... come to think of it, it's time Toby was up. I'm going to go and wake him. See you in a mo'.'

Toby had Nelle's undying sympathy at that moment.

She crossed the camp, passed the other tents, which were firmly closed for the time being, and stumbled over the dunes to the beach.

Her shoes attracted every bit of grit in sight, so she abandoned them half way to the boats. Brad had been right about the tide. The Inland Sea was once more lapping the shore, the water high until the tide turned and the process began all over again.

The boats looked pretty much as they had the day before, with the exception of Octopussy, who had her black awning raised up over part of the cockpit.

Nelle wasn't quite sure what she was going to say to Jack when she did see him. Half of her felt guilty for spending the night with Brad, but the other half felt that as Jack had made no effort at all to secure her comfort, he hardly had a leg to stand on if someone else had. But was that the point, and would it all cause a big scene? That was the last thing she could face just then.

Nelle hesitated on the edge of the deserted beach before stepping into the water and paddling over to Octopussy, which was bobbing up and down gently in the line of boats. Was that water cold! She couldn't haul herself on to the nose, so she followed the railing round to the side.

Thud, thud, thud came from the back of the boat. When she peered over, she saw Buster sprawled over the back seat which was now covered in black dog hairs. No sign of Jack.

Nelle put her hand out and stroked Buster, who rolled right on to his back and grinned at her.

'Where's your master, then?' she asked him quietly.

She glanced down the boat and through the open hatch of the small cabin she saw Jack. She also saw the thin frame of Camilla. Both appeared to be fully-clothed, covered only by a couple of beach towels and both were dead to the world. In fact, Jack was snoring.

Nelle pulled away sharply, not wanting to wake them or be anywhere near when they came to. Her first reaction was one of utter relief. It made her own secret so much easier to handle. Then several other reactions came flooding into her mind. What about Sandy?

Where was he? Was this normal behaviour? Did everyone wife-swap up here? Was she jumping to conclusions? They'd probably just fallen asleep chatting. Should she feel angry with Jack? After all, in theory, she was supposed to be the one sharing his accommodation. But that was ridiculous, because in practice, they hadn't shared that for several days. And then, who was she to cast the first stone anyway?

Time to wash. She yanked Brad's jumper over her head and bent down to splash her face with water. Good job it was so cold. Might just clear her head a bit.

'Morning, Nelle,' called Justin who was striding athletically towards her in his familiar shorts.

'Hi, Justin.' She patted her face as droplets slid down on to her fleece.

'Thought I might have a ski before breakfast. Great for hangovers and restoring the appetite. Where's Jack?'

Now what? How was she supposed to answer that? Maybe the truth was the best. After all, if Jack and Justin were such good friends, it probably wouldn't come as a shock to Justin to find Jack asleep next to someone else's wife. At least she wasn't Justin's.

'He slept on Octopussy,' she began. 'I didn't. It was too cold.' She felt the need for a little explanation of the situation. The rest he would have to work out for himself.

'Quite right. Besides, I know how Jack snores when he's pissed. I wouldn't share a room, let alone a boat with him when he's had a few.'

'Are the others awake yet?' asked Nelle. Anything to change the subject.

'Starting to be. I'm off for a swim first and then I'll fire up Just In. That should get Jack up. See you later.' And with that, he ran down the beach and dived head first into the water like something out of Baywatch. The only thing missing was his float.

Nelle picked up Brad's jumper and went back to the camp. When she got there, she found considerably more activity than she'd left earlier. Heaven knows who had slept where, because no-one seemed to come out of the tent they had brought, and if they did, their partner wasn't to be seen. It was a good job most of them had grown up together.

A few people smiled at her as they pulled on clothes, picked up rubbish or spread butter on bread. In the general hubbub of hangovers and delicate constitutions, no-one seemed to notice Nelle go to Brad's tent and unzip the flap. Or if they did and thought anything at all, Nelle was not aware.

Brad was still lying under his duvet when she peered into the tent. His hands were clasped behind his head and when he saw who it was, he just flashed her the most wonderfully reassuring smile which melted her to bits.

'Hi!' he said without moving.

'Hi,' she replied shyly. 'How are you feeling this morning?'

She wished she could capture that deliciously dishevelled look on film and store it away for ever.

'I've felt better.'

'So have I. I've just been down to the beach.'

'Have you? Come in for a minute. Did you find Jack down there?' he asked.

Should she tell Brad? She knelt down on the duvet beside him and he put his hand out to her.

'Yes. You were right about him sleeping on his boat.'

'Thought he would. But you aren't telling me something.'

'What do you mean?'

'Was Camilla there too?'

'You knew?' He'd taken her by surprise again.

'Not exactly, just guessed. They're very good friends.'

'What about Sandy?' Nelle was amazed that Brad was so matter-of-fact. Perhaps her life until now had been far too sheltered. Time she got out into the big bad world.

'Sandy and Jack are very good friends too. Don't look so worried. Nothing'll have happened. They probably just passed out together. Come here and give me a kiss.' He pulled her face towards his and their tongues united.

When she came up for air, Nelle gave him back his jumper and said: 'Thanks for this. I'm going in search of coffee if I can find some. Want some too?'

'Thanks.'

The first person she caught sight of when she came out of Brad's tent for the second time that morning, was Jack. He had obviously declined Justin's offer of a ski because he was bone dry.

'That's it!' he declared loudly. 'Alcohol is officially

banned as from today.'

'Speak for yourself, old boy,' laughed Sandy who had just mixed a jug of Bloody Mary. 'Hair of the dog's what you need.'

'Certainly not. I mean it this time. I will not touch another drop. Oh hello, Nelle.' He'd just noticed her.

'Hi, Jack,' she replied, trying not to sound awkward. The last thing she wanted to do was to discuss their respective sleeping arrangements in public.

'Where's our food, sweetie? I think I need to eat.' He acted as if everything was perfectly normal.

The camp was dismantled far faster than it had been established. Breakfast of sorts was consumed by those who could stomach it. Black coffees were poured out in large quantities, partly because no-one had remembered to bring any milk.

They were just having a final check round when Justin, who had more energy than the rest of the group put together, suggested: 'Who's on for a fishing trip this afternoon?'

'Sounds good to me,' answered Camilla, sneaking a look at Jack, who didn't notice. 'The children'll enjoy that.'

'Good for the kids, and the rest of us can do some Ginering. I must say, that sounds about right for today,' commented Sandy.

'What ... is ... this ... word, 'Ginering'?' asked Annette looking puzzled.

'Gina Lollo-brig-ering,' replied Justin as if she was utterly thick.

'Don't worry, Annette,' said Sophie, folding her rug. 'Lolling is a word we use for relaxing on the boats. Some people have their own language up here and it's not only foreigners who can't always follow it.'

'Oh, I see.' Annette, who felt out of her depth and didn't really see at all, laughed nervously.

'Anyway, getting back to the point, is everyone coming?' asked Justin, who had worn the same shorts since yesterday afternoon.

'Sure,' and 'Yes, OK, what time?' flew round the camp.

'Well, let's go and sort out the children and lunch them. What about, 2 ish, suit everyone?' suggested Justin.

'I've, er ... got a bit of work to do this afternoon,' announced Jack. 'Need to stay in touch with the office. Nelle, do you mind if you go out ... say, in Brad's boat today? I don't want you to miss the fishing on my account and I'm sure Brad'll look after you. You don't mind, do you, Brad? I promise you, she's better company than your nanny.'

'Yes, of course, there's plenty of room, Nelle,' replied Brad so casually, as if they were discussing the weather.

Nelle was just about to object to being organised without her consent, when she thought of the obvious appeal of spending the afternoon with Brad.

'You'll love his children,' winked Jack in Nelle's direction, unaware that Nelle had already met Luke and Annie.

Thinking she ought to at least be seen to have a say in

the arrangements and wondering what Jack was actually going to be up to for the afternoon, she asked Brad: 'Is that really alright?'

'Yes, that really is alright.' He smiled broadly. 'We'd love to have you along.'

'So that's settled, then,' said Jack. 'Make sure you bring back plenty of mackerel. Flora loves her grilled mackerel.'

Jack and the rest of the party went down to the boats.

'Brad, you know how yesterday I told you I couldn't ski?' began Nelle as she picked up Jack's cool-box.

'Yes,' he answered, taking a final look around to check they had got everything.

'Well, I'm not sure I can fish either.'

'Then I'll have to teach you.'

Big Rock loomed ahead as the boats slipped through the calm waters in the afternoon sunshine.

'Dr No, Dr No, this is Just In, come in ... over.'

Brad reached for his ship-to-shore and glanced over at Nelle, sitting in the passenger seat.

'Can I speak? Can I speak, Daddy?' enthused Luke from the back seat.

'Sit down, Luke, love, or you'll fall. Let Daddy answer it,' said Ruth.

'But I want a go.' Luke sulked back into his seat.

'It's not a toy, Luke,' Ruth told him, crossing her legs, over which she wore a pair of thick blue trousers. 'We'll be there in a minute. Be patient.'

'Go ahead, Just In, this is Dr No ... over.'

'Do you think we'd be better here, or just past the end

of Big Rock? ... Over.'

Before Brad had a chance to reply, they heard Kristian's voice: 'Just In, this is Over Hung. We came out here a couple of days ago and pulled masses out on the lines just past the rock. I suggest we go on a bit ... over.'

'OK, Over Hung. Why don't you lead the way and we'll follow you? ... Over.'

'Will do. This is Over Hung, out.'

Kristian's Jetstar snaked into the lead and the other boats fanned out in his wake. When he arrived at the right spot, Kristian turned off his engine and signalled to the others to draw up alongside.

'I'll shove an anchor out which'll hold us all if you tie up on either side,' he told them.

One by one, the boats lined up side by side, with Kristian and Juliet in the middle. Brad didn't seem to be in a hurry to take his place and finally cruised to one end of the line beside High Dive, where Marcus was busy tying on fenders.

'Shall I get our fenders out for you, Brad?' asked Ruth.

'A couple would be great, thanks, Ruth.'

Brad stepped up on to the front of the boat and called to Marcus: 'Let me have your rope and I'll put it round my cleat.'

Nelle didn't know how to make herself useful to the mooring operation and so turned her attention to the children.

'Do you like fishing then?' she asked them.

'Oh yes I do,' beamed Luke, looking the image of his

father. 'And I've got my own rod. Daddy bought me one last year and I caught loads of fish.'

'No you didn't!' Annie was quite advanced for her four years.

'Yes I did so!' he retorted indignantly. 'I did, didn't I, Ruth?'

Ruth was heaving a fender over the side between High Dive and Dr No and didn't answer.

'Anyway, it's not fair,' continued Annie. 'I want a rod too. If Luke has one, I want one.'

'Want one what?' asked Brad from the other side of the windscreen.

'I want a rod like Luke's.'

'Do you really think that's the way to get one, Annie?' He looked sternly at her.

'No,' she replied in a small voice, picking at the bobbles on the arm of her fleece.

'Did you stop to think that if you asked nicely, you might even get your own rod?'

'Please Daddy, can I have my own fishing rod ... please?' She spoke slowly and deliberately.

Nelle doubted whether anyone could resist that little freckled face, framed by those long golden curls. She certainly would have found it hard.

'That's better. Now give me a minute and I'll see what I can do.'

'Have you got one for me?' Things were improving all the time.

'I might have.'

'Ooh, Luke. Daddy's got me a rod. Daddy's got me a rod.' Her smile was infectious.

Along the line, fishing rods were appearing on most of the boats. Clothes were being discarded and there was a distinct smell of coconut sun cream as people were determined to make the most of the heat.

Very quickly, adults and children climbed from boat to boat, chatting and playing respectively. Nelle had only just worked out in her mind, who was married to who, so once everyone moved around, she lost track of which boat was which and whose children belonged where.

Savannah and Camilla had joined Amelia on the bimbo sun bathing deck of Just In, leaving their various offspring in the capable hands of the au pairs. All three had stripped down to bikinis and were supping cold glasses of white wine, trying to avoid having anything to do with the fishing at all.

Nelle felt overdressed and she also felt hot. While Brad sat up on the front, fixing the flies on to the children's rods, she took off her top and revealed a baby blue swimsuit with crossover straps at the back. Wising up to the havoc the wind played with her hair on a speed-boat, she had spent a few moments putting hers in a French plait before she'd left home.

'Check out Nelle's costume, guys,' called Justin from High Dive next door, whistling through his teeth.

Well, that of course attracted volumes of unwanted attention from all around, which made Nelle feel horribly self-conscious. Even a special look of approval from Brad didn't improve matters much.

'Thanks, Justin,' she smiled shyly from behind her fringe.

Fortunately, a loud scream from Justin's own boat diverted him swiftly.

'Get that over the side!' yelled Amelia to Amber, one of her twelve-year-old twins. 'Justin, sort that line out now.'

Amber, who had been standing on the bathing platform at the back of Just In, had just reeled in her line on which she'd hooked several wriggling mackerel, all fighting for their lives. She was waving them in her mother's direction with a great sense of achievement.

'Look, Mum. I've got six!'

The sun bathing was well and truly disturbed further when two of Camilla's boys, John and Joe, leapt over from Moneypenny for a closer look, dragging their own lines round with them.

'Stand back, everyone,' commanded Justin, taking control. 'Where's the bucket, darling?'

'I don't know where the flaming bucket is! You look for it and make sure you don't get any blood and guts over us,' warned Amelia, curling away from the rod in her white bikini.

Justin found his blue bucket in the cabin and proceeded to climb down on to the bathing platform. He grabbed each mackerel in turn, breaking their necks and throwing them into the bucket.

'Well done, Amber. Six on a line! Must be over a shoal here,' he congratulated his daughter and ignored his wife.

Nelle realised Ruth had been talking to her.

'Sorry, Ruth. What did you say?'

'Could you pass me the children's caps, please?

They're tucked down in the pocket beside you.'

'Yes, of course.' Nelle found them. 'Here they are.'

'Thank you,' she smiled briefly.

'Hey, Nelle, come up here and have a go,' called Brad.

Behind her, Ruth was hanging on to Luke and Annie who dangled their rods impatiently over the back of the boat, anxious for a bite.

As Nelle climbed out through the windscreen, she could see Marcus and Sandy light up a couple of long cigars on High Dive. It didn't look as if they were planning to fish for a while. Sophie and Annette had joined the mothers' meeting on Just In.

Brad's rod lay propped against the windscreen. He was checking to make sure the weight on the end of the line was securely attached.

'Now sit here with your legs over the side,' he told her, 'and I'll pass the rod to you.'

Still unconvinced that she wasn't about to fall overboard when balancing on the nose of a speed-boat, Nelle put her hand on Brad's shoulder to steady herself into a sitting position.

Brad perched on his haunches behind her and passed the rod forward. His arms went round her as he showed her what to do.

'Hold it here.' He picked up her left hand. 'With your right hand, you can wind out the line quite a long way. The water's deep enough.'

His arms stayed where they were.

'Do I have to cast up and down?' asked Nelle.

'You're not on a river, you know.' He laughed at her,

his face just beside hers. ‘All you need to do is gently move the rod up and down like this.’ He covered her hands and demonstrated.

‘And how do I know if I've caught something?’

‘You'll know because you'll feel a great tug and the rod'll bend.’

‘I hope it doesn't pull me in.’ She made light of her greatest fear.

‘If it does, we'll both go in,’ he smiled and released her hands.

‘Brad, sorry, but can you come here? I think Luke's caught something,’ called Ruth, turning round.

‘Coming.’ And to Nelle, ‘OK for a minute?’

‘I suppose so.’ She wasn't entirely sure.

As it turned out, Luke had not caught anything, or if he had, it had escaped from the hook and certain premature death.

Great whoops of joy could be heard periodically from other boats as more mackerel succumbed to the temptation of the brightly coloured feathers below the surface of the water. Only one of the nannies was prepared to take the fish off the lines and risk a shower of fish innards. That was Kelly, a buxom teenager with a strong Yorkshire accent, who was employed by Jamie and Savannah. As both her charges (Charlie, who was four, and baby Carly) were sound asleep in the small cabin on Jaws, it left her free to help the other children.

Brad rejoined Nelle with a couple of bottles of beer.

‘How are you doing up here?’ he asked.

‘Nothing so far. I don't think I've got the knack.’

‘Give it time. Here, have a beer.’

‘I think I'd better keep both hands on the rod or you might lose it over the side,’ she replied in all seriousness.

‘Brad, now Annie's got her line tangled. Can you come and sort it out?’ It was Ruth again.

‘Sorry about this,’ he told Nelle quietly, raising his eyebrows and jumping back into the boat to attend to his daughter.

Nelle didn't catch a thing! Despite her best efforts and a strong desire to impress both Brad and the assembled company, the fish just ignored her bait completely. The only comfort was that from what she could hear, she wasn't the only one.

‘Either of you two fancy a swim round the boats?’ Justin called over to Brad and Nelle from the stern of Over Hung where he was busy flexing his muscles.

‘Good idea,’ replied Brad without asking Nelle.

‘I think you should all have a race.’ Sandy inhaled his cigar deeply.

‘And I think you should put that cigar out and go too,’ said Camilla, who had undone the back strap of her bikini and was still lapping up the sun on Just In.

‘Feeling a bit sunburnt, my dear. You haven't been looking after my shoulders. You know how sensitive my skin is. In fact, come to think of it, where's my t-shirt?’

‘Sandy, would you like me to come and rub some cream into your shoulders?’ asked Tanya, whose boat was tied to the other side of High Dive. ‘Only there's no way I'm going swimming. I'd go all the way to the bottom, I'm sure.’

‘I’d be absolutely delighted, thank you, Tanya. By the way, Toby, do you mind me borrowing your wife?’ checked Sandy.

‘She's all yours, mate. I'm off for a swim. I've had enough of not catching anything,’ answered Toby who seemed permanently to have the weight of the world on *his* shoulders. But being married to Tanya, it was hardly surprising.

Tanya made a great exhibition of herself crossing from her boat to High Dive and Nelle suspected she much enjoyed being handled into the boat by both Sandy and Marcus.

‘Only thing is, boys, you'll have to keep those cigars to yourselves. I can't stand the smell when I'm pregnant. Now where's that cream?’

Tanya was starting to grate seriously on Nelle’s nerves. She was acting as if she was the only person ever to have been pregnant and was revelling in the attention.

Brad had taken the rod from Nelle and was winding in the line so that he could stow it in the boat while they joined the others in the water.

‘It's nice to see you out with Brad, Nelle,’ said Tanya arranging her ample self on the bimbo deck beside Sandy.

Nelle's mind flew back to that morning when she'd emerged from Brad's tent in full view of Tanya.

‘Jack's working this afternoon,’ she told Tanya quickly.

‘I know. I remember he said so this morning. But I'm so glad you found someone to bring you. It'd be a shame to miss out on a day like this. If Jack continues to be boring and work on holiday, you can always come out on our boat, you know.'

'Thanks for the offer.' Nelle wasn't comfortable with the disguised innuendos.

'Are you coming too, Nelle?' asked Brad who was just about to dive over the side.

Nelle had already decided she wasn't. Swimming was not her greatest achievement in life and the trouble with swimming out of your depth in the sea was, you never quite knew what was underneath you.

She was just about to decline when she caught a look from Ruth which, for some reason, was none too friendly and she quickly made up her mind that swimming with Brad might have its appeal after all.

'OK, you go first.' Was she really agreeing to this?

Brad flew into the water like a dart, with hardly a splash, and came up some way from the boat.

'Is it cold?' shouted Nelle.

'Refreshing's probably how I'd describe it,' called Brad, grinning.

'He means bloody freezing, darling,' smirked Tanya, massaging Sandy's back. 'I think you're very brave. We'll have the towels waiting for you.'

Nelle hated diving. She really didn't like going much below the surface. Instead, she climbed over the back seat, past Luke and Annie who were sharing a large multi-save bag of crisps and stepped on to the bathing platform.

Just after she'd sat down and was about to slip into the water, Tanya popped her head over the side of High

Dive and announced in a loud voice: 'Has anyone ever told you, you've got a figure to die for, Nelle? I'm going to simply starve myself after this baby comes.'

Nelle didn't hang around to answer. Tanya was right about one thing, the water was unbelievably cold.

'Keep swimming and then you'll get warm.' Brad appeared at her side.

A little way ahead she could see Justin swimming next to his youngest, Indigo, and not far away, she recognised Sandy's au pair, Roxanne, keeping an eye on John who was also seven.

Nelle and Brad swam level with Just In and they were beckoned over by the girls on the back, who were taking a little more interest in the proceedings than before.

'Hey, Brad,' called Camilla, enjoying the rest from her four children. 'Do you think I should come in?'

'Sure, why not?' He stopped swimming and put his arms over the bathing platform.

Nelle wasn't sure whether she was brave enough to carry on by herself or whether she would be better to wait for him. She decided to stop too.

'Oh, Nelle, I didn't see you there,' remarked Amelia, curling up her toes. 'Couldn't persuade Jack to come out this afternoon then?'

'No. He's had to work.' She was beginning to get fed up of accounting for Jack.

'Work my arse! He's probably in bed sleeping off his hangover,' laughed Camilla knowingly.

'Wouldn't surprise me,' agreed Amelia.

Nelle wasn't exactly enjoying herself at that moment

and Brad could sense she needed to swim on.

'We'll catch you in a bit. It's too cold to stop for long. We're going round the boats.'

Brad led the way and Nelle followed close behind. They swam a little way out so as not to encounter any of the lines which trailed out from the few fishing rods still in the water. They came across several others swimming round the opposite way and skilfully dodged Amber and Violet who were having a race. They trod water as they watched the girls pass; all eyes were on the competitive twins.

Under the water, Brad reached for Nelle's hand and squeezed it, which made her already goosepimply skin prickle all over, and she turned to him, very conscious of being discreet.

Brad looked even more attractive when wet, if that was possible. Droplets of water slid down his face from his hair. He looked so strong and yet so vulnerable that it was all she could do to restrain herself. Yet control herself she had to, because Jamie was almost upon them.

'Hi, Brad! Have you noticed those clouds over there?'

Brad turned in the water and looked up to where Jamie was pointing a long bony finger.

'I see what you mean.'

Just then, Sandy's voice could be heard from the back of High Dive.

'I don't wish to alarm anyone, but there's a front coming in, if I'm not mistaken. Perhaps we should think about wending our way back?'

‘He's right,’ said Brad. ‘Come on, Nelle, these fronts can come in really fast here.’

If she hadn't seen it with her own eyes, Nelle might have wondered if they were joking. It was extraordinary. Above them, the sky was a brilliant blue and yet a little way out to sea everything looked a ghostly grey. The more she looked, the nearer the wall of grey crept.

Panic was the best way to describe the ensuing scene. Dripping bathers scrambled on to boats and snatched up towels. Children were hauled back to where they were supposed to be. Husbands issued orders and no-one felt like challenging them.

The drama was unfolding.

On Dr No, Ruth had responded to the alarm and had both children dressed and zipped into their life jackets by the time Brad and Nelle arrived back.

‘Grab us some towels, Ruth,’ said Brad helping Nelle out of the water.

Ruth passed a large beach towel to Brad and one of the children's small ones to Nelle. It barely covered her bottom but it was better than nothing.

Brad tucked his around his waist and began to untie fenders.

‘Are we going to die, Daddy?’ wailed Annie.

‘No, Annie, of course we're not. We just need to get back to Rhoslown because this mist is going to make it hard for us to see soon.’

‘If we can't see, how will we know where to go?’ asked Luke.

‘We've got navigation equipment. Don't worry, we'll

be fine. Now, help Ruth put these fenders away will you? You're part of my crew.'

Nelle dried herself as best she could and pulled her fleece over her wet costume. She was shivering. As ropes around them were untied, the boats started to drift free from one another and one by one, the engines were fired up.

The mist rolled ominously towards them.

'I'm scared, Daddy,' said Annie.

'So am I,' agreed Nelle. 'Would you like to come and sit with me and we can be scared together?'

Brad threw Nelle a grateful look and Annie climbed on to her knee.

'I like it better in the front, Ruth.' Annie turned round.

'Hold on to her, Nelle. She tends to wriggle and bump around,' Ruth informed her.

'She'll be fine,' reassured Nelle, sounding calmer than she felt.

Someone was talking on the ship-to-shore and Brad tuned his radio so they could pick up the channel clearly.

'This is High Dive,' came Marcus's voice sounding more serious than Nelle had heard before, and taking charge of the situation he said: 'I've plotted a course on my GPS navigational system that'll get us all back safely to Rhoslown. If we take it nice and steady and you keep me in sight, we'll be back there soon. I'll lead the way ... over.'

Sandy replied: 'High Dive, this is Moneypenny. So glad someone went to the Boat Show this year. You'll have to share the secret of your new high tech equipment with us on our return ... over.'

Then they heard Justin. 'Moneypenny, this is Just In. Might I suggest you join us at the Boat Show next year? ... Over.'

'Don't tell me you've got a GPS system on board too, Just In. Some of us were too busy working at selling houses and making money to go this year ... over.'

'Put it this way, Moneypenny, stick close to me on the way back if you want to avoid the rocks ... over.' They could hear a few chuckles from the other boats through the mist.

'On a serious note, guys,' Marcus continued, 'I reckon we should make a move because these conditions are getting worse. We can't even see Big Rock now ... over.'

'Righto, High Dive,' said Sandy, 'we're on your tail. Out.'

The blanket of sea fog had folded around them in an amazingly short space of time. The other boats, which only moments earlier had been clearly identifiable, had become mere outlines. The air had chilled and gone was the reassuring sun.

'Gosh, I can't see anything!' said Luke excitedly.

'Let Daddy concentrate, Luke.' Ruth's voice rose above the engine noise.

'We're OK. That boat you can see just ahead is Uncle Marcus's and he's the best skipper there is. He's mapped out a course to get us back safe and sound,' Brad told them.

Nelle desperately wanted to believe him, but inside

she felt so out of control of the situation. She also knew it was important not to give anyone the impression she was frightened. Brad would get them home. She had to think that.

All they could hear was the drumming of boat engines. She could only just make out Marcus's boat ahead of them and even though she knew the other boats were nearby, she couldn't see any of them.

Then she did. But it wasn't a boat she recognised. It wasn't even a speed-boat. It was a small, wooden fishing boat which had once been painted blue but the paint was badly chipped. It lay only a few metres to their left. It wasn't moving. The colour drained from her face. The boat was empty. Abandoned. There was no-one aboard.

'Brad, Brad,' she whispered anxiously, 'there's a boat ... just there.'

But her voice was small and Brad couldn't hear her words.

'There's a what?' he called, over the sound of the engine.

'A boat,' she repeated, pointing to the place where she'd seen the boat.

'What boat, Nelle?' asked Annie, craning her little neck.

But the boat wasn't there any more. It was gone! Vanished into the mist. Nelle screwed up her eyes and looked and looked but all she could see was a blank screen of nothing.

Brad, who was busy keeping Dr No in High Dive's wake, flicked his eyes momentarily to Nelle and back again.

'Are you alright?' Nelle looked very strange, but Brad couldn't risk losing sight of Marcus.

'Must be seeing things.' She tried to make light of it, but something had made her feel very uneasy inside, somewhere deep within her.

'Maybe it was a bit of driftwood or a bird, because I didn't see anything?' suggested Ruth.

'You could be right.' Nelle wasn't convinced.

She tightened her arms around Annie who was beginning to feel sleepy from the fresh air and the slow, steady progress of the boats.

'Message for all boats following High Dive,' Marcus's voice crackled through the radio. 'Is everyone still with us? Has anyone drifted off course? I repeat, does anyone need assistance? ... Over.'

'High Dive, this is Bun In The Oven,' came the unmistakeable voice of Tanya. 'I, for one, am right behind you and I'm not budging ... over.'

'Bun In The Oven, this is Just In. Glad to hear you haven't strayed. For God's sake, don't go into production, will you? ... Over.'

'I'm not scheduling it at the moment, Just In. I'll keep you informed of any developments, though ... over.'

There followed various other confirmations of position and all seemed to be well. It was a weird feeling, knowing they were so near to five other boats that they could almost reach out and touch them, and yet they couldn't see anything at all to left or right. It took all Brad's concentration to maintain his direction.

'This is High Dive. I can tell you all that we've passed

Pound and Shilling beaches and we should have Rhoslown Bay coming up on the starboard side in a few minutes. High Dive ... out.'

The blankness and the silence were eerie.

'How's my crew bearing up?' asked Brad, not turning round.

'Where are the other boats, Daddy?' asked Luke.

'Very near us. It's just that you can't see them.'

'Annie's fallen asleep,' Nelle told Brad.

'I wish she hadn't. She'll be up till all hours tonight now,' said Ruth from the back seat.

Nelle felt like a naughty schoolgirl caught doing something she shouldn't.

'Sorry,' she found herself apologising. 'It just sort of happened.'

'I would've done it myself if I hadn't been driving,' said Brad. 'I feel like I've been up for days.'

'You probably didn't sleep properly when you were out last night,' said Ruth.

Nelle felt herself blush and buried her head into Annie's curls. She felt Brad turn the boat in a different direction. They must be near home by now.

The closer they got to the shore, the more shapes began to emerge through the mist. Lights, sounds of people shouting and finally houses, became clearer.

The ruined house - it was the first thing she recognised, tall and menacing at the end of the bay. Wait - was there a light on in the upstairs? But surely the house was empty and everyone was warned not to go there. She peered past Brad to make certain. But then she wasn't certain. There was no light. Had there even been one? And then the vision of that shabby little blue boat, floating all alone out to sea, flashed into her head. Was she completely losing her marbles? Her mind must be playing tricks on her. She was freezing cold so perhaps that was it. Or perhaps it was the guilt of her feelings for Brad? Or maybe it was sheer tiredness making her hallucinate. Whatever it was or was not, she longed to step off that boat and soak in a hot, deep bath.

As the boats approached the beach, they were set upon by an army of anxious parents whose offspring had obviously ventured out for what had been expected to be a glorious day on the water.

'Have you seen a white Dory out there? It's my son and his girlfriend. They went out without a radio.' And, 'Have you come from Shilling Beach? Is there anyone left there?'

'As if we could even see Shilling Beach,' said Justin under his breath, helping Amelia pack clothes into bags. 'And as for going out without a radio, good luck to them.'

'What can I do to help, Brad?' asked Nelle, wishing she knew without having to ask.

'Do you mind holding Dr No while I go for the trailer? I think Ruth had better get the children up to the house.'

'I'll do my best,' she promised, climbing down into the icy water, 'but I don't have a great track record when it comes to holding boats, remember?'

He grinned at her and said: 'I do remember. At least it's only Just In you'll bang into this time.'

'Do you mind? I heard that,' butted in Justin to their left.

Brad helped Ruth off the boat and then carried the two children to the beach. Nelle called 'goodbye' after them and Luke and Annie turned to wave to her.

'Won't be long,' called Brad as he and Amelia disappeared up the beach to fetch their respective vehicles and trailers.

Just as she was finally losing touch with her feet in the freezing water, Brad appeared with his trailer. He backed it into the water towards the boat. Horrified to be given yet further boating responsibility, Nelle was asked to take hold of Justin's Sea Ray, while he gave Brad a hand with the delaunch of Dr No.

At last, she was allowed to climb gratefully into the front of Brad's car, in which he had had the foresight to leave the engine on and the heater running.

When he'd secured Dr No on her trailer and reciprocated with help for Justin's boat, Brad joined Nelle in the welcome privacy of the car. It was the first time they had been alone together since the tent that morning.

'You look frozen.' He rubbed her bare leg.

'I am. Completely,' she admitted.

'I'm really sorry the day ended like that. It happens sometimes, but we're usually more prepared for it than we were today. I thought the weather was going to change tonight.'

'It doesn't matter, and anyway, I've really enjoyed today. It was great to meet your children properly. They're very like you, you know. I think they're lovely.'

'Thanks for that, you didn't need to say it.' He seemed almost embarrassed by her compliment.

'I wanted to.'

He hesitated as if on the brink of several thoughts, but he only said: 'Now what about tonight? Are you going to come back and have something to eat with us?'

She hadn't expected that.

'Brad ... I can't.' Damn protocol! 'You know I'd love to, but I really think I ought to go back and see Jack. I'm ... I'm in a difficult position.'

'I know.'

'Jack wasn't really working today,' she said quietly.

'Don't tell me. He went back to bed to sleep off his hangover, for the second day this week?'

'Something like that. He was really honest with me when we got back from Puffin Island. He told me he felt like death warmed up and just couldn't face going out and drinking more.'

'Mind you, I'm not surprised, judging by the way he looked this morning. But if he's doing something later that you don't want to, and providing it's not awkward for you with him, I just want you to know you could always come over. Ruth wouldn't mind cooking a bit extra.'

'I'm not so sure. I don't think she approves of me,' replied Nelle.

'Rubbish! She's just a different generation from the rest of us. She's like my mother. Take no notice. Besides, there's nothing to disapprove of ... yet.' That smile again.

Nelle couldn't hold herself back that time. All she could see before her was the boy behind the man, and the image she found was craving affection. There was something about him which seemed so lost, so hurt. She put her arms around his neck and kissed him, hoping to goodness that Justin had already taken his boat back to Flora's field.

He kissed her back with all the force of someone who had gone without for far too long, years in fact. In the fading light, they allowed their mounting feelings to flow.

'I have to go, Brad,' she whispered. It was the last thing she felt like doing.

He ran the back of his hand across his mouth: 'I'll drop you at the house.' He put the car into drive.

Brad left her on the beach in front of Flora's house, and after she'd watched him drive away with Dr No, she was about to turn and go to the back door. But she paused for a moment, her attention attracted yet again by the house at the end of the bay. Why was she so drawn towards it? Why her in particular? No-one else seemed bothered by it. She had to get this obsession out of her system. Perhaps the best thing would be to do a little of her own investigating on the pretence of taking Buster for another walk. The thought terrified and intrigued her at the same time, but if she got the chance, she was just going to have to steel herself and do it in order to satisfy her burning curiosity.

Chapter Nine

Friday, August 7th

That chance came, as if by fate, the very next day and she took it.

The front which had swept in with such ferocity the day before was in no hurry to move on. Poor visibility imposed a severe restriction on the day's potential. Boating, and indeed for that matter, golfing, were out of the question.

It was therefore seen as a good day for faffing. Boat admin, beach walking, trips out of town to stock up at the big supermarket and general catching up on lack of sleep. In fact, a day welcomed by everyone except the children, who had already rented all the films they wanted to see from the limited selection at the video shop and were promptly bored.

Flora had asked Jack to run her to the supermarket to do her monthly shop, as she didn't drive. He could hardly refuse. After all, they had already enjoyed almost a week of hospitality under her roof.

Nelle had been invited along too, but she had declined, seeing the opportunity she was looking for and using Buster's clear desire for a walk as an excuse. Besides, she thought it would be good for Jack to spend some time alone with his aunt.

Jack hadn't pushed the shopping trip but he did comment that if she carried on walking Buster so regularly, he might get too used to it. Dog walking apparently wasn't exactly Jack's thing, not on a daily basis anyway, which Nelle thought was a shame for Buster who appeared to put walks well up on his list of life's little highlights.

The previous evening had been considerably toned down socially. Jack, who had re-charged all his batteries during the afternoon, was about the only one in the mood to party. Everyone else was counting the minutes to bedtime. The result was that only the few with any stamina left, which included Justin, Kristian, Juliet and Sandy, joined Jack and Nelle for a low-key chicken in the basket in the pub. It did not include Brad. All were tucked up tightly by midnight.

Zipping up Jack's jacket which she had temporarily adopted, Nelle stepped out into the crisp morning air. How could the weather change so quickly? She could feel the odd tender spot of sunburn, and yet today, it was damp and miserable again.

Jack and Flora had already left and she was glad because somehow, she didn't want anyone to see where she was going. How absurd! She wasn't a criminal and why shouldn't she explore a bit? After all, she'd never been to Rhoslown before and naturally, she was curious to see more of the place. Or was her particular interest in that house natural? Was it plain stupid to set out alone, with the intention of snooping into a building that was clearly unsafe? Nevertheless, she just had to do it.

She set off down the road, Buster investigating smell after smell and leaving tiny drops of his scent on every one. Nelle was deep in thought. It would have been awkward, in fact impossible, for her to have seen Brad the previous evening. She could hardly have said to Jack, 'I'm off round to Brad's for supper. See you later.' She would have had to go into a whole round of explanation of something she had difficulty putting into words in her own head, let alone to Jack. She needed time to think it all over.

The best place to start unravelling the situation, she reasoned, was to examine the facts: after a year, when her hormones had been raging particularly high, she'd met a man, whom she couldn't deny she found attractive, but more importantly, he had found *her* attractive. Whether she'd been giving out such negative signals ever since she'd lost the baby that men had run a mile, she wasn't sure. What was plain however, was that she'd responded eagerly to the attention and the sympathy showered on her by Jack.

She had acted impulsively, agreeing to go on holiday with this new man. Whilst on holiday, she had quickly discovered ... no, perhaps she should be more truthful ... they had independently discovered, that although they liked each other as friends, she had been flattered by his attention and he had used her for sex. She stopped dead in the road ... was that it? Had Jack just used her for sex? How awful! She hadn't let that happen to her ever before. Best to forget that idea.

She continued to analyse the situation. As the

mismatch with Jack was beginning to dawn on her, she had met a good friend of his. This friend's wife was dead and he had two beautiful children to whom she felt inexplicably drawn. From what she'd been told, he had been close to his wife and had not so far been involved in another relationship, although he did appear to be the object of plenty of flirtatious attention.

So what therefore had happened in Nelle's case? Was the attraction all one-sided? Was she imagining it on his part? She forced her mind to picture the encounters with Brad since they had first met the previous Sunday. Had he just taken pity on her because he could see she was an outsider and that she wasn't having that great a time with Jack? But remembering the passion of his embrace in the tent on Puffin Island, that really didn't ring true. There was something more there than pity.

But where did that leave her now? What she probably ought to do was to go back to London and return to work, putting the last three weeks down to more of life's rich experience. But hell, she didn't want to do that! There was something about Brad which made her feel special. *He* made her feel special, by the way he looked at her without the need for words. By the way he touched her and by the way he'd already looked out for her in difficult moments during the week. Why should she turn her back on that? No man had ever made her feel quite the way he did and she liked that feeling.

What about his children? And the nanny, Ruth? She shuddered. Could she ever have a future in his life when his first consideration had to be his children?

And look how far apart they lived. She was getting carried away, thinking about futures with Brad! She hardly knew him and anyway, a grope and a cuddle in a tent hardly added up to any form of future commitment. Perhaps he would just want her for sex too? But somehow, that just didn't seem his style. He could probably have gone around bonking left, right and centre if that was his wont. He would certainly not have been short of admirers.

At the end of the day, it was best to think of it as a holiday fling. The most important thing was to avoid any confrontation or embarrassing situations. She had to remember she had come to Rhoslown with Jack, and sooner or later, if her 'holiday fling' was to continue, she would have to bring the subject up with him and they would need to air a few respective home truths. She would just have to take her chance that she'd read him correctly where his feelings for her were concerned and that a life-long friendship with Brad would not be severed because of her. That was inconceivable.

So lost in her own world was Nelle, that she almost had heart failure when a car horn blasted in her ear. She realised she had strayed into the middle of the road and Buster was heaven only knew where!

To make matters worse, she recognised the car as Brad's, with Ruth sitting in the passenger seat. He pressed the window down as she stepped to the side of the road.

'You were miles away,' he smiled at her, looking relaxed with his hands over the steering wheel.

'Sorry about that.' She looked up shyly.

'What are you up to this morning?' he asked, his eyes huge and questioning.

'I'm just walking Buster - or I was, but I seem to have lost him again. Jack's taken Flora to the supermarket.'

'I saw Buster a moment ago, going into that garden with the three sailing boats on the lawn.'

'Thanks, I'd better go and rescue him. He's probably kindling another romance with some dog there.'

'More than likely. Listen, we're off to Beaumaris to look at castles and museums.' He gave her a look which told her that the trip wasn't entirely his idea. 'We'll probably catch up with you all later, although I think this front'll take a while to move on.'

'OK. I have no idea what the plans are.' She stuck her nose into the car and said to Luke and Annie: 'Have a lovely time in Beaumaris. Hope you like the castle.'

Ruth smiled. 'I'm sure they will, thank you.'

Another car drew up behind Brad.

'See you later, then. Happy walking ... and watch where you're going!'

She sent a smile after him which he caught secretly in his mirror.

Did holiday flings leave you feeling like that, she wondered, as his car disappeared down the high street? It had to be more than that.

Nelle found Buster, much as anticipated, trying to mount a poodle. She yanked him out of the drive, refusing to be responsible for a litter of labrador/poodle crosses. Luckily, no-one was about and so Buster's amorous intentions seemed to have gone unobserved.

Fishing in Jack's pocket, she found a choke lead which she put on him. If she was going to venture where she intended, she preferred the idea of having Buster close to her. Not that he was likely to protect her. He had shown no signs of aggression to date. But why did she feel this inexplicably strange need to be protected? Protected from what?

'Now, my boy, you're going to have to put your love life on hold for five minutes, and what's more, I've had quite enough of you running off. We're going to have a look over here.'

They had come to the end of the village and drawn level with the house, set back from the road a little way. This was as near as she had been to it so far, and close up it looked so sad, so abandoned and so dilapidated.

She forced herself to go on.

'Come with me, Buster.' She pulled the dog through a gap in the low crumbling wall which surrounded the side of the house facing the road. But he wasn't having any of it. He sat down firmly and refused to budge.

'Come along, for crying out loud!' she said more forcefully. She wanted to get in quickly before anyone else she knew came down the road.

She tugged on the lead which wrinkled his skin and fur over his face and made him look pathetic. Added to that, he had an air of 'you must be joking if you think I'm going in there' about him.

The more he pulled back, the more determined she was to go in. She couldn't leave him there. Anyway, with his track record of obedience, he wouldn't stay.

She had no alternative but to go round to his back end and shove him forwards.

'It'll be alright,' she told him, sounding braver than she felt. 'We'll just take a quick peep and then we'll go for lovely walkies down on the beach. Now shift!'

Whether or not he understood that to get what *he* really wanted he had to do what *she* asked first, she couldn't tell, but reluctantly, he allowed himself to be dragged across an overgrown garden towards a porch which had seen much happier days. Humans could be so unreasonable.

Nelle stepped up to the front door. It had once been painted black, but in the passing of time and exposure to the elements, most of the paint had flaked away down to the bare panels of wood. She tried the door handle. It was locked. What did she expect?

She went to one of the windows and peered through the splinters of broken glass. Apart from a couple of tins of blue paint which, surprisingly, looked quite new, the room inside was dingy and empty. Very dark and very empty. Her spine tingled and she said to Buster: 'Let's just take a quick look through the mermaid's gate at the side. The back door might be open.'

Then she halted abruptly in her tracks! What was she talking about, mermaids and a gate at the side? She'd never been round that side of the house. It was the end which faced out to sea and was certainly not visible from the road. What on earth had made her think of mermaids?

With a new urgency, which was not shared by Buster, Nelle marched round the outside of the house, trying to avoid the nettles and brambles which grew unchecked in thick quantities and she turned the corner.

There, standing tall, was what would once have been an impressively ornate iron gate, but it was in a poor state of rusty repair. It was an unusual gate. Once upon a time, it must have been handmade to individual taste. Within the framework of it, she could make out the shape of two mermaids, each holding up a dish, with their tails fanned and curled to opposite sides. It made an immediate impression on her. It was something you would not forget.

It was also something currently designed to keep nosey parkers such as Nelle from trespassing any further, probably for their own safety. A strong padlock forbade anyone to enter.

Well, that was that. Front door locked. Side gate locked. Unless she planned to force entry some other way or risk tearing herself to shreds on the broken window panes, she would have to think of another way to play Sherlock Holmes. Or abandon the idea altogether, which was possibly more sensible.

Far from dragging his heels, once Buster got the message that further exploration of the house had been foiled, he positively sprang into a state of great excitement, reminding Nelle, in case she'd dared to forget, that walkies on the beach was next on the agenda.

Later that afternoon, as the credits of Gone With The Wind rolled up the screen and Nelle realised that the film had made her feel unexpectedly miserable, Jack asked her if she'd like to go to the annual Boat Owners' Association children's barbecue and disco, which was being held in the village hall that evening.

She must have pulled a face without meaning to, because he laughed at her and said: 'Really, it's not as dreadful as it sounds. Everyone'll be there. In fact, there's usually more adults than children.'

Would 'everyone' include Brad?

'Do you want to go?' she asked.

'We usually do.'

Did 'we' mean his friends or did it mean his appointed girlfriend for that particular year? Careful.

'OK then.'

'Good, because I got the tickets this morning,' he told her.

'Did you?'

'Yes. I was so sure you'd want to bop the night away with me and besides, they usually sell out by now.'

She asked: 'Why, is it that popular?'

'It's the social event of the year, sweetheart!'

If it really was the social event of the year, Nelle's first impression when they walked into the hall a little after seven, was that any subsequent events would struggle even for a mention in the Boat Owners' Association annual magazine, a copy of which she'd found in the loo at Flora's house.

Jack had been right. Everyone did seem to be there. She quickly scoured the room for Brad and found him sitting at a table chatting to Camilla, both of them surrounded by their children.

As if drawn by her across a crowded hall, he looked up when she came in and seemed to acknowledge her eyes on him. She couldn't swear to it, but she was certain he winked and then he broke into his famous smile, before returning his attention to Camilla. There was no doubt, he'd seen her.

'Oh, so you both made it, Jack, old boy. Great stuff!' Sandy came up in his beige cords and brogues and went through the usual kissing routine with Nelle.

'Yes. Sorry we're a bit late,' apologised Jack.

'I wouldn't worry. Apparently, Amelia's girls have been slapping on the makeup all day for this and Justin couldn't wait to get them out of the house. It meant we were all queuing as they opened the door. But you haven't missed much. Come and get some of this punch. God knows what's in it, it's like rocket fuel!'

They made their way over to the rickety trestle table which was acting as a bar.

'Hello, darlings! Have you had a super day together?' probed an over made-up Tanya.

Nelle held her tongue.

'My day is all the better for seeing you, sweetie.' Jack responded to Tanya's outstretched flabby arms.

'Hey, watch out, you're crushing Toby's freshly ironed shirt,' she giggled. 'Honestly, I couldn't get into a thing tonight. I think I must've grown during the day.'

'You look stunning as always, Tanya.'

Nelle watched Tanya swoon under Jack's compliments.

'I say, it's a bit of a hoot isn't it? Here we are, taking our child to a children's disco and it's not even born yet!'

'Nothing like starting as you mean to go on.' Jack tried to peel her off him. 'Hi, Brad. Hi, gorgeous,' he greeted Brad and Camilla, who had just come over to join the group.

Further kissing all round.

'How were the castles and the museums?' Nelle asked Brad, who had remained at her shoulder.

'I didn't know you were off sightseeing today,' interrupted Jack, who was next to Nelle on the other side.

'I saw Brad on the road this morning, as we were going for our walk,' explained Nelle quickly.

'Can't bear the roads in August,' said Jack. 'Too much riff raff going far too slowly.'

'They were certainly out in force today,' agreed Brad. 'Took us an hour to get to Beaumaris and then we had to queue to get into everything.'

'Did you have a good time?' Nelle asked Annie, who was dressed in her best sky blue party dress and was clutching her Daddy's hand.

'Yes ... and I got a dinosaur in the shop.'

'Did you?' Nelle laughed and looked at Brad.

'It was what she wanted.' He shrugged his shoulders and smiled easily back at her.

'Here's your drink, Nelle.' Jack passed her a cup of punch, with slices of oranges and lemons floating lifelessly on the top.

The barbecue consisted of rubbery burgers served between soft white baps, with shrivelled coleslaw and greasy chips. Various bowls of green salad looked more inviting.

Nelle was surprised and rather pleased to find that she'd made a hit with Annie. As they lined up for food, Annie begged her Daddy to let them sit on Nelle's table. It was very sweet, if a little embarrassing, but Nelle and Brad did their best to take it in their stride.

Jack collected his food just ahead of Nelle and left her spearing lettuce leaves, promising to find them all a big table.

By the time Brad and Nelle steered the children to Jack's table, he was already tucking into his meal.

'You get better food on 'planes,' he grumbled.

'Don't moan, Jack,' reprimanded Amelia, who had put on her snakeskin jeans for the occasion. 'What did you expect? This isn't your first year and the tickets haven't exactly cost you much.'

'That's right. It isn't the Ritz, you know, old boy' grinned Sandy, biting his burger and causing a blob of tomato sauce to escape gleefully on to his cords. 'Oh hell!'

'Come and sit here, Brad.' Amelia pulled out a chair, making it very difficult for him to go anywhere else.

'Thanks.' He set his plate down and made sure the children had somewhere to sit too.

Nelle took the free seat beside Luke.

'Where's Ruth tonight?' she asked Luke, noticing how much Amelia was already enjoying monopolising Brad.

'Oh, she hates discos. In fact, she hates it when Daddy and I put our music on loud at home too.'

'Not everyone likes loud music, Luke.'

'Ruth's really old. Old people don't like music. Can

you pass the ketchup, please?'

'Sure, here it is. Some old people like music, though.'

'You're not old. Do you like music?'

'Oh yes, Luke. All kinds of music.'

'Annie likes dancing. She wants to be a dancer when she grows up.'

'Does she? What do you want to be when you grow up?'

'A doctor, like my Mum.'

'Your Mum was a doctor?' Nelle had no idea.

'Yes, she was. She was the one who called our boat Dr No.'

'That's a good name.'

'She's dead now.'

'I know, Luke.' Nelle wasn't sure what to say, but somehow, the conversation just flowed naturally.

'She had an accident. I don't remember it. Actually, I don't remember her. She died when I was two.'

'I'm sorry.'

'We've got some pictures of her. There's one in our sitting room at home.'

'I'm sure she'd be very proud of you, Luke.'

'She's in heaven now. At least, that's what Daddy says. Annie thinks she's an angel. Ruth doesn't talk about her much. Nor does Daddy to other people, but he does to us.'

'She must have been very special.'

'Daddy says she was a great doctor. She was a children's doctor. That's what I'm going to be too.'

'I'm sure you'll be very good at it.'

The first record of the evening interrupted them and

thundered out across the room. Lights began to flash on and off.

'I want to dance, Daddy!' Annie was up from her seat in a second.

Amber, Violet and Indigo had already dragged a red-faced John on to the dance floor and were flinging themselves around him, in time to the music.

'That's my boy!' remarked Sandy. 'A chip off the old block at seven. Three birds at a time!'

The others laughed.

'I want Nelle to come and dance too.' Annie was most insistent.

Brad had been forced to his feet.

'Nelle hasn't even finished eating, Annie,' said Brad.

'Doesn't matter,' said Nelle. 'I've had all I want and I'd like to dance with you, Annie.'

That was it! Annie was hardly off the dance floor for the rest of the evening. She wore them all out. She wasn't shy about asking other friends of Brad's to dance with her either. At one point, she even had Jack on the floor. Nelle thought he secretly enjoyed it because he picked her up and danced round the room with her legs straddling his waist. The two of them laughed and laughed together.

'It's great to see Annie having so much fun!' Brad shouted into Nelle's ear, as they sat on the sidelines.

'She's a live wire, isn't she?' observed Nelle.

'She certainly is! She's mad about music and dancing.'

'Luke tells me she gets that from you,' she smiled.

'How about you coming for a dance while my

daughter's occupied?' His hand had strayed to her knee.

'I'd love to.'

Brad led her into the throng of heaving bodies. She could see Justin twirling Amber and Violet who were trying not to fall off their high heels. Amelia was jiving with Indigo, and Camilla was trailing around after Jack, carrying Junior on her hip and towing two-year-old James behind her.

Brad and Nelle were soon dancing as if they were only aware of one another. Although physically apart, their eyes never left each other for long. They danced close, often forced together by the volume of people. He stepped back and looked her up and down. Then he touched her, letting her go and admiring her, then touching her again. She felt sexy. She felt carefree. She loved every minute of it, throwing caution to the wind and responding to his touch. For a split second, she caught Jack's eye across the floor and then he was gone again. She could feel the music control them, beating faster and faster, until they were out of breath and Luke interrupted them: 'Can you get me a drink, Dad?'

They left the dance floor arm in arm, gasping for breath and happy. Brad had one hand on Luke's shoulder.

'Hold on there, I'll get us all a drink.'

Nelle flopped into a seat, knowing she looked horribly red in the face and probably quite sweaty. She prayed her mascara hadn't run everywhere.

'Crikey, you can dance!' Tanya had her arms folded

on the table. 'I thought Brad was good, till I saw you.'

'Sorry, I get carried away on a dance floor.'

'Hey, don't apologise. Go for it, darling! You make a great team. I always feel like I've got two left feet when I dance with Brad.'

It wasn't long before someone had the bright idea of bringing out a karaoke machine. It provided ample opportunity for those who rated themselves as singers and dancers or those who'd had just enough punch to shed their inhibitions, to really let themselves go.

Nelle couldn't remember enjoying herself so much for ages.

When the machine was first set up, of course no-one wanted to volunteer. There was a lot of 'I'll go, if you go,' bandied round the room, and in the end, Justin and Jack were persuaded to start the ball rolling. Actually, it turned out to be the perfect stage for two such professional exhibitionists. Anyone who didn't know them would never have suspected they had high-powered careers back in the City of London.

They opened with Make Me Smile by Steve Harley and Cockney Rebel and, oozing confidence after their first success, followed it up with A Kind of Magic by Queen, during which Justin did a brilliant impersonation of Freddie Mercury, which drew gasps of admiration from all around.

Initially, everyone sat at the tables to watch. Brad and Nelle were together with Luke and Annie on their respective knees. To any outside observer, they must have resembled the perfect family. But they weren't and Nelle was fully aware of it. She was also aware of a few questioning stares aimed in their direction. She was torn between being caught up in the euphoric excitement of a developing relationship and concern about what people might be thinking and saying. Especially Jack. A chat with him was becoming overdue.

Gradually, unable to sit still any longer, everyone got to their feet to support Justin and Jack who were in full swing.

It didn't seem to matter who danced with who. No-one remained with anyone in particular for long and soon Nelle was being twisted by Marcus, breathed on by Jamie, fondled by Sandy, tangoed by Toby and rock 'n' rolled by Kristian until she was in such a spin she had to stop - co-incidentally, near the bar and Brad.

'Where does all that impressive energy come from?' he asked, carrying a flagging Annie.

'I don't know, but I'm sure I'll pay for it tomorrow.'

'Listen, I'm going to take these two home. It's nearly eleven and they should really be in bed.'

'Oh, Dad ...' groaned Luke.

'It's very late, Luke.' He lifted his son's chin. 'The other children have nearly all gone home.' And to Nelle: 'We'll see you tomorrow.' He put his free arm around her and kissed her, not on the cheek but a far more meaningful and secretly passionate kiss on the lips.

Then he was gone, taking his two sleepy children back to their beds and leaving Nelle to watch Jack smooching awkwardly with Tanya on the dance floor.

Chapter Ten

Saturday, August 8th

Nelle found it very hard to sleep. She tried the old sheep-counting routine but quickly lost concentration and soon had no idea how many of the wretched animals had jumped the fence.

The wind howled making the windows rattle. She drew the duvet up round her chin to keep out the cold air which flowed in freely from outside. She drifted into a vivid dream and found herself on a television game show, where she, as the female contestant, had to choose the ideal male contestant. It had been narrowed down to two - with one she would ride slushily off into the sunset, while the other would be pushed backwards into a swimming pool, fully clothed! Surprise, surprise ... the two men left to choose between turned out to be none other than Jack and Brad.

She woke up with a start, sitting bolt upright. That was it! That was definitely it. She had to talk to Jack at once and not leave it a moment longer ...

In the end, she'd made her own way back from the disco the previous evening. After Brad left, the party just didn't seem to be the same for her. Jack had succumbed once again to the temptations of alcohol. Indeed the punch must have been strong because contributing to Nelle's insomnia was a head which felt as if it had been put through a mangle. Jack had appeared to be having the time of his life (once he'd returned Tanya to Toby) with several women hanging off his every word, not to mention parts of his body.

He'd been wonderfully understanding when Nelle had whispered to him that she was about to go home, but he had not offered to escort her. That didn't matter, however, because it gave her the chance to slip back into her own bed, even if she did have to share it with Buster whose loyalties appeared to be shifting with the tide.

Early morning tea ... that would be the way to embark on a conversation with Jack. It would be her best opportunity of capturing his full attention, even if he was still half asleep. She would have to take that chance. If she left it any later, her nerves might get the better of her.

Glancing at her watch and realising it was still only six forty five, she shoved Buster off the end of the bed and trotted down to the kitchen. She took out the cups as quietly as possible because she didn't want to disturb Flora and have to exchange lengthy pleasantries that early in the morning. Besides, she needed to concentrate her mind on just what it was she was going to say to Jack.

All her silent creeping came to nothing when she arrived back upstairs to find Buster scratching on Jack's door and whining pathetically.

'Hey, stop that!' she hissed. 'You're going to blow everything if you get him all cross before I start.'

She tried to push Buster gently aside with her foot, while transferring both cups of tea to one hand and opening the door.

Jack was already awake.

'I wondered what happened to Buster last night. Then I figured if he'd got any sense he'd find sleeping with you a more attractive prospect than sleeping with me, so I didn't bother to look too hard for him.'

'He was already on my bed when I got back and I hadn't the heart to move him,' replied Nelle, setting a cup down next to Jack.

'He's got great taste, my dog. Thanks for the tea, but why the early morning wake up call?' Jack propped himself up on his pillow.

'Couldn't sleep. I think it was because of the wind battering the window.'

'I know what you mean. Bad news is, I think this weather's here to stay for the day, but the good news is that it'll be so hot tomorrow, you'll think you're in the South of France!'

'Can't wait,' she enthused.

'Look, are you going to stand there all morning discussing the weather, or are you going to come in here and get warm? It's bloody freezing in this room. I must get Flora to do something about the heating up here.'

What to do? She *was* freezing and her silk dressing-gown barely covered her knees. However, remembering her mission, she knew she mustn't give Jack the wrong idea. Still, just climbing into bed with someone didn't automatically mean you were about to sleep with them. She would make sure of that.

'Thanks.' She got under the duvet and put her tea on the bedside table so as not to spill it all over the bed and ruin her plan. 'But most people don't have their heating on in the summer,' she told him.

'I know, but most people don't live in Rhoslown. Here, there are several occasions during each summer when you most certainly *do* need the heating on or you completely freeze your bollocks off, if you'll pardon the expression.'

Whether he sensed that she had come in for more than a casual cup of tea, and the signals she was giving off did not invite sex, or whether Jack wanted to get a few things off his own chest, wasn't clear. What was clear, was that he made no attempt at a pass in her direction and indeed, opened the way for her thoughts.

'So, one week on, how are you enjoying Rhoslown?' he asked, turning to face her.

Nelle fiddled with her dressing-gown tie. 'I'm having a great time, thanks.'

'Come on, there's a 'but' in there somewhere. I can tell by your voice.' His eyes seemed to narrow.

'No there isn't,' she laughed, all her rehearsed lines instantly forgotten.

'Yes, there is and I think I know what it is.'

'Well, what then?' She prayed he wasn't going to get too serious on her.

'That I've behaved like a singularly selfish bastard

who has got pissed most evenings and who you think has led you up here on utterly false pretences and you're livid with me.' Thank goodness his face broke into a guilty grin.

After pausing to digest his comments, she replied quietly: 'Really, I wasn't going to say it as bluntly as that. Don't put words into my mouth.'

'But it's true, I haven't been there for you like I probably should've been and I'm sorry.'

'Jack, you only asked me to come on holiday with you. I wasn't exactly expecting a marriage proposal, you know!' she told him.

'Yes, but still, cards on the table, I don't feel too clever about it all right now,' he admitted.

'Let's be honest, seeing as we've got this far. How shall I put it?' She began with a deep breath: 'I don't think we're exactly made for each other, do you?'

'Is that supposed to make me feel better?'

'If you want it to.'

'Does it excuse my behaviour? And why aren't you more angry with me?' he asked suspiciously. For once, Jack was at a loss. Nelle seemed to be holding all the cards.

'Far be it from me to deflate your ego, although I like you a lot, Jack, and I love your company – when I can get it, really I do, but I'm not *in love* with you, strange as that may seem.' She felt brave.

'You're not?' Again, his face creased into a smile and he pretended to be shocked, or was he relieved?

'Come on, I'm sure you wanted to hear that. I've studied you all week, Jack, and you're not nearly ready to settle down or commit yourself to any one person.'

'Settle down ... commit ... you're right, of course. Those are steps I find hard to imagine myself taking. Seriously, I admit I'm not the settling down kind and being totally frank, I think you need more emotional security in your life than I could ever offer you. Sorry, darling, but that's just the way I'm made.'

'I understand that. I know you've got a fantastic circle of friends and they all think you're great. You're very lucky. But then so am I, and I must tell you, it's got a lot to do with you that I've started to realise that just lately.'

'Don't shower too much praise on me. I'm not used to it,' he laughed.

'Will you shut up and just listen to me for a minute?'

'I do love assertive women!' His eyes danced.

'You were very sweet to me that day at Henrietta's. When she called me and invited me down, it was the last thing I wanted to do. But I'm so glad I went because meeting you was the first positive thing to come into my life for over a year. You've helped me to break down barriers that were so tightly round me, it would've taken the entire National Guard to get them down before.'

'Is this really me you're talking about, because I'm hugely impressed already?' he teased.

'Yes, it is. Now listen again. How about us just accepting our friendship for what I think it really is? OK, we've had a fling, but it was never really going to last for long. That's fine by me, honestly, and I hope you feel you've gained a friend out of it to add to your harem.' She took a deep breath.

His hand closed over hers on top of the duvet.

'Sounds like you've got it all worked out, sweetie, but are you sure you're not mad at me?'

'No, I'm not mad at you! Have you been listening to anything I've just said?' She left her hand where it was, under his.

'Yes, I have, and it was beautiful ... apart from the harem bit, but I guess I had that coming.'

'Let me ask you something, and I want you to answer me honestly.' She was in full flow now.

'What?' His face was blank.

'Do you want me to go back home? Am I cramping your style by staying on here?' she asked him.

'Are you what? What do you take me for? Some kind of sex machine? Of course you're not cramping my style! Believe it or not, I like having you around. You're fun and to give you your due, you've slotted in really well down here and believe me, sweetheart, not everyone does. This is experience talking here.'

'I do believe you.' She knew just what he meant and allowed herself to wonder for a second, how differently she might be feeling at that moment if she'd never clapped eyes on Brad.

'I asked you up here for a fixed period of time and unless you desperately want to go, I would love you to stay until next Thursday as planned.'

'OK, then I will, if that's really what you want ... and thanks too for saying that, because for some reason, I don't feel ready to leave. I suppose the break is still doing me good and to tell you the truth, I'm really enjoying myself too!'

'Added to which, Flora has really taken to you and while she's happy, believe me, I'm happy. You're really good with her, you know.'

'I'm not sure I am. All it takes is a little of your time so she gets the chance to talk to someone. Her trouble is she's got no-one around on a regular basis to chat to.'

'But you seem to have her eating out of your hand. Perhaps I should be thinking of settling down and marrying you, after all.' He turned on his side to face her.

'I hope you're joking.' She reached for her teacup.

He continued in a quiet voice: 'Besides, I don't think I'm the only one here who would prefer you to stay.'

Nelle nearly choked on her tea and only just managed to put the cup down in time. She wiped her mouth.

'What are you talking about?' Her heart began to thud.

'Come on, darling, it would take a blind person not to have noticed.' He looked her straight in the face and she found it hard to meet his eyes.

'Notice what?' Why did she have to blush at all the worst possible moments? It always confirmed her guilt.

'Are you going to make me spell it out for you?' he asked.

'I don't know what you mean,' she said quietly.

'Well, all I do know is that I haven't seen him look at any woman, the way he looks at you, since the early days with Jane. I'm talking about Brad, of course.'

Just what had he seen?

'There's really nothing in it,' she said quickly, trying to make light of the situation because she wasn't sure she was ready to talk to Jack about it in any detail. But part of her was relieved in a way, to be able to talk to someone, and who better than a good friend of Brad's? She was also becoming more certain that Jack would prove to be a good friend of hers too.

'That's not the case from where I'm standing.'

'How do you mean?' Where was Jack standing, anyway?

'Last night's disco for one thing. The air was electric when you two hit the dance floor together. And then there was Puffin Island and even back as far as that day on Shilling Beach, the chemistry was becoming obvious.'

'Obvious to who?' The implication of what he was saying was horrifying Nelle.

'Don't look so worried, it's not the topic of local gossip if that's what you're concerned about. It's just that I've been through enough relationships myself to know about chemistry when I see it.'

'I didn't think you had any idea.'

'Well, oh serious face, that just shows how wrong you were. And before you start to feel bad or guilty or anything else where I'm concerned - that is assuming you were about to - relax, we've rather been over that one and I can't think of anything that Brad needs more right now, than a stable relationship. You know? The kind I'm not very good at?'

'Oh Jack, underneath it all, you're a real brick!' She almost felt on top of the world.

'He's had a miserable time since Jane died. What with those two children to bring up and that nanny in charge at home. I can't think of a nicer guy for you and hear me out on this, I also think he'd be pretty damn lucky to have a girl like you around him! In fact, looking at the whole situation, I think I'm due for some credit round here!'

'Hang on a minute, for someone who's so commitment-shy himself, you're certainly trying to pair me off conclusively,' she remarked.

'Not really, more steering you in the right direction. You could do an awful lot worse than Brad.'

She paused again. There was something she had to tell him. It was important to her.

'Jack ...' she began.

'Yes? Why another serious look?'

'I haven't slept with Brad. I wanted you to know that.'

'I hope that wasn't due to fidelity for my benefit. Anyway, if you haven't, I would guess it's only a matter of time. I just assumed that that night on Puffin Island ...'

'I know I shared his tent, initially because you completely failed to bring us anything to sleep in or under and also because I didn't know where on earth you'd disappeared to ...'

'I'd better stop you there and add it to my list of humble apologies. I did bring sleeping-bags though, remember? I wasn't to know Buster would soak them with sea water. Anyway, I don't remember a lot about that night but I do remember Camilla and Sandy having a row and her asking me to go for a walk with her. I swear, the next thing I remember was waking up with a stonking headache on the boat, with her fully-clothed next to me. Hey, you're making me think now. I hope it was only a shoulder I offered her to cry on.' He looked pensive. 'Must've been because Sandy seemed fine the next day. I really am going to stop drinking, you know. Anyway, where were we? I think we were talking about you and not me, if I remember rightly.'

'What did you think when you saw me coming out of Brad's tent in the morning?' She needed to know.

'I thought, the lucky sod, he's had his leg over Nelle!'

'Oh God, I hope other people didn't think that.' Nelle put her hand to her mouth. 'Because he hadn't. He was just ... really, really ... nice.' She blushed.

'Stop worrying about other people. You're both free agents. It's not like either of you are pinching someone else's spouse. It's not some great scandal. Truthfully, I think he needs someone like you. He's probably forgotten what to do with it after all this time.'

'Jack!'

'... and if he has, take it from me, you can show him.'

'You're embarrassing me!'

'Not intentionally.'

'He's a really good listener.' Now the subject was in the open, Nelle felt the need to talk more about Brad.

'What, better than me?' asked Jack, trying to look offended.

'Certainly as good as,' she informed him.

'Have you told him about your baby last year?'

The subject was becoming easier to handle each time it came up. Ghosts were being exorcised.

'Yes, I have,' she admitted.

'Good, because I think he'd be understanding about something like that, being a father himself.'

'Jack, what was Jane like?' she asked suddenly.

'She was small and blonde. In fact, everything you're not because you're tall and dark.'

'Was she outgoing, lively, or was she quiet and reserved?'

'She was quieter than some up here. She was a doctor, you know, and I always felt like she looked on people as potential patients. Rather a professional type really. Not nearly as much fun as you, darling.'

'Don't compare us because this is probably going to amount to absolutely nothing.' She tried to play it down.

'Not judging by your starry-eyed look.'

'But even if something comes of it, it would all be a bit hopeless because of where we both live and Brad having the responsibility of his children to think of.'

'He wouldn't be the first widower and father to have an affair and, as for the distance, I'm sure that could be overcome depending on how much you ended up caring for one another.'

'But how do I find out what he thinks of me? Perhaps this is totally one-sided.' She fished for reassurance.

'Take it from me as someone looking in from the outside, there is nothing one-sided about what I have noticed.'

'But how does one ever bring something like this into the open? I mean it would look like such a mess to everyone else. Here am I, on holiday with you and I meet a friend of yours and fall for him. That's going to make me look like some kind of man-eater.'

'What's more important? What other people who've only just met you think, or what the three people actually involved think?' he asked firmly.

'I suppose you're right, if you put it like that.'

'I am, and taking it a step further, we've already aired our feelings about our relationship, which would seem to pave the way for you and Brad, if that's what you both want. Don't you think I saw this coming when I suggested you go on Brad's boat for the fishing trip on Thursday?'

'And to think I fell for the nursing another hangover story!' she exclaimed.

'Well, there was an element of that too, I have to admit.'

'So, are you saying go ahead and see Brad with your blessing?' Life had such a strange way of working out.

'Absolutely. But mind you still let me take you out for dinner here and there, when we get back to London.'

'You're special, you know that, Jack?' She kissed him lightly on the cheek.

'Hey, watch out or we might end up back-tracking on that relationship of ours.' He put his arm round her and gave her an affectionate hug.

'Can I ask you another thing? Back to the subject of Jane, Sophie told me something when we went riding the other morning. You know that old ruined house at the end of the bay? Well, apparently it used to belong to relatives of Jane's years ago. Did you know that?'

He thought for a moment.

'Come to think of it, I'm sure someone did mention that to me once. Perhaps it's what brought Brad and Jane up here for holidays initially? I'm not really sure. I guess Brad's the best person to ask about that.'

'Maybe you're right.'

'Why the interest in that house anyway?'

'I've absolutely no idea, to tell you the truth. It sits there, looking so run-down and it's in such a prime position on the bay, you'd think someone should live there.'

'Everyone says it's haunted. I wouldn't want to share my house with a ghost, would you?'

'Probably not,' she had to agree.

'You don't sound convinced.'

'It's not that. It's just I always think ghosts must be so lonely and miserable. I mean, all the stories you read say that the reason ghosts are there in the first place is because something tragic happened to them in life and they can't rest in peace.'

'You don't really believe in all that stuff, do you?'

'I think there must be something in it because why else would so many people say they'd seen ghosts and describe them in such detail?'

'You've got me there. Perhaps they're sensationalists seeking attention?' he suggested unconvincingly.

'What, all of them? I doubt it, in some cases, maybe, but it can't be true for them all. Often, historical facts back up specific sightings anyway.'

'My, you have got a thing about this.'

'I know and I'm sorry. I just seem to have a morbid

obsession with the past and I don't know why or where it comes from.'

'In that case, I think you missed your vocation. You should have been an archaeologist or something. Mind you, it's not too late to make a career change.'

'Now you're taking the mickey.' She laughed at him.

'How I love that laugh!' He took back his arm and stretched, before swinging his legs over the side of the bed. 'Well, as we appear to have put the world to rights, how about breakfast?'

'Good idea.' She was famished.

'And then, I think this looks like the perfect day to go musseling down the coast.'

'I don't think I like mussels.' She wrinkled up her nose.

'Doesn't matter. It's the fun of collecting them, not to mention getting the cars stuck in the mud and towing each other out.'

'You're a load of big kids, you lot.'

'Sure are.' He patted his hair down. 'And then it will be back to someone's house to cook them in oodles of garlic butter.'

'Sounds horrible!' She made a face.

'Trust me, you'll love it!'

Nelle preferred to reserve judgement on that.

'You keep telling me to trust you, and my mother once told me never to trust a man with dark brown eyes.'

'I'm sure she was right. What a good job Brad's are blue.'

The sound of Jack's mobile suddenly interrupted them

from across the room.

'I'd better get that and then I'm going to call out on the radio to see who else is awake and on for musseling today.'

Nelle tucked her dressing gown round her and went for a shower. The last thing she heard Jack say was: 'Candy, darling, how simply lovely to hear from you so early on this Saturday morning ...'

Jack would never change and she was glad because she liked him just the way he was.

As the water drummed down on her head and cascaded over her curves, Nelle felt as if a weight had been lifted from her shoulders. Jack had been marvellous, wonderful and far more generous than she'd dared to hope for. Yes, had she had high expectations of a lasting romance with him, she would've been upset by his lack of attention and sensitivity towards her. But as it was, she had come to Rhoslown not really knowing what it was she wanted, and one week on, it was becoming clearer and clearer to her, that she did now know exactly what she wanted and more importantly, who.

Chapter Eleven

Sunday, August 9th

'But when is it time to start making my sandcastle?' whined little Charlie to his mother, who was busy trying to mop up baby Carly's regurgitated breakfast.

'Oh Tanya, I really am sorry about this,' apologised Savannah for the fifth time, frantically wondering how to get tomato ketchup stain out of thick cream shagpile carpet. She ignored her son.

'Don't worry, Savannah,' said Toby. 'I always thought we should've gone for a darker carpet and anyway, I'm sure we'll be clearing up after our own baby before too long.'

Tanya looked secretly furious.

'Mummy ... Mummy ... sandcastle.' Charlie tried again, tugging at her sleeve.

'Once and for all, Charlie, the sandcastle competition is not until lunch time and if you don't stop whingeing, you won't be taking part anyway.' Where the hell was Jamie?

This had the predictable effect of producing loud wails from Charlie, sending Savannah's already high stress factor soaring to boiling point.

Luckily, Brad had just arrived with Luke and Annie

and swiftly came to the rescue. He swept the distraught child up into his arms.

'What's all this then, tiger?'

'Want to make my sandcastle now,' sniffed Charlie, his face deadly serious.

'I'm sure Luke and Annie do too, but if you made it now, the tide might come up and flatten it and then you'd have to do it all over again for the competition.'

Silence from Charlie. That took some thought.

'How about you coming over here and sitting with Luke and Annie and starting off with breakfast? That would help to pass at least a bit of the time until lunch.'

Maybe it was a good idea.

'Thanks, Brad,' said Savannah gratefully, squeezing her cloth into a bucket of soapy water. 'Not the greatest morning so far. Have you seen Jamie?'

'Yes, he's up at the boat field with Jack, who's lost one of the rollers off his trailer and the metal has carved a groove in his hull.'

'Bloody typical! Jamie would have to disappear, just as I've given Kelly the morning off. Still, I suppose I should be glad that Jaws is still working. It is OK, isn't it?'

'Sounded fine when Jamie started her up a few moments ago. Listen, can I get you a coffee?'

'Thanks, but I've already had one.'

Tanya had just noticed Brad and made a beeline for him.

'Brad, darling, I'm so glad you could all make it. Come over here and have some brekkie. Your adorable children can use the kitchen table. Come along, my pets.' The children trotted obcdiently over to the table where they were soon spotted opening all the mini cereal selection boxes and trying a bit of each.

Tanya continued, fluttering her long, curled eyelashes as she spoke: 'The others are through here. Of course Nelle's had to come without Jack because something's happened to his wretched boat. I'm sure he and Jamie'll be along soon. Do help yourself, darling, there's simply masses! Toby's been cooking since eight.'

Brad followed Tanya and the smell of fried food into the dining room where he found several people tucking into bacon, egg, sausage, beans and black pudding. He piled various things except for the black pudding on to a plate and looked around for Nelle.

Several greetings later, he found her in the corner of the room, chatting to Sophie and Annette. He dutifully kissed them all and perched for a moment on the arm of Nelle's chair.

'How did those mussels go down yesterday?' he asked her with a smile.

'Well, put it this way, they did stay down, but I wasn't convinced that they would when I ate them.'

'They're pretty gross if you stop to think what you're eating.' He sawed his sausage in half.

'Now you tell me. Thanks a lot!' She put her hand on his leg and then withdrew it fast in case Sophie noticed. Just having him beside her made her heart pound and her knees turn to jelly. It was important to act casual.

'Jack's boat's got a problem with the hull,' she told him.

'I know, I've just been up there. I'm not sure he's

going to be able to use it as it is. He's talking about trying to get a Sea Ray mechanic up here to check it over, but it is Sunday.'

'Very bad luck about Jack's boat, isn't it?' said Sophie. 'Just as the weather's turned nice again, too.'

'Could happen to any of us,' said Brad.

'I know, only too well!' Sophie spoke from experience.

Justin and Sandy turned from the table to join the conversation.

'We've just been talking about going up the Straits today and over to the mainland for lunch. Would you be on for that, Brad?' asked Justin.

Nelle's heart sank. She didn't want Brad to go off for the day leaving her stranded in Rhoslown because Jack couldn't take his boat out. But then she told herself to get a grip.

'Sounds great to me. The children are doing this sandcastle thing over lunch, but Ruth'll be there with them.'

'Our line of thinking was to go while the children are occupied, although I think we might find Amber and Violet coming with us. Can't exactly see them building sandcastles. Might break their nails,' said Justin.

Oh well, Nelle would simply have to find something else to do. Jack wasn't going to be the greatest company with a hole in the hull of his boat. He'd already snapped at her when she'd suggested leaving it for a while and coming to Toby and Tanya's breakfast party.

'I know, I can get Roxanne to do lunch for all the

children if I leave it out for her,' said Camilla. 'They can come round to our place for the afternoon.'

'Roxanne can do me for lunch anytime,' laughed Justin.

'Steady on, I'm ahead of you in that queue,' announced Sandy.

'Boys, boys, she can hardly even speak English!' Camilla reminded them.

'It's not the lingo we're interested in, dear,' grinned Sandy. 'Anyway, back to Jack, shall we call up the old boy and see what the news is with Octopussy?'

'Might as well,' agreed Justin. 'Take your mind off your au pair.'

'Octopussy, Octopussy, this is Moneypenny ... over.'

The radio crackled and Jamie's voice could be heard back through the airwaves: 'Moneypenny, this is Jaws. Octopussy's in the middle of a delicate operation in his engine ... over.'

'His engine? We thought the problem was with the hull, Jaws. Anyway, we were wondering whether Octopussy was going to be seaworthy today ... over.'

'Judging by the look I've just been given, I think possibly not ... over.'

'I'm very sorry to hear that, Jaws, because we've just made a decision to head on down the Straits for lunch today ... over.'

'Right, I'll pass that to Octopussy. Stand by, Moneypenny ... over.'

A few seconds later, Jack came on the radio.

'Moneypenny, this is Octopussy. The groove in the hull is looking quite deep. I think it may well have to be repaired before she can go out again. I'm going to see if I can get someone to look at it but as it's Sunday, I might have a problem ... over.'

'I'm sorry to hear that you may be forced to be Beached Whale today, Octopussy. Should you decide to come out without your craft, there would be plenty of room for you and the lovely Nelle on Moneypenny ... over.'

'I appreciate the offer, Moneypenny. I'll have to let you know. By the way, how are the provisions looking? We thought we might come round soon ... over.'

'Bun In The Oven's just signalled that she'll have something fresh on for you when you arrive ... over.'

'Then tell Bun In The Oven that Beached Whale has had enough of pratting about with his boat for now and is coming right on over as soon as he possibly can. Out.'

'What a shame,' commented Camilla. 'Let's hope it's not as serious as it sounds.'

Gradually, plates were cleared and people began to drift off to fuel boats or make preparations for both the lunch expedition and the children's sandcastles.

Ruth had appeared at the door but refused to come in, saying she wanted to collect the children to take them to buy flags and other decorations for their sandcastles. She seemed to be taking the competition very seriously.

Nelle said her 'thankyou's' and her 'see you later's', not certain that she would. She wanted to wait for Brad but as he was deep in conversation with Marcus on some boating issue, she thought it a bit too obvious if she hovered and so she stepped outside without him.

'Goodbye, darling,' called Tanya from the doorway. 'I'm sure we'll see you later. Remember, if Jack can't get the boat out, there's always room on ours. Or of course, Brad's'll be empty, if you prefer.'

Tanya definitely suspected something. Who else did?

'I'll be fine, thanks,' smiled Nelle as sweetly as she could manage.

'You must come. It'd be a ghastly shame to miss an outing like this. It's not every day the weather's up to it, as you might have gathered. Anyway, better go and see to the mess inside. 'Bye for now.' She turned, almost tripping over Amelia's Jack Russell who scooted out with a fat sausage hanging out of his little mouth.

Nelle was just going down a footpath between two houses which led to the road, when Brad caught her up. He grabbed her and pulled her into his arms, kissing her with a force which took her by surprise.

'I've wanted to do that since Friday,' he told her once they paused for breath.

'What if someone sees us?' She felt a pang of guilt.

'They won't.' He put his hands on her shoulders and with his head slightly to one side he said: 'Look, I won't have the children today. Why don't you come down to the pub with me if Jack has to stay behind? I can't bear the thought of you stuck here all day.'

'I'm so glad you said that. I've been miserable ever since the idea came up and I thought you'd be out there today and I wouldn't.'

'Come here.' He kissed her again and when she

opened her eyes, the sun behind him shone down directly through his hair and fell warmly on her face.

'Just one thing,' he continued.

'What's that?'

'Please don't take this the wrong way ...'

What was he about to say?

'... I know Jack suggested you came with me the other day, but you know better than me the way things are between you two. Will it be a problem with him?'

'I was going to talk to you about that. I never got the chance yesterday because there were always so many people around.'

'It gets to be a bit of a problem up here sometimes. Anyway, go on, what were you going to say?'

'Jack and I had a big talk yesterday morning.'

'What about?' he asked.

'Well, we both kind of agreed that there was never going to be anything in it for us, beyond good friends.'

'So you both felt the same way?'

'Yes, I think so. I had a pretty good idea that he felt like I did because of the vibes I'd been getting for most of the week.'

'And so you both agreed to leave it as just friends?'

'Yes. He was really sweet, actually.'

'I told you he was a nice guy, as long as you weren't looking for a steady relationship.'

'There's something else we talked about.' She chewed on her lower lip.

'What was that?'

'You.'

'OK, how did that go down?'

She suddenly felt very nervous. She didn't want to say the wrong thing, make assumptions and blow the situation apart. Brad took his hands from her shoulders and shoved them into his pockets.

'He said he'd noticed we'd become quite close and that it was alright as far as he was concerned.'

'I guess I owe him one.'

'He sort of implied that as well!' She giggled nervously.

'Right, that settles it then.' He kissed her on the nose. 'You're coming out with me today and we'll go now and see how Jack's getting on so we can tell him.'

She followed him down the footpath.

'It won't be like rubbing his nose in it, will it?' she worried.

'Not from what you've just told me.'

'No, you're right. He said we had his blessing.'

'Well there you go then.' They had reached the road.

'How's it going, Jack?' called Brad, once they arrived at the field.

Jack's face appeared over the side of the boat. Nelle could see he had on his dirty blue overalls and beads of sweat trickled down his oily face.

'It's difficult to tell. I think there may be more damage than you can see from the outside. I also think I've got a fuel problem. It just wasn't running quite right the other day. I don't think the fuel's getting through properly.'

'How frustrating,' sympathised Brad.

'Yes. I just can't believe I didn't notice the roller'd

come off when I winched her on to the trailer. God knows where it went to. Anyway, I've managed to get someone from ABC Marine over on the mainland to come across but I don't know what time he'll get here. I guess I'm lucky to get him at all today.'

'Just something you don't need.'

'Listen, are you going down the Straits?' asked Jack, wiping his forehead on his sleeve.

'Yes, I planned to,' Brad told him.

'I don't blame you. Rude not to, on a day like this.' He managed a smile. 'But what I wanted to ask you was actually another favour. Would you take Nelle too? I can't think of anything worse than being stuck here all day, in this sun, with a boat that's going nowhere.'

Nelle caught Jack's eye and she knew that although the boat problem was genuine, Jack was working the day to her advantage and she loved him for it. She mouthed a secret 'thanks' from behind Brad.

There was no way the relationships between the three of them were about to come out into words because those had already been discussed enough.

Instead, Brad flicked his eyes northwards and then nodded his head, smiling. 'Yes, of course I will.' He put his arm casually around Nelle's shoulders and added quietly, looking up at the boat standing high on its trailer: 'Thanks, Jack.'

'It's fine. Really, it is,' replied Jack ambiguously.

'Can you throw me a life jacket, Jack?' asked Nelle.

'Yes, hold on, I'll get one.'

He disappeared into the cabin and they heard his

mobile go. He returned after a moment and passed down the jacket.

'Samantha? Is that you?' he said into the 'phone. 'What's that? Dinner when?' He raised his eyebrows and put up his hand, waving after Brad who strode off to fuel Dr No.

The sun beat down, high in the sky. The wind had dropped and the boats bobbed gently in the water, waiting for the off.

Six speed-boats had been launched and Toby was just about to make it seven when Tanya finished levering herself up the rear ladder.

The children on the beach were all thoroughly absorbed in creating castles fit for royalty and hardly seemed to notice their parents sneaking off for a trip without them. Au pairs and nannies hovered offering advice and tried not to get their charges disqualified by assisting too obviously. The competition was seen as very important. Reputations were at stake.

Nelle buckled her life jacket and tried to keep a low profile in Dr No. There had been several offers for her to join other boats, for which she'd been grateful. However, no-one had appeared too surprised when she told them she'd already accepted Brad's offer. After all, he was on his own and she had been seen on his boat the previous Thursday.

'Come on, Tanya,' called Sandy from the helm of Moneypenny. 'I'm getting a thirst on here.'

'Look, darling, you try hauling this thing around with you and see how fast you get about,' replied Tanya, pulling the straps of her life jacket to their maximum length.

'Don't upset my crew,' added Toby. 'We might hold you up even longer.'

Sandy took Moneypenny up alongside Toby's boat which Tanya had aptly named Lovey.

'Are you comfortable and ready now?' asked Sandy, blowing Tanya a kiss.

'I don't know about comfortable, sweetie. Ask me that one again in two months time. As for ready, I'm as ready as I'll ever be.' Then she put up her arm and called to Brad: 'Hi Brad! Well done for bringing Nelle along.'

Brad acknowledged her with a smile and steered Dr No's bow out to sea.

Nelle turned to Brad as they pulled out of the bay. 'Why did Tanya have to say that?'

'Don't take too much notice of her. She thrives on gossip and tends to make it up if she can't find any.'

'But she keeps making comments to me about you. And the other thing I haven't told you, is that she knows where I spent the night on Puffin Island because she saw me come out of your tent.'

'So, she's probably cottoned on to the fact that I find you hugely attractive!' He turned to face her momentarily but she couldn't read his eyes behind his dark glasses.

She hadn't expected him to say that.

'You're making me blush.'

'Really? I thought it was your sun tan.'

She caught sight of the now-familiar ruined house

and it drew her attention away from Brad. As they snaked out of Rhoslown in a flotilla of speed-boats, Nelle could see the mermaid's gate for the first time from the sea. It was wide open. Why was it open now? Who had opened it and what were they doing in the house? She glanced back at Brad. Was she seeing things? She turned again. It was definitely open, but there was no sign of anyone about. She was dying to bring the subject of the house up with Brad but found it difficult to talk about anything to do with his wife. Besides, it wasn't the right moment because he'd just opened up the engine and they started to fly through the water, hair streaming out behind them. She gripped her seat and pushed her feet hard down into the floor. Would she ever feel totally safe on a boat?

The Straits consisted of the strip of water running between the island of Anglesey and the mainland of Wales and the journey to get there lasted about twenty minutes. After a while, they throttled back the engines and the radio banter began in earnest yet again.

'Just In, Just In, this is Moneypenny ... over.' Sandy came across loud and clear.

'Go ahead, Moneypenny ... over,' replied Justin.

'I don't think you've got it all quite there under the hood today, old boy,' teased Sandy.

'I've been having a problem with my fuel this week, Moneypenny, rather like Octopussy, otherwise I would've been creaming past you ... over.'

'I'm sorry to hear about your fuel problem, Just In, and look forward to putting you to the test once you've had a play with your engine ... over.'

'Moneypenny, this is Just In's crew,' came Amelia's voice. 'If Just In spends any more time playing with his engine, he might just find he hasn't got a crew ... over.'

Brad and Nelle laughed. Amelia was on form!

'That's a great shame, Just In,' continued Sandy, 'because I was going to ask him to give me a hand with an oil change later ... over.' Sandy loved to wind Amelia up and she usually bit like a salmon.

'Moneypenny, I think it's about time you learnt to do your own oil change ... over,' suggested Amelia.

'Is that something else they teach you at the boat show, Just In? ... Over,' asked Sandy.

'Moneypenny, this is High Dive ... over,' interrupted Marcus.

'High Dive, how nice to hear from you. I'm sure you're good at oil changes ... over,' said Sandy.

'Can I recommend a Power Boat course, Moneypenny? You'd be amazed what you'd learn ... over.'

'Yes, all right, thank you, High Dive. Now, my crew here is requesting a photograph and was wondering if all boats could oblige? ... Over.'

'Moneypenny, this is Bun In the Oven. Would you like my left side or my right? ... Over,' asked Tanya.

'How about a full frontal fly past, Bun In The Oven? ... Over,' replied Justin for Sandy.

'Anything for you, darling - and we've got plenty of front to offer you, Just In ... over,' replied Tanya.

'Remind me to take you up on your offer at a later

date, Bun In The Oven. This is Just In assuming position. Out.'

Sandy sped ahead of the others, who had all slowed down to listen to the conversation. Moneypenny rose up, on to the plane as she carved a perfect 'V' shape through the thick treacle water. They could see Camilla kneeling on the back seat facing the others, camera in hand.

The remaining six boats spread out across the Straits and began to give chase to Sandy, who was far enough ahead to slow down again.

Camilla clicked away with her camera as the boats advanced upon her. Adrenalin flowed as most people stood up behind their windscreens and waved at Camilla's lens. Even Nelle could feel a surge of excitement as the engines roared and the wind whipped past their faces. On the banks to either side, trees, fields and sometimes houses all merged into one long scene which flowed away from them in the opposite direction.

'Isn't it great?' Brad shouted to her, one hand on the steering wheel and the other on the throttle.

'It's a beautiful feeling,' she told him, smiling at Justin who was level with them on their port side.

Her eyes flicked from boat to boat as they divided to pass the now stationary Moneypenny. Three passed on the port side and three on the starboard. All the while, Camilla continued to shoot her film.

'She should have some good pictures,' said Brad. 'We'll have to get some copies.'

'I think I'll have to have one, just so that when I get

back home I can look at it and reassure myself that all this wasn't just a dream,' laughed Nelle.

'I promise you, you're not dreaming,' he told her, and she really hoped he was right.

They got to the Crabshell Inn a little after one, and as the space on the pontoon was already taken up by a number of boats, they had to moor up side by side and climb from boat to boat.

The sun continued to offer them a welcome contrast from the weather of the previous couple of days and a unanimous decision to eat outside was reached on arrival at the pub.

As there were a number of them, they pulled a few tables together, and once the drinks had been bought and the food ordered, one end of the table launched into in-depth boat talk and the other, into fashion (sunglasses in particular), wandering husbands and other gossip. As none of this really inspired Nelle, she contributed little, listened to a lot and risked several longing looks at Brad, who unfortunately, was not seated as near to her as she would have liked.

Three lagers later, Nelle hatched a plan to escape to the loo where she had a confidence crisis. Perhaps she was wrong to pursue a relationship with Brad after all. Perhaps she didn't fit in with his life and his friends. But then what was more important, him or his friends, she could hear Jack say?

As she was drying her hands under the electric dryer which had the strength of a breath of fresh air, in waltzed Tanya, 'For my tenth pee of the day, darling!'

After she had listened to what Tanya had to say on the subject of Brad, she felt infinitely happier.

'Gosh, it's a jolly sight cooler in here than it is out there,' announced Tanya. 'Being preggers through the summer, what a mistake!' She approached the mirror and started to examine her chin. 'Look at that! That spot's erupted during the morning. Take my advice, sweetie, don't ever get pregnant. It does the most appalling things to your body. Quite unexpected things.'

Nelle tried flicking the water off her hands, determined to forget about her own pregnancy at that moment and certainly not to discuss it there and then with Tanya. It was far too private.

Then Tanya made her stop in her tracks.

'Actually, I'm frightfully glad I caught up with you in here, because there's something I've been utterly bursting to talk to you about.' She pulled at her vest top, trying to stretch it further over her leggings.

'What's that?' Nelle was intrigued. To hell with the dryer, she wiped her hands down her shorts.

'Are you aware ...' she began slowly, in the most maddening fashion of someone withholding a juicy bit of gossip and stringing it out as long as possible in the telling. 'Are you aware, that ... your skipper for the day is madly in love with you?' There ... she grinned triumphantly.

Nelle struggled to remain calm and tried to appear shocked.

'What, you mean Brad?'

'Yes, of course I mean Brad. Who else did you think I

meant, for goodness sake?' she snapped.

'What makes you say that?'

'I can't believe you haven't twigged. Darling, his eyes are all over you like a rash! I honestly don't think he's listened to anything anyone has said to him all through lunch out there. I knew it the minute I first met you outside the supermarket. I was so sure you were with Brad when I saw you two together that I nearly accused you of lying when you said you'd come up with Jack.'

'Jack and I are just good friends,' said Nelle, wishing it didn't sound so horribly corny.

'Where have I heard that before, sweetheart? Anyway, what I wanted to say was that you're simply so lucky to have the two best looking men in the whole village eating right out of your hand.'

'Don't talk rubbish!' Nelle could feel herself getting hotter and redder.

'It's quite definitely true. What makes it all the more remarkable is that Brad's such a catch and no-one seems to have managed it since his wife died four years ago. But it's positively happened now.' Her eyes were gleaming.

'Tanya, you are seriously exaggerating.' Secretly, Nelle was lapping up every word and storing them for private analysis.

'Not a bit. Look, I've been around these boys for quite a long time and I know them well. What I want to know is what you're going to do about it? It's so brilliantly exciting!'

'I wasn't planning to *do* anything. Why, what would you suggest?'

'First of all, you've got to decide which one you want. What a choice! Once you've made that decision, you've got to make it blastingly clear to both, otherwise you'll end up in a sort of awkward threesome. Mind you, that sounds pretty exciting too, come to think of it.'

Little did Tanya know that the course of events had already taken care of that decision for Nelle. Tanya might be perceptive but she was several steps behind.

'I think you've blown this totally out of proportion. I really do,' protested Nelle.

'Gosh, how can you act so casual? I'd be in such a state if I was in your shoes.'

That's just what Nelle was trying not to be.

'I'm not really sure what to say.' Nelle didn't want to give anything away at that stage.

'I know which one I'd go for if it was me.'

Nelle didn't really think she wanted to hear any more. It was all getting a bit out of hand.

'Tanya, I really think you've got this all wrong.'

'Stuff and nonsense! You go out there and see what I mean. You've got them on a plate, I tell you.'

'Look, I don't think you're right for a moment, but can you please keep your thoughts to yourself? It's difficult enough trying to fit into a crowd you hardly know, let alone causing a scandal in the midst of it.'

'Of course. Count on me to be discreet.' Tanya winked at Nelle and put her finger to her nose. 'But you enjoy it while it lasts. Married and pregnant, believe me, that's where the fun ends.'

'Right. I'll have to take your word for it.' Nelle rapidly decided that listening to the girls outside seemed more appealing at that moment than pursuing this subject with Tanya. 'Now, I'd better go back out or they'll think I'm ill or something.'

'Yes, I understand, not to mention lover-boy who'll be missing you like mad!'

Nelle chose to ignore that.

'And please don't forget, if you ever need a little chin-wag, I'm always available,' added Tanya.

'Thanks, I'll bear it in mind.'

Sometime, never.

Mid-way through the afternoon, the seven boats floored their engines and flew out between the marker buoys which indicated the start of the Straits.

The sun laid a golden passageway across the sea, in the direction of Rhoslown. Nelle felt deliriously happy beside Brad and her only regret was that, as usual, there were too many other people around and they couldn't just relax in each other's company and be themselves. They had so much of each other to explore.

The information which Tanya had shared with her in the loo had been welcome, even if it confirmed that other people had begun to notice something going on between Brad and her. If it was to continue, it was inevitable that all would come out into the open and they would have to deal with it. At least they would be able to deal with it together, secure in the knowledge that they had Jack's approval. She tried to put to the back of her mind the nagging fact that she was due to return to London on Thursday with Jack, and that life might get incredibly complicated on a practical level after that.

A short way down the coast, Brad glanced over his shoulder and suddenly swerved Dr No round in a tight circle which immediately wiped the smile off Nelle's face.

'What are you doing? What's wrong?' she asked quickly.

'It's Kristian. Look over there. He's got a problem with Over Hung,' he told her, steering straight for the stricken boat.

Sure enough, Over Hung had stopped and smoke was billowing out of the engine hatch.

'Are they OK?' Nelle had visions of boats exploding, preferably not theirs.

'It's probably just overheated. She's quite an old Jetstar and Kristian's had problems with her before.'

One or two of the other boats had also stopped and Nelle could see them turning to come and investigate the situation.

'Overheating again?' called Brad as he came up alongside Over Hung.

'Yes. One minute we were going fine and the next the temperature gauge rocketed up,' replied Kristian, shrugging his shoulders.

'That's it! You are definitely getting rid of this boat. I'm sick of having to be towed back almost every time we take it out,' stormed Juliet, her dramatically short, asymmetrical black hair making her look really quite fierce.

'We'll give you a tow,' said Brad, getting a rope out.

'What's the matter, bro?' called Justin, who had also

returned to the scene.

'It's this bloody overheating again,' Kristian told him. 'I'm going to have to get it sorted properly this time.'

'Get it sold, more like,' snapped Juliet, standing up with her hands on her hips.

'We'll drag you back in, if you like,' offered Justin.

'It's OK, actually Brad said he would.'

'You did it last time,' Brad reminded Justin.

'Well if you're sure, I think Amber and Violet do want to get back to Rhoslown to preen themselves for some do tonight.'

'That's fine. Ruth'll be with the children. Could you just let her know we'll be back a bit later for me?' said Brad.

'I'll pop round to your house,' promised Amelia. 'Juliet and Nelle, do you want to come back with us?'

'Do go if you want to,' Brad told Nelle. 'We'll be a while getting back.'

Nelle was quite content to be a while with Brad, anywhere.

'No, I'll stay and keep Brad company,' she called over to Amelia. 'But thanks anyway.'

'Well I've had enough of this boat. I'm going back, Kristian.' Juliet was steaming.

In the circumstances, everyone seemed to think that was the best idea.

Juliet clambered across into Just In and the boats turned, one by one speeding off in the direction of Rhoslown, getting smaller and smaller until they became mere dots on the horizon. They left Over Hung and Dr No to slosh about in their wakes.

The rope had been secured to both boats and just before they set off, Brad cracked open some beers and passed one to Nelle and one over to Kristian, who didn't appear to have any on board.

'Thanks, mate,' replied Kristian. 'I'm really sorry to end your afternoon like this.'

Brad looked at Nelle for a split second before he replied: 'It's not a problem. We've got nothing special to rush back for.'

Nelle wasn't worried about Jack and she knew that news of what had happened would filter through to him once the other boats were returned to the field. Besides, everything that was important to her at that moment, was right with her on Dr No.

They couldn't tow Over Hung much faster than a walking pace. Both Brad and Kristian had to steer but other than that, it was a chance to relax and enjoy the sun which still had plenty to offer them.

The flat water was hauntingly quiet and perfectly still, apart from the ripples which ran out to left and right as the boats slithered through it. A few seagulls dared to spy on them but soon left in search of more likely sources of food. One or two boats could be seen in the distance but none came near enough to identify. It was just Brad and Nelle, and a little way behind and out of earshot, Kristian.

Fate worked in mysterious ways.

'We might as well catch some of these rays,' said Brad, stripping off his t-shirt and chucking it on to the back seat.

'It's a beautiful day, isn't it?' commented Nelle,

pulling her shirt off over her head to reveal a low-cut black costume.

'It's certainly beautiful from where I'm sitting,' smiled Brad, admiring Nelle's ample cleavage.

She felt herself colour up as she returned his smile and reached in her bag for her sun cream.

'Do you want any of this on?' she asked him.

'Only if you do it. I hate getting my hands greasy.'

'You probably don't need it because you're brown already but I was always told you burn on a boat from the reflection of the water.'

'Whether or not it's true, I'm looking forward to going through the motions of preventing it,' he grinned at her.

Nelle stood up and squirted a blob of cream into her palm which she mixed into her other palm before taking up her position behind Brad and massaging it into his shoulders.

With both hands, she rubbed gently down one side and then moved slowly across his back to the other side. She had to stop for more cream to fold seductively into his upper arms, before leaning over him and running her fingers down his chest. She lightly kneaded the lotion around his collar bones and slipped further down until she could feel the hairs around his nipples.

He took hold of her arm and pulled gently until her face was level with his and he was able to find her mouth with his own. She could feel herself burning up with desire which was reciprocated by him through the passion of his kiss. Her vulva began to tighten and it took all her self-control not to put her free hand down onto his shorts, where she knew he would be waiting for her. Maybe it was the time, but they both knew it wasn't the place.

'Much more of that and I'd have no choice but to make a dishonest woman of you.' He wiped his forehead.

'Sorry, I got a bit carried away, and I forgot about Kristian too.' Nelle glanced to the boat behind them.

Kristian's attention was taken up by his mobile, into which he was frantically punching numbers. Nelle settled herself back into the passenger seat, but turned it sideways so she was facing Brad.

'Do you think he saw? What would he think?' she asked.

'If he did see, I'm sure he was insanely jealous and will shortly be demanding your services with the sun cream!'

'You're laughing at me.' She squinted as the sun fell across her face.

'Only teasing. But is it such a big deal if he did see anything? I think someone's bound to connect something soon.'

Nelle wondered if she should tell him about her conversation with Tanya and then decided against it because she didn't want to rush things. Everything was happening quickly enough. It was, after all, only that same day that she'd started to be secure about the way Brad felt about her. She didn't want him to think she'd been discussing the two of them behind his back with Tanya.

'They're your friends, Brad. My biggest concern was

Jack and we've covered that.'

'I think they're old enough to cope with the news as and when they find out.'

What exactly was the 'news', Nelle wondered? And what would he say to his children? And Ruth? Did Ruth really have to know too? But there she went again, trying to move too fast.

As if he'd read her thoughts, he startled her by saying: 'I'm not sure whether Ruth has put two and two together yet.'

'Ruth?' She tried to sound casual. 'Will it matter if she does?'

'I doubt it. But she'll probably think I'm having some terribly irresponsible holiday romance and disapprove strongly.' He laughed.

But his words struck an uncertain chord within Nelle and his unintentional flippancy made her nervous. She tucked her toes under his leg on the seat and clasped her knees.

'To tell you the truth, Ruth makes me nervous.'

'Ruth's fine, really she is. She means well, it's just that she can be a bit abrupt sometimes.' He put his hand on her knee, as if offering her reassurance and regretting his words of a moment earlier.

'But it's the way she looks at me,' continued Nelle, not letting it drop.

'She looks at everyone like that, so don't take it personally. I don't think she enjoys the scene up here too much and I can see why. After all, she belongs to the 'old school' of nannies, with different values to our generation. But she's been devoted to our family for years. She was my nanny when I was young and when I had my own children, she seemed the obvious choice for us as we were both working unscheduled hours. I guess she was glad of the job too, as older nannies are rather out of date these days.'

'She certainly does seem very fond of you all,' observed Nelle.

'I guess it goes deeper than just the job. She's been very loyal over the years and has never had her own family to divert her attention.'

He took a swig of beer, before continuing: 'She's been an important part of our lives since Jane died. I probably wouldn't have managed the children without her.'

Nelle wished he hadn't been wearing sun glasses the first time he'd mentioned Jane to her, because she just couldn't read his eyes the way she wanted to at that moment.

'I suppose there was a degree of stability there for you all, as she was already working for you.'

'It was probably slightly less of an upheaval for the children, yes,' agreed Brad. 'But then again, they were very small at the time and have grown up accepting life without their mother around.'

'Do you think they look on Ruth as a mother figure?'

'Inevitably, she fits into that role to an extent because she's the constant female presence around them, but I try to keep Jane's memory alive for them as far as possible.'

'Of course,' agreed Nelle.

'Actually, she treats me like one of the children too

sometimes.' He smiled at her.

'I didn't like to say so,' she told him. 'But perhaps you do need some looking after as well,' she added.

'I don't think many men would say no to that, depending on who was offering of course.' He took her hand.

'Do you worry about the children growing up without a mother?' she asked, hoping she wasn't prying too deeply.

'Yes, of course. Particularly in Annie's case. I think the relationship between a mother and daughter can be so special and sometimes I feel she's been robbed of her birthright. Naturally, I do try to be all things to both of them and in that, I've got no choice. At the age she is now, it's not as difficult as it may be later on.'

'I'm sure you'll cope. There's plenty of time.'

'Thanks for the confidence, but we'll have to see what transpires.' They were interrupted by Brad's ship-to-shore which he'd left on the dashboard.

'Dr No, Dr No, this is Just In. Are you reading me? ... Over.'

Brad reached for his hand set.

'Go ahead, Just In. This is Dr No ... over.'

'Just calling up to see what progress your rescue mission is making ... over.'

Brad looked at Nelle and replied: 'Steady progress confirmed, Just In. Over Hung, scenery, company and beer all doing well here ... over.'

Nelle blushed as she knew he was being deliberately ambiguous.

'Delighted to hear it, Dr No,' came Justin's voice. 'So

you're not too bored or anything? ... Over.'

'Not in the least, Just In. There's plenty to occupy us at the moment, thanks ... over.'

'So I guess you won't be requiring my boat to do a fly past to entertain you? ... Over.'

Brad and Nelle could hear Amelia's agitated voice in the background saying: 'Justin, Justin, don't be ridiculous! The girls want to get back and that's a total waste of fuel.'

'Doesn't sound as if your crew would approve of that, Just In,' said Brad, putting his arm round Nelle, who now perched next to him, leaning against his chest and resting her feet on the passenger seat. 'Besides, we're quite enjoying the quiet ... and the sun ... over.'

'Good for you, Dr No. Would hate to crowd you so we'll just delaunch as planned. The weather seems to be holding out so make the most of it and we'll look forward to catching you later. By the way, if my brother is in earshot, tell him that Juliet's looking forward to riding in his new boat, when he gets it ... over.'

'Just In, he's on the 'phone at the moment, so perhaps she'd better tell him herself when we get back ... over.'

Nelle turned to look at Kristian who raised his beer bottle by way of recognition.

'Probably wise, Dr No. This is Just In ... out.'

Nelle settled herself back, her head against Brad's shoulder while he slowly inched down the coastline back to Rhoslown and they chatted easily together. She felt truly happy and contented, not to mention secure, with his arm draped comfortably around her. If the world had ended there and then, with the two of them drifting gently along in that boat and with Kristian preoccupied behind them, then she couldn't have wished for a better way to go.

But the world didn't end there and then, and the difficulties of trying to weave their developing relationship into their already complicated lives loomed over them like gathering clouds. She tried to prolong that oasis of calm for as long as possible and to enjoy it for what it was. She felt more at peace with her life and with herself than she had in a long time. So much so, that she was totally unprepared for what was about to happen to her in the middle of the night on that same day.

Chapter Twelve

Sunday Night, August 9th

Brad and Nelle had returned to Rhoslown with Kristian shortly before six. There was an enthusiastic welcoming committee waiting for them on the beach in the form of Luke and Annie, who were bursting to tell their father how they had won the sandcastle competition and desperate for him to admire their creation, before it was lost to the threatening tide for ever. Ruth's presence on the beach had made Nelle feel a little edgy, despite what Brad had said about her.

Brad had thrown Nelle an apologetic look once they'd delaunched the boat, when it became clear that his attention for the time being was to be engulfed by his children. That was only right after he'd been away from them for most of the day, and she understood unconditionally that she had to melt into the background for a while.

When she returned to the house, she had found Jack in the garden with Sandy, Camilla and Amelia sipping Pimms and nursing his sun burn which had apparently, been self-induced, as he hadn't bothered to use any sun cream. Nelle soon learnt that Justin was with his parents preparing for their 'open house' drinks party that evening, to which anyone remotely acquainted with the family had been invited.

Jack had been in buoyant party mood all night, determined to make up for lost time as he'd missed out on the day's social activities. He lavished his attention on anything in a skirt, while Nelle hovered, making polite conversation with a number of people she'd never met before, wondering frantically where Brad was and why he hadn't come too.

She had eventually discovered the answer when she overheard Tanya broadcasting to anyone caring to listen, that both Ruth and Annie had been violently sick that evening and wasn't it a shame that Brad had had to miss the party? She even declared that she'd offered to babysit for a bit so Brad could get out, but then realised that the last thing she needed in her delicate condition was 'some vile tummy bug'.

Nelle's mind had started to work overtime at that moment. She wanted to run round to his house and see if she could help, but her feet were rooted to the spot. Damn Ruth, she'd thought. If it hadn't been for her, she wouldn't have hesitated. But something about Ruth made her feel uneasy and she just couldn't face going round that night. She would wait until the morning and then go over.

From then on, Nelle was just waiting for a chance to escape the drinks party, which showed no signs of ending. She'd lost Jack in the throng of people but the truth was that she'd never really had Jack with her since they'd arrived at the party. But she couldn't blame him for that. He didn't owe her anything.

Escape she eventually did, not only from the party, but from the leering advances of a man old enough to be her father, whose wife kept glaring at her across the room. Enough was enough. She'd had a wonderful day with Brad and, even though she had hoped they would have been together in the evening too, circumstances had intervened and she was confident that it would not change the way they felt about each other. Tomorrow was another day.

She had sprinted all the way back to Flora's house, not even sure of why she was in such a hurry. Maybe it was just the desire to get to bed quickly so she could wake up to the excitement of seeing Brad for another precious day. She hadn't bothered to find Jack and she knew it wouldn't occur to him to be worried about her anyway. If he'd stopped to give it any thought at all, he would probably have assumed that she was with Brad. If only ...

She climbed quickly into bed and curled herself up under the duvet. In her mind, she pored over the day - what they had said and what they had done and, most of all, different pictures of Brad drifted into her mind - all of which should have been the perfect recipe for peaceful sleep. But it was not.

'Wake up, wake up.' She could feel someone shaking her with a terrifying urgency. It was dark. So terribly dark. Outside the rain lashed against the windows of the turret and the wind moaned as if in dreadful pain.

She fought the need to wake up. It was so much

easier to bury herself deep in that long, safe tunnel. But she wasn't to be allowed to stay there. Inch by inch, she was being dragged, sucked up and the ghastly realisation that it was all so familiar was gradually beginning to dawn on her. It had definitely happened before. But how many times? And how many times would it go on happening?

'Come on!' It was a command and one she always had to obey. The choice was not hers and never would be.

'You're needed. We're needed ... right now. For God's sake, wake up!'

She was expelled from the tunnel like a ball from a cannon and, once again, there would never be any way to return. This time it was more real than ever before. This time everything she saw, everything she touched and everything she heard was so very vivid, as it had never been before. If only she could try to understand, then perhaps it might not happen any more. And then everything went quiet.

But not for long. There was more shouting. Desperate, urgent shouting. More than one person this time. What did they want of her? Why couldn't they manage without her? Why did she always have to be there too? Why her? What was she doing there at all? She frantically searched her mind for the answers and all the time the shouting and the drumming and the beating of the rain droned on and on. It never stopped. It never gave her a moment's peace.

It was very, very cold. She shivered uncontrollably as she desperately pulled and pulled until her arms ached. She longed for the night to go away, for the day to come and for everyone to leave her alone. But that would never happen, not until they were all safe. But how could they all ever be safe again?

Now the ice was washing over her. It was all around her and she couldn't breathe but she had to find a way. She stretched out, reaching and stretching until she felt she would burst. But it was not enough. It was never enough and she didn't know why. Why, for once, when it kept on happening over and over, could she not have made it right? It wasn't lack of effort because no-one could have tried harder. Once she recognised her role, her well-rehearsed role, she put her body and her soul into it. Perhaps that was the problem. Perhaps she put too much into it and that was why she could never get out of it.

Just when it all seemed utterly hopeless and everything seemed lost, she saw the boat. That wonderful, beautiful blue, serene little boat. For a second all went calm. The storm abated and the shouting reduced to a whisper. Or did it? Was that all in her head too? She struggled to reach the boat. As usual it was empty. It was always empty, but she couldn't get there. Just as she got near, it always seemed further away and she was fading fast. If only she could get to the boat, everything would be alright. It was always alright in the boat. But to her horror, she knew that this time it was different. Even if she got to the boat, it would never be alright again. Everything had changed. Two had become one and one could not survive alone and whatever she tried to do, there was nothing she could do to reverse it.

She still could not remember why it was happening again. She searched desperately for the reason, sensing that if only she knew that, everything could be changed. But it was much, much too late. She was sinking, down, down and no-one even knew. No-one was there to bring her back this time. If only she could find a way to let them know she was there. She had to try, just one more time before it was over. She was soaked to the skin, but that didn't matter. She was more exhausted than she'd ever been, but that didn't matter either. Her head throbbed and she no longer felt as if it was part of her body, but that didn't matter. Her limbs were numb and she knew she was no longer in control of them, but that was only to be expected. And then something did change. She mustered every last ounce of her ever-decreasing strength before that, too, floated away on the water and she screamed! She screamed as if the very life force was being choked from her body. She screamed as if the sound of it would split her in two. She screamed and she screamed and she sobbed and she sobbed ...

'My God, Nelle, what the hell's the matter?' She was being shaken again, but this time, the familiarity was friendly. 'Are you OK? You're wet through!' Jack, dressed only in his boxers, had come flying out of his room at the sound of her screams, followed by Buster with his tail between his legs. Jack thought she was being murdered!

She opened her eyes wide and in the dim light from

the landing, Jack could read the fear through her tears.

She tried to sit up as Jack bent over her, his hands on her arms.

'Hey, there, there, it's OK, darling. It's me, Jack. You're alright.'

'I ... I must have been dreaming.' She began to come to, wiping her eyes on the back of her hand.

'Some dream! I thought at the very least you were being attacked in here.' He sat gently down on the edge of the bed.

Her t-shirt was soaked and clung to her body as beads of sweat trickled down her face.

'Let me get you some water. Hold on there a moment.' Jack went in search of a glass.

Nelle ran her fingers through her hair and forced her eyes to focus on the room. She knew she had been very frightened but could not remember for the life of her, why. No-one had ever told her before that she screamed in her sleep and so she presumed it wasn't a regular occurrence. Sure, she had had her fair share of bad dreams, and quite a few of those since she'd lost the baby, but this was different. This had really been scary.

Jack returned with the water and a face cloth he'd found in the bathroom.

'I thought you might need this too,' he told her, dabbing her face while she clutched the glass.

'Thanks, that's really sweet of you. What time is it?'

'Haven't a clue, sweetheart. I didn't exactly stop to study the clock when I heard you back there.'

'I guess not.' She managed a small, sheepish smile.

‘What was going on in that dream of yours to make you yell out like that? You sounded terrified!’

‘That's just it, I can't remember a thing beyond feeling really frightened. I don't know what happened or why I felt like that. I'm just sorry that I woke you up.’

‘I'm surprised even Flora didn't come bounding up the stairs. You probably woke most of Rhoslown. That's quite a pair of lungs you've got there when you need them.’

‘How awful! I'm really embarrassed.’ She put her hand over her face.

‘Not on my account, I hope. Anyway, I'm just glad I was here to get you out of it or who knows what might've happened.’

‘Jack ... will you do something for me?’ she asked hesitantly.

‘Yes. What is it?’

‘Will you hold me and just talk, for a little while? I'm not sure I can face the dark on my own again yet.’

‘To tell you the truth, I'm so wide awake now that I don't think I could sleep even if I wanted to, and I think I can be trusted. Well, just about anyway. Let me know if I overstep the mark, won't you?’ he teased, as he slid under the duvet and gathered her into his arms.

‘You're really good to me, Jack. I don't know what I would have done without you tonight.’ She lay against his shoulder.

‘I actually didn't know if you were here when I got in. I thought you might be with Brad.’

‘Ruth and Annie both got sick and so he wasn't able to get away and come to the party.’

'Really? I didn't know that. But come to think of it, I didn't see him there tonight. I suppose I just assumed you two love birds had sneaked off together.'

'No, we never got the chance.'

'What made them ill then? Was it something they ate?' he asked her.

'I really don't know. I haven't spoken to Brad since this afternoon. I only heard about it from Tanya.'

'That figures. She would know. Maybe it was the water? People always seem to get sick from the water here. Something to do with the way the sewage is disposed of.'

'Oh, don't! I can't bear to think about it.' Nelle shuddered and added: 'Will you do something else for me?'

'I don't see why not. Might depend on what it is, though.'

'Will you keep it to yourself about my dream? I don't want everyone to think I've gone raving mad, even if I have.'

'What do you take me for? My name isn't Tanya, you know. But you were in quite a bad way when I came in. Do you dream like that often?'

'No. At least, I don't think so. I don't remember it being like that before.'

'Perhaps you ought to look into some kind of 'dream therapy', if such a thing exists.' She couldn't tell if he was being serious and his words brought Brad back into her mind and the 'therapy' they had shared in his tent on Puffin Island.

Jack interrupted her thoughts. 'Were you thinking

about Brad?'

'Was it obvious?'

'Frankly, yes. I recognised that twinkle in your eye. Are you going to tell him about tonight?'

'I don't know. He might go right off me if he thinks I'm some kind of hallucinating lunatic. Would you tell him if you were me?'

'I probably would. I don't think there's much danger of him going off you because of some nightmare. After all, we don't exactly have much control over what we dream, do we?'

'I've often wondered about that. Many times I've been able to tie bits of my dreams into happenings in my life. Only this one seems completely unrelatable.'

'I'm not aware of dreaming much. Probably too damn tired most of the time - or too sozzled.'

She took another sip of water, beginning to feel more together.

'There's something I've been meaning to ask you, Jack, and never quite found the courage.'

'I'm intrigued,' he said.

'This holiday in Rhoslown - I met you two weeks before you were due to come down here, right?'

'I guess that was about it. Why?'

'Well, your infamous reputation where women are concerned leads me to wonder whether you were planning to break with tradition and come here unaccompanied this year, or were you on the lookout for someone to bring when we met and I just happened to fit the bill?'

'Ah ...' He pushed his hair off his forehead and

looked up at the ceiling, as if in search of the best way to deal with such a delicate question. 'The truth?' He met her eyes again.

'I think in the light of everything that's happened here, I can probably handle it, yes.' She braced herself for his reply.

'You remember when we met at Hen's, I mentioned some 'commodities' I had to take care of? Well, the particular one I was referring to was a lady by the name of Claudia. Delightful for a while, but it all got a bit hair-raising when she started walking me past jewellery shops. I got frightfully nervous at that stage, as you can imagine.'

Nelle nodded and thought she could predict what was coming next.

'I can't deny that I had sort of mentioned her coming up to Rhoslown with me, but to be perfectly honest with you, sweetie, I was desperately looking for an 'out'.'

'And is that what I was? Your 'out'?' Nelle pretended, unconvincingly, to be hurt.

'You did just have a teeny bit to do with it, I must admit.'

'So did the fact that you suggested us having dinner on the Wednesday allow you time to put Claudia off first?'

'You're really asking for the details?'

'Not all the details, but I am curious.'

'If you must know, I have learnt to always allow two days for breaking off a relationship.'

'Two days? What for?'

'Well, on the first day you do the dreadful deed and then you need to keep a second day free to allow for any repercussions that might take place before you embark on a new relationship. At least that's the way I play it. All up front and plenty of honesty - usually keeps relative peace.'

'You're impossible, Jack!' Nelle giggled and propped herself up on her elbow so she could see his face more clearly. 'And were there any of these ... repercussions ... in Claudia's case?'

'Luckily, not too many. I'd already made several excuses to avoid seeing her in the previous week and so I only had a couple of tearful 'phone calls to deal with. I think she'd started to get the message. Could've been much worse.'

'No wonder so many women get emotionally destroyed over men, when there are people like you around!'

'Steady on. I did at least put her in the picture. It's not like I was seeing you and her at the same time.'

'Am I supposed to be grateful for that?'

'Yes, and so should she be.'

'And if we'd never met, would you have brought her down here anyway?'

'Oh God, I hope not. She would've been a crashing bore and she'd have hated it! No shops to flash her plastic in. She would have suffered from retail withdrawal symptoms after about two days. The moment I met you, I knew you'd be far more fun.'

'Even though I was miserable that day at Hen's? But poor Claudia,' remarked Nelle. 'How long had you been seeing her?'

'Don't feel too sorry for her. We'd been going out on and off for about two months, which actually isn't bad for me. But she was a bit of a gold digger and besides, she had really smelly feet ...'

'She *what*?!' Nelle couldn't contain herself as they both hooted out loud.

'That's good, to hear you laugh again,' said Jack, giving her an affectionate hug. 'Yeah, her feet became a real problem for me. But changing the subject back to you and Brad, you had a good day today, did you?'

'It was lovely just being with him,' she admitted, trying not to feel guilty for saying it.

'Even when Kristian's boat broke down?'

'Especially when the boat broke down because it gave us a rare chance to talk on our own. For once, I wasn't worrying about other people seeing us together.'

'You worry too much.'

'You said that before, but you're probably right. I just feel so at ease with him, like I've known him for much longer than a week.'

'Perhaps it's the path of true love.'

'You're teasing.'

'No, honestly, I'm not. If anything, perhaps I'm envious. It's a path that seems to have eluded me to date - present company excepted, of course.'

'When you're ready for it, I'm sure you'll meet the right girl.' She felt their roles reversing.

'Yes, but will I ever be ready?'

'Only you can answer that one.'

'Who knows? Anyway, have you talked about where

you two go from here?'

'No, not really. I think we've both been avoiding it, but I'm not looking forward to going back on Thursday.'

'Well, if you both feel the same, you'd better get working something out quickly because the last thing I can stand to think of, is you moping around in London, missing Brad who's moping around up North, missing you! What a waste that would be. Besides, I'd have my work cut out just cheering you up. So will you do me a favour and get round to discussing it? You've got three more days.'

'As you know, it's not that easy to be alone together here,' she replied.

'Don't make that an excuse. Take the bull by the horns and get out there with him tomorrow. The weather's supposed to be great, so make the most of it.'

'What are you going to do about your boat?'

'Oh God, don't worry about me too - you worry enough for the entire village! I'm trying to forget that just as the weather settles for a couple of days, my boat gets a hole in the hull. Besides, I'm going to sod off on to the golf course tomorrow and take it out on the balls. So you see, you'll need to occupy yourself anyway.'

'You have a really weird way of being incredibly nice, Jack!' She reached up and pecked him on the cheek. 'But what if Brad doesn't want to go out with me tomorrow?' she added, as an afterthought.

'There you go again! Of course he will. Every person who has a boat wants it out in good weather. Why else have one?'

'But there's the children, and ... Ruth.'

'I thought you said they were sick?' he said, as if she were inventing problems.

'They are. Or at least Ruth and Annie are.'

'Well, there you go. They probably won't feel like rolling around in a boat in the sun tomorrow. Anyway, try not to think about it too much now. Things have a funny way of working out. Go round to Brad's tomorrow and see how they are and take it from there.'

'I guess you're right.'

'I know I am.'

As they lay there, totally comfortable with their newly-established, platonic friendship, nothing stirred in the house. The distant sound of the sea permeated the window panes and the darkness just went on and on. The morning was still far away.

Soothed by their companionship, they drifted to sleep, heads facing in opposite directions, each with very different thoughts circling their minds.

As the dawn began to break over the horizon, they were rudely awakened by the sound of Jack's mobile 'phone ringing out from his bedroom.

'Who the hell is calling me at this time?' he moaned, extracting his arm from beneath Nelle.

'You won't know till you answer it.' She turned over.

'True, but why on earth did I leave it on through the night?' He sat up on the edge of the bed, his elbows on his knees and his face in his hands, trying hard to focus.

'Don't you always leave it on, just in case?'

'Just in case what?'

'Just in case that all-important lady tries to call.'

'Now you're teasing me.'

'I know.'

'I guess my 'phone's never far away, is it?' He looked round at her.

'Aren't you going to answer it then?' she asked.

'Yes, I am. My head's just busy establishing whether my legs can hold me and then I'll be right there.'

Recent events flooded back into Nelle's mind and she pulled the duvet round her, trying to blot out the fear of the night. Jack stumbled over the corridor, back to his room and she heard him pick up his 'phone and say sleepily: 'Hello? ... Claudia, darling! I've been meaning to call. Sorry you beat me to it ... What? ... Oh, no, dreadful time. Weather's ghastly. Spending all the time on the 'phone to the office as predicted, so good job I came down on my own after all ...'

Nelle chuckled to herself. He really was every woman's nightmare - the truth always dangling conveniently at arm's length. But she couldn't help liking him. Friends like that just didn't grow on trees and now that everything was in the open and their friendship was secured, she felt eternally grateful to Henrietta for having introduced them.

Jack closed his door after that and she heard no more. She didn't want to hear any more. After all, she had no hold over his life. She closed her eyes and started to plan what she would say to Brad when she saw him in the morning. Tomorrow was the first of the three days she had left, and those days would slip away all too fast.

Chapter Thirteen

Monday, August 10th

Bang, bang, bang! Nelle floated up from oblivion to the sound of repeated rapping on the back door. Then she heard a voice which made her leap from her bed and grab her dressing gown, forcing herself to face a day which had already begun several hours earlier. She heard him call her name again.

She took the stairs two at a time, desperate to get there in case he went away again, and not stopping to wonder why Jack or Flora hadn't got there first. Perhaps they had gone out?

She flung open the unlocked door and, without pausing to think, threw her arms around the bewildered figure on the doorstep who was dressed in shorts and a t-shirt.

'Hey,' laughed Brad, when he got the chance to come up for air. 'Have you missed me that much?'

Nelle suddenly became aware that the events of the previous night had not left her looking her best and that, in contrast, Brad was even more desirable than ever.

'Sorry, I'm just really pleased to see you.'

'Don't apologise. It's great to see you too. That's why

I came round. Sorry I didn't make the party last night.'

'I heard about Annie and Ruth being ill. How are they, by the way?'

'Ruth's fine but I think it must be a bug because Luke's woken up with it too this morning.'

'Poor thing. Is there anything I can do? I was planning to come over this morning, only I've just woken up, as you can probably tell ...' She pulled at her hair which badly needed brushing.

'As a matter of fact, there is.' His face creased into a huge smile and she felt herself tingle all over. 'You can take their father away from it all for a bit because if he has to empty one more sick bowl, he might just end up joining them.'

'Oh, yuk! I know what you mean. Anything to oblige, of course. Did you have something particular in mind?' she flirted, narrowing her eyes and looking up at him.

'Actually, I did.'

'And that is ...?'

'I thought that before we got roped into whichever beach expedition is generally being planned for today, we might launch the boat and take off with a bottle of wine. There's something I want to show you.'

'How can I refuse when you put it like that? How soon do you want me ready? Do you want to come in, by the way? I have no idea where Jack is.'

'I think the sooner we go the better. They're all sleeping back at the house and it was Ruth's idea that I get out for a while. She said she'd cope.'

Nelle led the way into the kitchen. 'So she didn't

mind then?'

'Who? Ruth? No she didn't mind a bit.' Then as if to reassure Nelle, he added: 'She really *is* OK, when you get to know her.'

'I know and I'm sure you're right. I'm sorry. Want a coffee? I think I need bump-starting this morning.'

'Don't tempt me!' He grabbed her round the waist and their lips locked.

When she went to the fridge for the milk, she found a note pinned to it by a magnet which looked like a small plastic can of baked beans.

'It's from Jack.' She read it aloud as she stirred the milk into the coffees.

Nelle

Morning, sweetie. Hope you don't mind, but gone to vent boat frustration on golf course with Marcus. Did look in on you, but you were sleeping like a baby! I know Brad'll look after you today. Great day for boating - (lucky sods). Hope you're feeling better now. See you later!

Hugs and kisses ...

Jack

'Thanks for the coffee,' said Brad. 'What did Jack mean about feeling better now? Were you ill too? I hope we haven't passed this thing on to you as well.'

'No, it's nothing like that, honestly, I'm fine. But I'd better go and have a shower if you want to get off soon,' she said, changing the subject quickly. 'Won't be long,' she called over her shoulder as she went towards the stairs, leaving him standing in the kitchen re-reading Jack's note.

When she came out of the bathroom, she found Brad in her room, staring out of the window. He seemed lost in thought and didn't turn round when she came in, rubbing her hair on a towel.

'Great view from here, isn't it?' she observed.

'Sorry?' He spun round, as if she'd pulled him back from some far off place. 'The view? Oh, yes. I hope you didn't mind my coming up. I haven't been upstairs in Flora's house before.'

'No, of course I don't mind. But excuse the mess. I haven't got around to putting anything away for a few days.' She picked up her comb.

'I didn't notice. I was just interested to find out what you could see from up here.'

'You can see that empty old house quite clearly. It's a bit of an eye-sore isn't it?' Her hair was enjoying a subtle fight with the comb.

'Did I tell you that Jane's family originated from Rhoslown and that, apparently, they used to live in that house years ago?'

He took her by surprise and she stopped combing altogether.

'No you didn't, but someone else did. I think it was Sophie. Yes, that's right.' She thought for a moment. 'It was when we went riding last week.'

She could tell they had veered on to a subject that was obviously painful for him, and memories of her own pain were rekindled. Neither pushed the subject of Jane and her family. It was as if they both recognised the need to drop it for the time being.

'Do you want me to bring anything?' She had to break the silence which she found too heavy. It worked because he seemed to close that door and open the next.

'For a start, you need to come here because I haven't kissed you for at least ten minutes ...' To hell with the combing ... '... and now you need to put on some clothes and maybe find your sun glasses and let's go.'

'Where's the boat?'

'It's hitched up on the beach, at the front ... and before you ask, the wine's already on board, chilling nicely.'

'You'll be able to see it from Jack's room then.' She took him across the corridor and even before they went into Jack's room, they knew who was in there from the thud, thudding noise which came from the bed. Buster was delighted to see them, needless to say.

For a reason she didn't feel inclined to discuss with Brad, Nelle was pleased that fate had brought him round to the house and up the stairs, so he could see for himself that she and Jack were not sharing a room. It was important to her that he knew he could trust her and that everything she'd told him about her and Jack being 'just good friends' was true. After all, it was.

They peered out of Jack's windows and saw that predictably, all the 'bunnies' had scurried out of their warrens again, and already boats were being launched left, right and centre.

'Come on.' He took her hand. 'We need some time together and I want to show you something special.'

'Can't wait!' Her heart was racing and her skin prickled with excitement. 'See you, Buster. Sorry you can't come, but I'm sure Jack'll be back soon,' she called.

Buster didn't lift his head, but he followed her out of the room with his big brown eyes and seemed resigned to a long nap on his master's bed. Nothing he wasn't well-used to.

They drove the boat down to the water's edge where they couldn't avoid Amelia and Camilla who stood, toes in the water, looking out to sea with cigarettes in hand.

Nelle felt as if she'd been caught red-handed in the act of sneaking off somewhere, but Brad took the whole thing in his stride. The girls both greeted him with open arms and pink Christian Dior lips, flicking their ash into the sea and holding in their stomachs. Then they noticed Nelle and she got a watered-down version of the same greeting.

'What a fantastic day! Any luck with Jack's boat, Nelle?' asked Amelia.

Nelle thought it was a bit of a loaded question to which she must have already known the answer.

'Not good news, unfortunately. They're going to have to re-seal the hull before he can take it out again and I don't see that happening today.'

'Poor Jack. What hellishly rotten luck! So you're all going out with Brad then, are you?' continued Amelia who was dressed head to foot in Ralph Lauren.

'Jack's gone to work off his frustrations on the golf course,' Brad replied for her.

'That's right,' remembered Camilla. 'He must've gone with Marcus, because Sophie's riding this morning.'

‘Well you two are certainly off out early,’ fished Amelia. ‘Our lot aren't nearly ready to go yet.’

‘I promised Jack I'd teach Nelle to ski, only she doesn't want to do it in the bay,’ said Brad calmly.

Nelle nearly choked and prayed they hadn't noticed.

‘I don't blame you,’ Camilla told her. ‘If I was learning to ski, I'd want to do it as far away from everyone else as possible too.’

Nelle couldn’t imagine Camilla skiing. She looked as if she might disappear under a wave, never to be seen again.

‘You couldn't have a better teacher,’ Amelia informed her, putting her arm round Brad.

‘I know. I've seen him in action,’ answered Nelle, trying to keep up what she sincerely hoped was just a pretence.

‘I don't know what the plan is for us today yet,’ continued Amelia. ‘We've come out for a quick fag. Mind you, we did remember to re-introduce our husbands to their children before we left. Justin and Sandy have made themselves scarce since first thing this morning.’

‘I've left Roxanne making up 'Danish' sandwiches and using virtually every ingredient in the kitchen in the process. God knows what we'll end up with,’ added Camilla.

‘Talking of children, how are yours, Brad? We really missed you last night at the out-laws' drinks do,’ continued Amelia.

Not half as much as I did, thought Nelle.

‘They're not too clever today. That's why we thought

we'd make the best of the sun now, so we can get back and see how they're doing.'

'Good idea. There's nothing worse than being stuck indoors holding a sick bowl when it's hot outside. That's always a job for the au pair in our house.' Amelia made a face and took a long, deliberate drag on her cigarette.

Nelle buried her thoughts behind her fixed smile.

'Anyway,' continued Amelia, 'we'll keep in touch on the radios and you must come and join us when you're tired of skiing.'

Nelle was feeling more and more uncomfortable.

'Sounds good to me. We'll catch you later,' answered Brad, going round the front of the tractor, ready to back the rig into the sea.

'Have a great time, Nelle, and good luck with the skiing,' said Camilla.

'Thanks,' replied Nelle, wishing they were anywhere but there at that moment.

'Yes, you'll have to treat us all to a demonstration later,' added Amelia with a chuckle.

As they pulled out of the bay and Amelia and Camilla's forms shrank on the shoreline, Nelle secured her life jacket and breathed a huge sigh of relief.

'That was a loaded sigh,' remarked Brad, standing at the helm.

'Why did you have to go and tell them you were teaching me to ski? I nearly died when you said that!' She frowned behind her shades.

'It just came to me on the spur of the moment.

Seemed like a good thing to say at the time.'

'Thank God that's all it was,' she answered, relieved.

'Mind you, we could always do it, if you wanted to.' He sucked on his bottom lip.

'What do you think?' she asked, pretending to be indignant.

'I think you'd make a great skier and there will be plenty of time to teach you, but perhaps not today.'

'That's OK then. So what is it that you want to show me out here?'

'Wait and see when we get there. It's a surprise.' He wasn't giving anything away.

'I love surprises! I can't imagine what it is.'

All she knew was that they had turned to the right coming out of the bay and Nelle could feel herself tensing up with anticipation. For just that moment, her life was perfect. She shut her mind to everything except for Brad, his boat and the huge expanse of flat, calm water which they slipped through and spat out in their wake.

She picked up his radio absent-mindedly and put it to her ear.

'Is it switched on?' she asked him.

'No.'

'Shouldn't it be?' She had yet to step into a boat where the radio was not the centre of attention.

'No.'

'But didn't you promise the others you'd keep in touch on the radio, so we'd know where they've gone?'

'Yes, I did, but that was then. This is now and everyone I want to know about is right here on Dr No.'

He patted her on the bottom, as she stood beside him behind the screen, relieved that for once, the radio would not interrupt them.

After a while, she realised he was making for a headland which jutted far out into the sea. She still didn't know why they were going that way, or what he could possibly want to show her. He pulled back the throttle and slowed the pace which enabled them to talk rather than shout. The headland was still a little further on. To the right of them, long empty beaches stretched between jagged rocks and hedged fields disappeared upwards, away from the coast. The occasional farmhouse formed a blot on the landscape while to the left, the sea rolled on to eternity. The only other boat she could see was a long, dark shape on the horizon which she presumed was a tanker.

'Are you sure you're OK?' He broke her train of thought.

'Yes, of course. Why shouldn't I be?'

'It's just Jack's note has been bothering me. What did he mean? Are you having second thoughts about any of this?'

'No, definitely not! I wouldn't be here now if I was. Brad, you've got to believe me, this is the best thing that's happened to me in ... God knows how long. It's really nothing like that at all.'

'Then what is it?' He wasn't going to leave it until he knew.

She realised she'd have to tell him. It wasn't really such a big deal and one thing she'd always hated in relationships was secrets. Secrets blew up into lies and lies usually hurt. Hurt a lot.

'I didn't think I'd mention it because I didn't want you to think I was mad. I just had some kind of nightmare last night and Jack heard me call out.'

'What was it about?' He looked concerned and tucking his hand into the back pocket of her shorts, pulled her on to his knee.

'I really can't remember. Sounds stupid, doesn't it? That's another reason I wasn't going to tell you.'

'Nightmares aren't stupid. They usually happen when you're uptight about something.'

'I've tried to work that one out this morning, but I'm not getting very far. If anything, my life's turned a huge corner recently and there shouldn't be any cause right now for bad dreams.'

'Can you remember anything at all?'

'The only thing I know for sure is that I was totally terrified of something. I woke up screaming and Jack just seemed to be there. He said I'd woken him.'

'I'm glad he was there for you, but I wish it'd been me.' She squeezed his hand. 'No-one should suffer nightmares alone,' he added.

'You sound like you're talking from experience.'

'I've had my share.'

'I suppose I have too, but never like that as far as I'm aware. Heaven knows what brought it on. I felt completely ridiculous afterwards, but Jack was very sweet and understanding.'

'If only I'd made it to that party. The whole evening could have been very different.'

'I know, but it was one of those things. It couldn't be

helped and maybe I had it coming anyway. Let's change the subject,' she said trying to sound bright and cheery. 'You've brought me all the way out here to show me something. We've slowed down and I'm not sure why. Are we getting close?'

He threw her a mischievous look but didn't answer. They were not far from the headland now and the protruding rocks loomed ever closer.

'What are you doing?' she asked puzzled, as he switched off the engine and opened the screen, climbing up on to the nose.

He didn't need to answer because she soon saw him throw out the anchor. Overhead, the occasional seagull squawked and flew on. They were quite alone as the sun beat down and the tiny ripples on the water gently rocked them to and fro.

Once he was sure that the anchor had bitten, he came back to where she was sitting.

'Close your eyes,' he told her, smiling mysteriously.

'Why? What are you going to do?' She could feel her pulse throb.

'You ask too many questions,' he told her, guiding her to the back of the boat which had spun round as it settled on the anchor. 'Sit down here.' He positioned her on her knees at one end of the back seat, facing the rocks, and she could feel him next to her with his arm around her back.

Half of her couldn't wait another second and just had to open her eyes and look, but the other half wanted to keep them shut and savour the moment for ever. No man had ever made her feel so special and so safe, the way Brad made her feel just then. She could hear the water splashing and the occasional gurgle but that was all.

'Now ... open them ...' he ordered triumphantly.

Almost reluctantly, she did as she was told and immediately her face broke out into a huge grin. There, sitting bold as brass on the rock, barely a few metres away from them, was a seal with an adorable face, huge brown eyes and wispy whiskers!

Brad was watching her, gauging her reaction and she felt tears of pleasure prick her eyes.

'He's gorgeous ...' she declared, 'and ... Oh, there goes another one.' She pointed as a second seal rolled out onto a rock. 'Their faces are so sweet. They remind me of Buster!'

'They're not always about but I decided it was worth the gamble to bring you out here.'

'I'm so glad you did. I don't think I've ever seen seals up this close. Not wild ones, anyway. Look how big they are!'

He was touched by her child-like enthusiasm which helped to emphasise everything he knew he was already feeling for her.

'Is this the only place around here you can see them?' she asked, totally fascinated by the wriggling creatures before her.

'I've only seen them here, usually on hot days. That's when they seem to come out of the sea to bask on the rocks.'

'I wish I could take one home! How many do you think there are? Look ... look ...' She almost fell overboard with excitement, as three more heads bobbed in the water.

'I don't know.'

'They seem so tame, so unperturbed by us being here watching them.'

'They must sense we're not going to harm them.'

'How could anyone ever harm something as cute as that?' she asked, outraged.

'Money. Sealskin probably fetches quite a bit on the black market.'

'Well I think it's barbaric! I wish I'd brought my camera. I can feel a whole feature on protecting wildlife in the sea coming on.'

'I'm glad you like them and I'm glad they were here for us.'

'It wouldn't have mattered, you know, if they hadn't been. I would've just had the best time anyway.'

'I was hopeful they would be here and I just didn't feel like coming over with all the other boats too.'

'Might've scared them, having too many of us around.' Then she laughed. 'Oh do look, Brad! That one's flapping around on the rock. I think he's about to dive in.'

She pulled up her knees and leant back against Brad, who sat on the seat behind her. He cradled her with his arms clasped around her front as she sighed and announced: 'This is just perfect! Thank you so much for sharing it with me.'

He entwined their fingers. 'Happy then?'

'Mmn,' she murmured, 'deliriously.'

She looked at the seals once more, lying peacefully in

the sun, opening and closing their eyes and oblivious to the bobbing boat which was no threat to them. She looked down at her fingers, locked securely in Brad's and she knew for sure what she wanted. The time was right. Nothing had been rushed. They had built a foundation upon an acquaintance and now it was time to move on. Time to go a step further. A huge and important step.

She could feel them both stirring and she knew she was ready. She slipped her fingers free but kept hold of his hands which she slowly slid up her shirt and over her breasts until she reached the point where her shirt was unbuttoned. She put his hand inside and started to melt as he felt her breast through her swimsuit, and very soon her nipples responded, aching with anticipation.

She squirmed round to face him and rising to her knees, stripped her shirt over her head and flung it to the front of the boat where it would not be required for a while.

Sitting back down she opened her legs and tucked them round him, as she lifted off his t-shirt and put her arms around his bronzed body. He clasped her face on either side and drew it to his own, burrowing deeper and deeper into her mouth, as their flames of passion were fanned. He pressed her to him and she arched her back, thrusting her head back as he fingered the straps of her costume and pulled them carefully off her shoulders. She looked down on his tousled blond hair as he cupped her breasts with his hands and explored their contours with his tongue. The moisture on her skin felt cold in the warm sea breeze and she stroked his hair and rubbed her hands down his back, bringing them together towards his front and the buttons of his shorts.

The coarse hairs around his tummy button wrapped over her fingers as she fumbled with the buttons, tearing them apart, her breath coming stronger and stronger as he worked his way down her body, pulling her costume as he went.

She could feel him hard and urgent as she reached deeper and he sucked in air through his teeth. He was momentarily paralysed. She slid down the seat, fighting with the remains of her shorts and costume, as she lowered herself under the weight of his mouth on hers.

Unable to contain their need for one another for much longer, she raised her knees and he slid between her legs, finally entering her firmly - but she was more than ready. She gave a little gasp and he covered her mouth, sharing in her pleasure. Their bodies began to move rhythmically and Brad held her tightly as he closed his eyes and pressed further and further inside her. Tears trickled from the corners of her eyes and splashed on to the white seat. She clasped his buttocks, digging her nails into his warm skin.

Their moments in paradise were numbered and each savoured them for as long as they dare, before the climax was finally upon them and they came together in united shudders of ecstasy, their two bodies acting as one.

He collapsed, gasping on top of her and she held him

as his breath came in rapid waves.

'Wow!' he managed after a while. 'You alright?'

She nodded her head, her lips felt totally numb.

He raised himself to his elbows and stroked the hair from her face, smoothing it away and running his forefinger down her nose.

'Why the tears, Nelle?' he asked quietly.

'I don't know,' she whispered, feeling useless.

'You don't have regrets do you?' He frowned in concern.

'Not one,' she assured him, rubbing her eyes. 'I just get like this when I feel emotional.'

'God, you're beautiful!' he said, gazing at her, his hair falling forward and shielding her from the sun.

'I think I'm falling in love with you, Brad,' she told him, her voice barely above a whisper as she forced her lips to form words, with more tears springing from her eyes.

'You're just ... beautiful,' he repeated slowly.

What seemed to Nelle like hours later, but probably wasn't, he suggested they open the wine. It just seemed like a good idea. She put on his t-shirt, which happened to be more at hand than her shirt, and took the glass which he offered her.

'Thanks.'

Brad sprawled himself over one end of the seat and she tucked herself in beside him.

'I can't bear the thought of going home on Thursday,' she began, remembering Jack's advice.

'It's not something I'm exactly looking forward to

either,' he agreed.

'I wish we didn't live so far apart.'

'I know, but we'll just have to work something out because I'm not about to let you drive out of my life when you go back on Thursday.'

'I don't know what we'll be able to sort out.'

'Neither do I, but don't think about it now. We'll take it as it comes. Let's not allow it to spoil today.'

'You're right,' she agreed. 'Today's special. Nothing must spoil that.'

'But I feel I should talk to you about something else.' He suddenly changed his tone and she looked at him, surprised. 'Now that we've come this far, I think it's time I made myself open up to you about Jane. It's a huge chapter in my life which I usually find really hard to talk about, but that's not fair on you now.'

'Brad, you don't have to if you don't want to ...' He didn't let her finish.

'I didn't want to before, but I do now.'

'Well perhaps it might make it easier for you if you were able to talk about her,' she suggested.

'I'm sure you're right. There are a lot of demons that need exorcising before I can really face the fact that she's not here any more. I think that by keeping her inside me all this time, I've found it hard to focus on anyone else. That was, until I met you.' He paused.

'Go on. I think you do need to get it off your chest,' she urged him.

'That's the problem. Talking about her is so damn difficult. It's been far easier to hold it all in. You see, I really miss her, Nelle, all the time ... still ... I miss her voice, her touch, even her smell. I miss her tea in the mornings, I miss her cuddle at night and I miss that awful old Doctor's bag she used to carry everywhere with her ...' He tried a smile.

'When you've had the kind of relationship with someone that I think you must've had with Jane and it's cut dramatically short for whatever reason, I'm sure it takes a lot of getting over. You're so lucky to have had each other. I guess lots of people never find that kind of love.'

'You must've realised you're the first ...' His voice tailed off.

She finished his sentence: '... girl you've made love to since Jane died?'

He nodded.

'It's OK, Brad. We've both got skeletons of different kinds in our closets. I'm just so glad that we had the chance to meet.'

'I haven't been looking for anyone,' he said.

'Maybe you chose me because when you met me, I was in an even bigger emotional mess than you were. Maybe I still am and that's why I'm having nightmares.'

'Part of the reason I wasn't looking for anyone is because ever since Jane died in that road accident, I've always dreaded meeting someone new, someone like you, who hasn't been married before and hasn't any children of her own and having to blurt out the fact ...' He sighed deeply before continuing: 'The fact that I can't have any more children.'

She spun round to face him, digesting the significance of his words rapidly, as he went on: 'I've steered clear of all relationships and of getting involved until now. You see, Jane and I decided that we had enough on our plates with Luke and Annie and I felt that as she'd gone through so much having the children, it was up to me to do my bit and so I had a vasectomy. After Jane died, I was afraid of getting involved again and reaching the part where I have to let someone down with a bump, which is exactly what I've probably just done to you.'

He glanced at her, trying to weigh up her reaction and to his great surprise, he found her smiling intently at him, with fresh floods of tears streaming down her face. But he read the messages wrongly because he said: 'I shouldn't have told you. I shouldn't have led you this far, it's totally unfair on you.'

But she grabbed his hands and forced him to be quiet.

'Will you please shut up and listen to me! Just stop rambling on for a minute and hear what I have to say because now I can say this! I've never been able to before and you've changed all that.'

'What?' It was his turn to look puzzled.

'What I told you in the tent on Puffin Island that night, about losing my baby last year, remember?'

'Yes, what about it?'

'Well, I didn't quite tell you all of it. There's more ... I had some kind of medical complications after the baby was born and they had to operate on me fast, so they told me afterwards, to save my life. The end result of that left me unable to have any more children either.'

'Oh Nelle, how have you coped with that one?' His heart went out to her.

‘I haven't coped at all well until recently. Like you, I haven't felt able to tell anyone.’

‘What, no-one at all?’

‘No-one at all. I didn't think anyone would want me after they knew about that, so I pushed them all away until I met Jack. You see, I was fighting this guilt thing, a feeling of not being worth anything to anyone. Then, through Jack I met you, with two adorable children of your own already, and I've been wanting to tell you, but couldn't find a way until now. I've been praying it wouldn't be such a problem for you, as you already have Luke and Annie.’

‘Of course it's not a problem for me! It's one hell of an enormous relief to be able to bring everything out into the open and not to have to worry about the consequences.’ He held her tightly and gulped his wine.

‘I can't tell you how much better I feel having told you,’ she beamed. ‘It's like removing a vast weight from my mind.’

‘So no more tears then, eh?’ he asked, kissing her tenderly on the mouth.

‘Definitely no more tears,’ she promised, hardly daring to believe all that was happening to her in such a short space of time.

‘Rhoslown's quite a place for different reasons, you know,’ he declared a few moments later out of the blue, as they watched the seals playing in the water not far from the boat. ‘We always used to holiday here even before the children were born. Jane liked coming here because she always said it felt like going back to her roots.'

'I suppose she would feel that if her family originated from here.'

'I think that's why I still come back with the children and rent a house each summer. It helps me to feel I'm keeping them as close to their mother as possible. We've also got a good crowd of friends here, of course, and it's great for all the respective children to meet up and make friends too.'

'How did you meet everyone here in the first place, seeing as they all seem to hail from different parts of the country?'

'Through Jack. Jack knows everyone, everywhere he goes. He's a bit like the Pied Piper in that he seems to collect friends and followers.'

'I had noticed,' she laughed.

'I think most of the others come here mainly for social reasons and because the boating is good, providing of course, you get the weather. But I would say that on the whole, my reasons are a bit different.'

'I'm not sure I could keep up with the social pace of life here, year after year,' remarked Nelle.

'You learn to adapt. They're all really nice people, individually especially, but I do recognise how cliquey the group can be when we're all together and it can become a bit stifling at times.'

'Hence the need to escape like this every so often?'

'Exactly. Except that in this particular case, I had other motives than just escape on my mind.' He kissed her again.

'I know what you mean about crowds becoming all too much,' she continued, after a pause, 'but I agree that everyone up here is very friendly. I've also learnt never to criticise friends because it always ends up back in your face in no time at all.'

'Really? I can't imagine someone as nice as you criticising anyone,' he teased.

'You'd be surprised,' she assured him. 'We all say and do things we're not particularly proud of.'

One and a half bottles of wine later, Brad reluctantly checked his watch. Neither felt like going back and both could have soaked up the sun, and each other, quite happily for the rest of the day, but duty called. Duty in the form of two sick children and their nanny.

Tan topped up, Brad hauled in the anchor and turned the boat around so they were heading in the right direction.

'Do you want to come up to the house with me when we get back?' Brad called to her, over the roar of the engine.

The wind tugged at her hair and she held tightly on to her seat. She nodded. 'Sure.'

'I don't want you to catch anything, though,' he shouted.

'I wasn't planning on catching anything. I think I've already caught everything I want,' she replied and he smiled back at her. 'Besides, I might be able to help.'

'Jack'll probably be still up at the golf club.'

'He'll be fine. He told me to come out with you today as you know, so he'll have an idea of where I am.'

‘We might have to play it by ear as to whether we can get out on the water again today. It'll depend on how the children are.’

‘I totally understand. Let's take it as it comes.’

‘I thought that was my phrase!’

‘I just pinched it. Hope you don't mind.’

It was early afternoon by the time they delaunched the boat and pulled it dripping from the sea. Slimy green clumps of seaweed hung off the trailer and Brad decided to leave the boat on the beach, hitched to the tractor, in case they were able to use it again that day.

They walked hand in hand across the warm sand, towards Brad's beach house. Part of Nelle felt wary of this public display of their growing affection for one another, but Brad seemed very at ease with it and so, she reasoned, she should try to be as well. So far, they hadn't met anyone they recognised.

Families sprawled across the beach, some behind the privacy of stripy wind-breaks. Sopping wet costumes were draped over posts, and lobster-skinned, freckle-faced individuals slumped in ageing deck chairs and pretended to look comfortable. Naked children munched their way through sandy sandwiches, watched over closely by drooling dogs and anxious parents with sun creams and sun hats. Both were waiting to pounce.

Defeated windsurfers lolled on their boards in skin-tight rubber suits, just in case the weather broke and they were able to get out on the water. In the middle of the beach, an energetic game of volleyball was underway, with enthusiastic youths leaping high into the air and trying not to land in the dog dirt which no-one was owning up to responsibility for.

As they approached the house, Nelle looked up at the first floor windows and her attention was immediately caught by the face which stared down at them. Partly hidden behind a fading velvet curtain, for a fleeting second, Nelle knew that she had seen Ruth watching them. She also knew that Ruth had a pair of binoculars in her hand. How long had she been there? What had she been looking for? Had she been just generally watching the activities on the beach and the comings and goings of the boats on the sea, or was there another reason for her staring out of the window, with such a fixed and distant look?

Nelle decided that whatever Brad said about Ruth and however much he tried to reassure her, Ruth would always slightly unnerve her. But Brad had other things on his mind as he strode purposefully towards the garden gate, still holding her hand. She didn't think he'd seen Ruth, or at least he didn't mention it if he had. She decided it wasn't her place to mention it either. They would see her in person, soon enough.

As she passed in front of Brad, through the gate which he held open for her, she sighed a private sigh. The vision of those wonderful seals, which part of her would always thank for bringing Brad and her finally together, crossed her mind. Their little faces, their playfulness and their peacefulness had all made a lasting impression on her. She envied their free spirits and wondered if her life would ever mirror theirs. Would all the complications which continued to surround her ever truly be ironed out?

For now, she could only follow her own advice and take everything as it came. Time would tell, for after all, destiny ultimately takes its course in life and what will be, will be.

Chapter Fourteen

Tuesday, August 11th

'But I'm so out of practice!' protested Nelle weakly, when Brad told her how he'd arranged for them to play tennis with Sandy and Sophie in less than ten minutes time.

'Doesn't matter,' he assured her. 'We're probably all a bit rusty.'

'Bet you're not,' butted in Jack, taking a break from playing James Bond on Luke's Game Boy. 'I've never noticed anything rusty about your tennis before.'

'There you are!' Nelle seized the point. 'Why don't you play instead of me ... please Jack?' she begged.

'Not today, darling, if you don't mind. I think Marcus's invitation to Bloody Marys at his house is more up my street.'

Brad stood up from the window-seat in Flora's kitchen and said: 'Come on, we need to make a move. Have you got the right kind of shoes, Nelle?'

'I suppose I'll have to find some if I'm not going to be able to get out of this ...'

'Which you're not,' interrupted Brad, winking at Jack over Nelle's shoulder.

'Don't forget you promised to pay me to ball boy for

you, Dad,' reminded Luke, zipping up his Game Boy case.

'You've recovered pretty fast, haven't you?' Brad pointed out.

'You promised ...' repeated Luke.

'I know, I know.'

'Quite the little businessman already, isn't he?' observed Jack.

To which, Brad just raised his eyebrows.

'Well, shoes it is.' Nelle resigned herself to looking a complete idiot in precisely five minutes time, and went upstairs.

'I don't know what you were worried about,' grinned Brad as Nelle smashed another lob, cross court, which landed on the base line, just out of Sandy's reach.

'I guess it's come back to me,' she admitted, starting to relax and enjoy the game.

'I say, it was a great night down the Straits last night, wasn't it?' commented Sandy, stooping to flick a ball on to his racquet.

'We were lucky that the weather held out for us,' agreed Sophie. 'We certainly couldn't do it again today, now that that wretched wind's got up again.'

Nelle presumed that the white sun visor Sophie wore was designed more to keep her greying hair from flopping over her eyes, as there was a distinct lack of any sun around.

'Set to get worse as well, judging by the forecast I heard this morning,' continued Sandy, panting a little from the exercise his body clearly wasn't used to.

'I thought we'd do supper round at our place tonight,' said Sophie, taking a ball from Luke and tucking it into her knickers. 'Nothing elaborate, just a lasagne or something.'

'Great idea, Soph!' enthused Sandy, who was always keen to party. 'Count us in.'

'OK, will do. You two'll come, won't you Brad?' she asked, stretching for a spinning ball.

Brad glanced at Nelle and without pausing, he replied: 'Sure, we'd love to. Thanks.'

'That's settled then,' decided Sophie. 'I'll tell the others. Could you mention it to Jack for me?'

In a very short space of time, it seemed to Nelle, word had spread that she and Brad were becoming an 'item' - what a ghastly expression! Acceptance of them was seemingly infectious, but she couldn't help having doubts about the way a certain few might be viewing the idea. She found it hard to tell if people were gossiping about them, but one thing was certain, if they were, it wasn't blatantly obvious. Thanks for most of that had to lie firmly at Jack's door. He'd been a real brick! He made no attempt to conceal his seal of approval of them and had gone out of his way to see that she and Brad had sat together at dinner the previous night, without making an issue of it. He'd also hitched a lift with Justin, enabling Brad and Nelle to go alone together in Dr No.

On the way back from the Straits, Brad and Nelle had reached the difficult decision to go their separate ways for the night, only for the sake of the children. The last thing Nelle wanted to do was to force her way into their lives and they both recognised the need to let Luke and Annie in on the relationship gently. Finding her in Brad's bed with very little prior warning would hardly have been subtle. Besides, Nelle felt awkward about the idea of sharing Brad's bed under the same roof as Ruth, but that was something she would have to overcome if things were to continue.

'Shot, Nelle,' praised Sandy as he dived for and missed her cross court return. 'You've got a lot of power in that right arm of yours.'

'And to think she was trying to get out of playing,' Brad told them. 'Remind me not to partner anyone else in future.'

That was something Nelle had no intention of letting him do.

'It's a fluke, really it is. I honestly can't remember the last time I played.'

'Dad, I'm bored and it's starting to rain,' wailed Luke from the edge of the court.

'He's right,' agreed Sophie. 'Looking up there, I think we're in for a downpour.'

'Best get back before it happens,' said Sandy. 'I hope those boys haven't finished the Bloody Mary by the time we get there.'

'Not much chance of that, Sandy,' Sophie told him, putting her racquet into its case to protect it from the gathering rain. 'Marcus was mixing enough for an army when I left.'

'That's what we like to hear,' chuckled Sandy, happy to move on from the tennis.

The afternoon dissolved into an alcoholic haze of videos and sleep. All ideas of giving up drinking and smoking were forgotten by those whose intentions had previously been strong. The rain drizzled on ceaselessly and no-one felt particularly inclined to venture out into it, preferring to continue to accept the warm hospitality offered by Marcus and Sophie.

Brad had a pang of conscience over the children about mid-way through the afternoon and he and Nelle went off to entertain them with several games of junior Monopoly. It wasn't the easiest game to play because Luke cheated like mad and Annie cried every time she had to spend any of her money. That probably had a bit to do with the fact that she was still recovering from her tummy bug and had so far refused to eat anything except for fruity ice-pops.

Nelle didn't care. She found herself fitting in happily with Brad's children and loved that feeling. They seemed to accept her as a friend of their father's, asking no awkward questions and treating her as if they had known her for years.

Brad felt himself knot up inside as he watched Annie climb on to Nelle's knee and giggle gleefully when Nelle tickled her. He enjoyed seeing Nelle on the floor surrounded by chipped wax crayons and colouring books, helping the children with their pictures. She seemed so natural and carefree, and he thought again, how cruel life could be and what a wonderful mother she would have made, had her baby lived.

Ruth had been given the rest of the afternoon off, once Brad and Nelle returned home.

Nelle stayed on at Brad's house and helped him with bath time. This involved Brad getting into the bath with both the children and the majority of the water ending up on the floor. Nelle had wondered if it ought to have been a private time for him to be with his children and whether she should go home, but when she mentioned it to him, he seemed keen for her to stay. No doors were closed, no barriers were put up and still no questions were asked. Nelle sat on the end of the bath while three naked bodies blew bubbles, squirted water and laughed until they ached.

Finally, with only half an hour to go until they were expected at Sophie and Marcus's, Nelle told Brad that she really had to get back to change before supper. She still wore the skirt which she'd played tennis in and she was in desperate need of a shower.

She said 'good night' to Luke and Annie who, rather egged on by each other, both insisted on hugs and kisses. Brad interrupted the story he was reading to them and followed her to the door.

'I'll see you there, shall I?' she asked.

'OK. In about half an hour?'

'I think I can make myself presentable in that time.'

'You don't have to go anywhere to make yourself presentable for me.' He took her in his arms on the doorstep. 'Listen, thanks for everything with the children today. They've really taken to you, you know.'

'They're lovely! A real credit to you,' she replied. 'I've enjoyed myself. Children are much more accepting than adults.' She didn't quite know why she said that, because she wasn't aware of any of the adults giving them a hard time.

'Will you come back here tonight?' he asked her softly.

'What, after the party you mean?'

'Yes.'

'Do you think I should? What about the children though?'

'I'd really like you to.'

'I'd really like to too, especially as Thursday's looming over us.'

It was as if he was about to say something else and then he thought better of it, because he simply kissed her and said: 'See you in a bit.'

She tried to go back via the beach but the weather had taken a turn for the worse and having battled with the wind for a short distance, she veered left and opted for the road route. The sky was starting to darken and the tide was creeping ominously up the beach.

When Nelle got to the party a while later, it appeared to her that some of the men hadn't distinguished between the afternoon and the evening and had simply allowed the two to merge. Jack was one of them. Poor Sophie had had to do the cooking, top up the drinks, lay the table and prepare to entertain while stepping over bodies and listening to guns blaring and people shouting on the television. Nelle thought she was a saint-in-the-making, and immediately offered to do the salad for her when she caught sight of the ingredients sitting idly on the kitchen table.

'Nelle, you're a darling! Thanks for doing that. I've

no idea how many we're catering for because Marcus seems to have forgotten who he's asked and who he hasn't,' she announced calmly.

Nelle admired her unflappable nature and wished she could sometimes be more like Sophie in that respect.

'I think you're marvellous having everyone round this evening when some of them have been here all day too,' Nelle told her.

'It's not really a problem. At least I'm past the stage of having young children to worry about.' She spooned some dips into ramekins and emptied a box of Pringles into a bowl, taking the chaos around her in her stride. 'Talking of children, are Luke and Annie over their bug now? I saw you two leave early this afternoon and hoped it wasn't because of the children being ill.'

Nelle found it strange listening to Brad and her being referred to as 'you two', but she was getting to like the idea more and more.

'They're much better, thanks. Luke was fine this morning and Annie will be OK by tomorrow, I'm sure. She just needs to get back into eating again.'

'That's good. Tell me, are you going to have time to fit in another ride this week?'

'Probably not, to be honest. I have to get back to London on Thursday. Sorry about that.'

'Never mind. There's always next year.'

Was everyone assuming Nelle would be returning next year?

Most of Jack's friends turned up for the party, with the exception of Kristian and Juliet. Whether they fell in the Marcus 'forgetting to ask' category or whether they were busy elsewhere, didn't quite become clear to Nelle for a bit.

The party seemed to be going with a swing. Sophie had put together just about every table she could find in the house and people were perched on everything from bathroom stools to small step-ladders, but no-one really cared. The wine flowed, the talking and the laughter rose above the howl of the wind outside, and several of them shared cutlery, which was in short supply.

Nelle was glad to have Brad on one side of her, while on the other, Sandy kept her amused with tales of some of the extraordinary characters he'd encountered while trying to sell houses. There were times when Nelle wasn't entirely sure whose hand was on her knee and whose feet were rubbing up and down her calf. She wanted to believe it was only Brad, but she had her doubts and decided it was best not to think about it too much.

The table was littered with dirty plates, an assortment of glasses and shreds of paper napkins. Sandy was just asking Marcus when he was going to produce the port and said that if he didn't actually have any, then he, Sandy, had a good selection at his house, when they heard a loud knock on the front door.

Before anyone had a chance to answer it, the door flew open and Kristian stumbled in, followed by Juliet, both doing admirable impersonations of drowned rats. However, it became apparent straight away, that this was not a social call and something was badly amiss.

'Hey, you guys, you're wanted down on the beach

right now. There's a phenomenal tide tonight and all the sailing boats are getting washed away. They need every hand they can get down there,' Kristian told them, drying his unshaven face on a napkin.

Nelle knew that most people who sailed in Rhoslown (and there were a large number of those each August) who did not own their own garden, parked their boats at the top of the beach. At that time of the year, normally tides were not a threat and although vandals did strike from time to time, many people found it the most convenient place to leave their boats.

Very quickly, Nelle had learnt that for any faults her new friends might have, one thing they were all very expert at was rallying round in a crisis.

Dinner was abandoned as everyone leapt to their feet. They pulled on jackets and fleeces and rushed to the door. Nelle thought she ought to follow suit, although she wasn't entirely sure how much use she'd be at saving stricken boats. Luckily, she'd come out in Jack's waterproof jacket, which she now grabbed and followed the general flow through the door and in the direction of the beach.

Brad waited for her, the rain already plastering his hair to his face.

'You sure you want to come?' he asked her.

'Yes, of course. If I can help, I will,' she called through the darkness.

'OK, stick close to me then. Come on.' He pulled her by the hand and they ran across the road, trying to shield their faces from the driving rain.

Once they got down to the beach, they found scenes

of chaos. Some people had torches. A couple of others had managed to park their Range Rovers on front lawns and had switched on their headlights to help with the rescue operation. One of the main problems was that it was so incredibly dark ... and then there was the water.

Nelle took off her shoes and followed Brad barefoot on to the sand. Very soon, she was ankle-deep in icy sea water which bit into her skin and numbed her toes.

All around them, people were panicking and screaming: 'Help me with this one,' or 'That one's stuck fast!'

Boats collided into each other as the sea rose up and vented its anger on the townspeople. Sounds of wood splitting, metal clanking, masts creaking and people yelling were carried on the wind which whistled into every nook and cranny.

Overhead, the sky exploded into bright, jagged lines of light and for a moment, everything around Nelle became clearly visible. Then, like the sound of bombs being detonated, the thunder crashed over them, as if it would divide the earth in two.

Beside her, Brad was called to help drag to safety a fishing boat which was keeling over at an alarming angle. Just as she was about to go with him, a voice a little further up the beach shouted at her: 'Can you come and secure this one to that metal ring for me, love, while I fetch another?' It was an older man, someone she had never seen before, but in an emergency, everyone becomes a friend. She hurried over to assist, stubbing her toe on a small rock and tripping over a rope she just hadn't been able to see.

She would worry about the pain later.

When she'd tied the tightest knot her freezing hands were capable of, she turned to look for Brad, only to find he was no longer there. He must have been drafted in to help with another boat, because the fishing boat had been successfully hauled on to a lawn.

'Hi, Nelle!' She turned to find Jack and Buster wading through the knee-high water towards her. 'You're shivering. Go back, there are plenty of us here and just between you, me and the wind, I think everyone is over-reacting somewhat.'

'Yes, but all these boats ...' she began. 'They're everywhere ...'

It was true. There were still a good number of boats which were floating in all directions, being tossed by the tide like peas in a can.

'Where's Brad?' asked Jack.

'I don't know. He's here somewhere.' She looked around again but the noise was deafening and she couldn't make out anyone she recognised in the darkness.

'Why don't you at least go back to our house and put something warmer on? You're wet through,' Jack urged her.

'So are you.' She looked down at his cords which he'd rolled up to his knees and then she felt a pang of guilt when she remembered she was wearing his waterproof. 'Do you want your jacket back?'

'No thanks, I'm fine. Go back along the beach to Flora's and I'll find Brad and let him know where you are. We'll come and get you once this madness is over.'

Her teeth were chattering and a searing pain shot up her leg from her ankle. She realised that she'd probably twisted it when she tripped over the rope.

'OK,' she agreed, trying to feel her fingers and toes. 'I'll go and wait for you there.'

'Good girl. Oh, and could you take Buster back for me too? He's getting in the way.'

'Of course. Come on, Buster. See you in a bit, Jack.'

She pulled the jacket collar tightly round her neck and stumbled down the beach in the direction of Flora's house. She had to weave her way round bobbing boats and anxious rescuers and all the while, the thunder clapped in her ears and the lightning leapt across the sky, out of control.

She made it to the front door and yanked her hand out from her sleeve. Her fingers slipped on the round, brass door knob. It wouldn't turn. She tried again. Either her grip on the wet metal was the problem, or it was locked. She was just about to go round the side of the house to the back door, when something further on caught her attention. There it was again. A light was flashing in the old ruined house.

She stood still and stared. Somebody was definitely there this time and, although her head told her to forget it and concentrate on drying off and getting warm, she found herself rooted to the spot. She couldn't turn away, feeling compelled to investigate. After all, it was only just a little further down the beach. She could easily get that far if she took it steady. She had to find out once and for all, what was happening there and why it was having such a disturbing effect on her, before she went completely mad. Something peculiar was going on and she was determined to get to the bottom of it – injured ankle or not!

Taking slow, deliberate steps and trying to keep the weight off her bad ankle, she headed for the house. Her pulse was thumping, her breath coming quickly. She was frightened but still she had to go on. Wheeling round, she suddenly had the sensation of being followed. But that was crazy because everyone else was occupied with helping rescue the boats. Peering into the blackness, she saw no-one. It must have been her imagination playing tricks.

The nearer she got to the house, the more evil it looked. It seemed to spring up out of the ground, a menacing, dark silhouette. Periodically, the light flashed again. It was upstairs. Yes, definitely upstairs. When she was only a short distance from the razor-sharp rocks which led up to one side of the house, she began to be aware of muffled cries. She told herself to get a grip. She knew no-one lived there. They couldn't possibly stay in such a place, but the cries grew stronger and stronger.

'Help ... over here ... help ... where are you?' She looked around, once more suddenly struck by the feeling of being watched. But as before, there was no-one there.

Then she remembered Buster, who, yet again, she was supposed to be in charge of, and as usual, she had no idea where he was. She thought that perhaps it was he who was following her, so she called out his name:

‘Buster, Buster ... come here, boy.’ But her words were lost to the hostile wind.

She climbed the rocks slowly, trying to avoid their saw-like teeth and starting to wonder if she needed her head examining as well as her ankle. She was drenched. She had pains darting all round her body. She was terrified and yet she was unable to stop. The voice came again, more desperate this time: ‘Please, will somebody help me?’ She was convinced it was coming from inside the house and it sounded like a young girl.

‘I'm coming. Hold on there,’ she called, having no idea if anyone could hear her. She came to a wooden gate which seemed to fall open when she pushed it, and went on through.

At that moment, the house was illuminated by the lightning and the glassless holes, where the windows should have been, glared at her like hollow chasms. She said a quick prayer and promised Him up there that if He would only see her through this ordeal and help her save whoever it was who had summoned her there, then she would promise to up her charity work considerably when she got back to London.

Crash! She jumped and spun round as the wooden gate flew back on its hinges and smashed against the wall. The light had stopped flashing upstairs and the cries had ceased, but she had to go on until she found whoever it was who needed her. What if they had become unconscious?

Again the lightning flashed, showing her the way to the back door across the sodden springy grass. She wondered if it would be locked. Would she have to climb through those perilous window holes to get in? But, to her relief, it was open and as she soon discovered, thoroughly rotten. She felt her way through the door in the darkness, wishing she'd brought a torch. But, for one thing, she didn't own one and also, this visit was in no way planned. She would just have to rely on touch.

Stopping to wonder for a second just what on earth she would do if she did stumble upon someone who was unconscious, she heard a crunching sound outside, as if someone had just stepped on glass. There was plenty of that lying around the house from the broken window panes.

'Hello,' she called out. 'Is anyone there?'

But no-one answered and she thought she might have imagined it. She made her way across what must have once been the hall and turned the corner to find the stairs. How did she know where the stairs were? It almost seemed to be instinctive and yet she knew she'd never set foot inside the house before. She decided to worry about that later and to make one final big effort to go up the stairs and check to see if she could find the person behind the flashing light and the cries for help. If not, she would bolt back down the stairs and make her way to Flora's house as fast as she could possibly hobble, because after all, Jack and Brad would probably be heading back there by now.

At the top of the stairs, another glare of lightning lit up four doors off a central corridor, but again, for some bizarre reason, she already knew about those. She groped her way into the first room which appeared to be totally empty and shadowless. Relieved, she stepped across the wooden floor boards to the window. She looked out over Rhoslown and could make out the lights of torches flickering about on the beach. Obviously, not all the boats were secure for the night yet.

She heard a creak and swung round. Nothing. Again she called out: 'Hello? Is there anyone up here? Do you still need help?' She had no idea who she was talking to, if anyone at all.

Tip-toeing down the corridor, she looked into the next two rooms, or at least tried to. She could feel the dampness like a suffocating blanket around her. When she reached the last room at the far end of the house, she paused for a moment. A face flashed through her mind and then it was gone. It was not a face she recognised, but the face of a young woman, her head covered in a dirty, torn cream shawl, and she was dripping wet, rather like Nelle herself.

'Who are you?' she asked. Then she realised she was being absurd talking to visions in her head and made up her mind to talk to Henrietta about therapists when she got back to London. Hen was bound to know a few. Someone needed to work out for her just what was going on in her head, because she certainly couldn't. Her imagination was running riot.

Half of her wanted to flee the house there and then, but that was impossible on two counts. One, she knew that her ankle was considerably swollen by now, and two, she would never forgive herself if she didn't check this last room before she left, just in case it was the one where someone was in trouble.

She felt her way round the walls, following the direction of the wind which was flowing in through a window. The wall seemed to bend in a curved shape and she decided she must be in the room with the turret. Her suspicions were confirmed when she came across wooden boards which were fixed over what must have once been a window. But there had to be another window in the room, she decided, because she could feel the breath of the wind on her face and it toyed with her rain-streaked hair.

Suddenly the door of the room banged shut behind her and she heard a key turn. She froze to the spot with fear. 'Who's there?' she managed, her voice barely above a whisper. She knew she was no longer alone. There was a shadow in the room with her, shifting slowly round the walls, but she could not make out who it was. 'What do you want?' She tried again.

No answer.

'If it's your house, I'm really sorry I'm trespassing, but I thought I heard someone up here calling for help,' she said, nibbling her lip and clenching her fists.

No answer.

'For God's sake, you're scaring me. Talk to me!'

No answer.

'Look, I'll just go, OK? I'm sorry I disturbed you and now I'll just go right back home.' She was getting desperate, as her eyes struggled to focus on the figure in the turret.

'Foolish girl,' croaked a voice she immediately

recognised.

'What are you doing here?' she gasped with surprise and horror.

'Everyone knows it's dangerous to come here, but you still had to come, didn't you?'

'I saw a light up here and I heard someone crying for help,' she protested, not daring to move.

'But there is no light, is there, and there is no person needing help. Why couldn't you leave it all alone instead of stirring up things which were none of your business?'

'What are you talking about?' She bit on her nails and hated herself for doing it, excusing herself at the same time, due to extreme circumstances.

'You came up here with one, but that wasn't enough for you was it? You wanted more and you had to get in my way and ruin everything. Everything I have ever worked for.'

'You're not making any sense. I haven't ruined anything.' Her fear ebbed a little and she felt angry and indignant.

'Yes, you have. It's happening all over again.'

'What is, for goodness sake?'

'You see, I can't allow it. I won't ever allow it!' Nelle heard a horrible cough.

'What do you mean?' Her skin prickled and the hairs on the back of her neck stood up.

'They're mine. All three of them. They're not yours and you're not having any part of them.'

'Why are you telling me this?'

Nelle backed across the room as the figure crept

threateningly towards her, out of the turret.

'You see, I always win in the end, Nelle.'

'This is crazy! Please just let me get away from here.'

'*NO*!' A scream, as Nelle reached the other window in the room. 'You see, they'll all think you overbalanced and fell in the dark. It couldn't be more perfect! An opportunity not to be missed,' screeched Ruth, suddenly rushing at Nelle like a wildcat pouncing on its prey. She grabbed Nelle by the throat, pushing her back, squeezing the breath from her lungs.

Nelle flailed her arms and tried to kick out with her foot, but found herself unable to stand on her bad ankle. Ruth's grip was so firm and, struggle as she did, it was no use. She couldn't shake her off.

A nasty, evil laugh chortled from Ruth's mouth as her eyes flicked wildly from side to side.

'You cannot have him,' she spat. 'Goodbye, darling Nelle.'

With that, Nelle felt herself being shoved backwards by a force far stronger than her own. She tried desperately to cling on to anything she could, but the skin on her hands was shredded by the broken splinters of glass, still attached to the window frame.

As she fell, she screamed with every last ounce of breath in her body, and her final vision was of Ruth, leaning triumphantly out of the window as the lightning ignited the house for one last time.

Down ... down ... she went, to that place of eternal night, where all pain is extinguished.

Simultaneously with Nelle's scream, the rotting, locked

door of that upstairs room succumbed to the frantic pressure of an almighty kick from the corridor. Panels of the door spewed across the room and Brad flew in after them. He realised straight away that something had happened and stopped in his tracks when he found Ruth, calmly standing by the window, as if nothing was wrong. But he knew now for sure that it was - desperately wrong. He had occasionally wondered about her, but he'd always buried his head in the sand and never allowed himself to believe it to be possible, and now it might all be too late.

He grabbed Ruth's arms and confronted her: 'What the hell's going on, Ruth? And where are my children?'

'Brad, darling, you're hurting me,' smiled Ruth. 'And don't worry, of course our children are fine.'

'Where's Nelle?' he demanded, peering out of the window and seeing nothing in the darkness.

'She's gone.'

'What do you mean, 'gone'? I heard her. Where is she?'

'She's not here,' she told him, truthfully.

'Where did she go?' He glared at her.

'The point is, Brad, she can't just waltz up here from her fancy job in London and take over you and the children, threatening *my* life and *my* job. Brad, you're not hers to have. You're mine! You've always been mine, ever since you were a tiny baby,' hissed Ruth venomously, changing her tone.

'What are you talking about, woman?' He increased his grip on her.

'I've taken care of it all. Don't you worry. I've

always taken care of everything,' she announced, proudly.

'Tell me right now, just what the hell you've done.' He shook her violently.

'I was only trying to protect you from her. She was evil, Brad. I did it for you and the children ... all of it. Everything I've ever done has only been for you and our children.' Her voice softened again.

'Oh, my God ...'

Down below, something soft, gentle and sticky was bothering her. Her eyes flickered. All sensation was lost except for that steady wetness.

It would be so much easier not to respond but she wasn't to be allowed to leave it at that. Nelle forced her eyes to open and her first impression was that she'd come face to face with a black, hairy, threatening monster. Then it began to dawn on her that only part of that was true and that it was in fact none other than her faithful friend, Buster! He was standing over her, water trickling down his glistening flanks, licking her face and whimpering pathetically.

She tried to move. In her mind, she needed to get up. She needed a shower because she was colder than she could ever remember being in her entire life, and she had a splitting headache in urgent need of pills.

But she couldn't move a thing except for turning her head, which simply gave Buster a larger surface area to work on. The ground under her head was gritty and she tried to focus on the sand on which she lay. She could hear the wind and she could smell the sea and slowly she began to remember where she was but certainly not why. And then she heard a voice. Oh, how she loved that voice at that precise moment! There it was again.

'Buster? Buster? Where the devil are you now, you stupid dog? Have you any idea what's going on? Losing Nelle on a night like this is disastrous enough, but now we've lost you, too!'

If she never did another thing in whatever was left of her life, she would find the strength to answer Jack.

'Over here ...' she called out weakly. 'Jack ...'

'Nelle? Is that you?' A torch flashed in her direction.

'Yes, Jack ...'

'What on earth are you doing down there?' He sounded alarmed as he rushed towards her, not yet realising that she was hurt.

'I'm not sure ...' she managed.

'Now don't panic and don't move. I can't really see you too well, but there's blood all over your hands. What happened to you?'

'I think I fell from a window ...'

'Look, you probably shouldn't be talking either. Get off, Buster.' He pushed the dog roughly aside.

She tried to take a deep breath but it hurt too much. 'Be nice to him,' she whispered. 'I think he brought me round.'

'Right, don't panic ...'

'You've ... already said that ... and ... I'm not,' she said with an effort, wishing her head didn't pound quite so much.

'I'll call an ambulance. I've got my 'phone here ...'

'Surprise ... surprise ...' She tried to smile.

'What? Oh yes, of course ... wait, I'll dial 999 ... hang on in there.' He fumbled in the zipped pocket of his fleece and pulled out the 'phone. By the light of his torch he managed to dial the numbers and convey the message that an ambulance was urgently required on the beach at Rhoslown.

'They'll be here soon, sweetie,' he reassured her. 'Don't you worry.' He took her hand and then laid it carefully on her chest when he felt what he suspected were fragments of glass embedded in her skin.

'Where has Brad got to?' he asked himself out loud.

'Is Brad here?' She tried to stir.

'He's about somewhere. We were worried about you when we got back to Flora's and found you weren't there. We decided to split up and look for you, but I can't see him anywhere. Maybe he's gone to check Sophie's to see if you went back there.'

'I'm ... so sorry, Jack.' Big tears started to roll out of the corners of her eyes. 'I've made ... such a mess.'

'Hey, worse things happen, you know. I still can't imagine what you were doing in this place tonight, of all nights, but maybe you'll remember soon enough.'

'Maybe.' She turned her head to the side.

'Look, I'm going to take off my fleece, which is wet but it might just help to warm you up a bit, and then I'm going to go to the road so I can direct the ambulance men here. That OK with you?'

She nodded.

'That's my girl. I'll leave Buster here with you and I promise I'll be back in a sec. I'll call round on the 'phone and find Brad for you too. Don't go away.' He bent over and kissed her on the forehead.

'As if ...'

She watched him go until she couldn't see him any more and in his place, Buster lay down beside her, his head on her stomach, doing his best to comfort her.

Some sixth sense told her to put her hand in her pocket. Her fingers felt stiff and sore but still she managed to slide one hand in. She felt something small and it puzzled her. Her vision started to blur and the pain racked her body, but she had to find out what was in that pocket. Slowly, she took hold of the object, using all her powers of determination not to let it drop, and she pulled her hand out, moving it slowly towards her face.

Ordering her fingers to co-operate, she screwed up her eyes so she could see what it was she had found. Then recognition flooded through her mind and all at once, she felt at peace. It was the cowrie shell that Brad had given her on Shell Beach for good luck. A calming wave of relief washed over her and she surrendered to the pain, clutching Brad's shell and passing out cold, there on the sand.

Chapter Fifteen

Wednesday, August 12th

The next thing Nelle was aware of was a smell. It was a clinical, detergent sort of smell and it was firmly wedged up her nose. It badly made her want to sneeze but something told her that that would be a big mistake because it would hurt a lot. But why should sneezing hurt?

Like slowly rising to the surface of a deep, icy pool, Nelle began to sense her weightless body floating upwards. It seemed to be taking for ever to get there. Why did it take so long?

Somewhere in the recesses of her mind was a baby. There was a cliff and there was water, but she could not connect the three. Whose baby was it and why was there always so much water everywhere? Then there was a voice, ringing in her ears, calling her name: 'Nelle ...?' Did she mishear or did he call her Ellen? Then she heard it again: 'Where are you, Ellen? ... Everything is going to be OK. I'm here for you, Nelle ...' It was a voice she knew, a voice she loved and was not afraid of. But just who was Ellen?

She needed to respond to that voice. It was a lifeline and it had been thrown to her to lift her out of that freezing water.

Nelle opened her eyes and tried to focus on the face beside her. She was muddled and travelling in time. She thought at first it was Roger-the-Rat, but that wasn't right because she knew he hadn't ever been there for her.

All at once, the veil of confusion began to drift away and she recognised the smile, the blond hair over the eyes and the bronzed skin. Returning the smile, she tried to move her hands but they felt so heavy. When she looked down, she realised they were thickly bandaged and then she remembered cutting them on glass. What glass?

'Hi,' said Brad softly. 'I thought you'd never wake up. They gave you some strong painkillers last night.'

'Where are we?' she asked, not familiar with the stark white walls.

'We're in hospital. You were brought here last night.'

'Was I? What time is it now then?' she asked.

'Almost eleven.' He checked his watch.

'Did you come here last night as well?'

He nodded. 'Yes, I came with you.'

'So have you just been sitting there all that time? You must be exhausted!' She tried to sit up but every bit of her body hurt.

'You went into casualty first and it took them most of the night to clean you up and do the X-rays ...'

'X-rays?' she interrupted him. 'What did I have X-rayed?'

'Just about all of you,' he replied, stroking her forehead.

'I can't take in what you're saying. I can only remember tiny things about last night. What happened? ... and what's wrong with me? I feel a complete wreck.'

'... and you probably will do for a bit. Apparently, you've cracked some ribs, broken one ankle and sprained the other, lacerated your hands and banged your head quite badly.'

'Crumbs, no wonder I feel so lousy. But I will live, won't I?'

'Yes, you certainly will, thank goodness, and probably will make a complete recovery, providing you take it easy for a bit.'

'Doesn't sound like I'm going to have much choice, does it? What with cracked ribs and a broken ankle. What a mess, Brad.'

'I'm just so relieved it wasn't worse. I would've thought that most people who fall out of a first floor window break much more than you did. Mind you, you were so lucky it wasn't any other window in that house, or you wouldn't have landed on the sand, which must've broken your fall.'

'Parts of it are coming back to me gradually. It was the old ruined house, wasn't it?'

'Yes, it was.'

'But why was I there?' she asked herself.

Brad didn't answer, but he stopped stroking her face and suddenly became very serious. She also took in the fact that he looked about as rough as she felt. He was wearing the same clothes he'd worn to dinner, which she now recalled was at Sophie and Marcus's house, and the events of the night had left him somewhat bedraggled. Stubble had begun to appear on his face, but those blue eyes, which had had such a blinding effect on her little more than a week ago, were just the same.

'Why that look?' She was worried and frightened at the same time.

'Just what do you remember about last night, Nelle?' He had his head in his hands, avoiding her eyes.

'Bits and pieces,' she replied, wishing he would look at her. But when he still didn't, she continued: 'I remember dinner at Sophie and Marcus's. I remember it was raining hard and we all ended up on the beach, but I'm not sure why. I know I went to the ruined house for some reason, but I don't know what that was. Then I remember feeling very frightened and falling from a window. And then the next thing was Jack ... and I think Buster was there too. Yes, he definitely was. For some reason, Jack went away again ... and then there's a gap, until just now.'

Brad listened and didn't interrupt. He had to know for sure how much she could remember for herself, before he told her the truth. In the beginning, he'd made up his mind to keep that from her, if she couldn't remember what had happened. But that changed when he realised she would find something out soon enough, and then might not forgive him for holding bits of the story back.

'Brad, say something. You're scaring me ...' With a big effort, she moved her bandaged hand and touched him.

'I'm so sorry, Nelle ...' he began.

'Sorry about what, for heaven's sake?' She was becoming even more afraid. 'I don't understand.'

'... sorry that I've put you through all this. Sorry that you were in so much danger because of me, and sorry I wasn't there in time for you when you needed me. You never deserved any of this.'

'Are you going to explain to me what you're talking about before I completely freak out?' she demanded.

'Yes, I do owe you that.'

'Well ...?'

'It was Ruth ...' he started, but stopped again.

'Ruth? What did she have to do with anything? I thought she was babysitting the children last night.'

'She was supposed to be, but she left them at home on their own, mercifully asleep, and they were none the wiser. Anyway, once she realised everyone was on the beach, I'm afraid she came looking for you.'

'Wait a minute ...' The penny started to drop. 'Are you telling me that Ruth had something to do with what happened to me?'

He nodded and raised his eyes from his lap and met hers at last. 'She pushed you, Nelle ...' he confessed quietly.

Nelle thrust her head back into the pillow, which made it hurt more. Tears filled her eyes, but they stung too. She stared up at the ceiling.

'But why, Brad? Why did she do it? What did I do to make her hate me so much, that she wanted to do that to me?' she sobbed.

He pulled a Kleenex from the box beside her bed and

wiped the tears from her face. 'She did it because … she was completely obsessed with possessing me ... and the children ... and she couldn't bear the thought of sharing us with you ... apparently, in her sick mind, she saw you as some kind of threat to her job … and her future with us.' The words were so hard for him. '... at the end of the day, she'd been with our family for way too long. She never had her own children and first I became a substitute for that, and then Luke and Annie followed suit ...'

'When did you find all this out?' asked Nelle, turning her head back to face him.

'She told me last night.'

'When, last night? Do you mean at the old house? Were you there too?'

'Unfortunately, I arrived in the room just a moment too late. When Jack and I got to Flora's house and you weren't there, we got worried and came looking for you. I remembered you mentioning the old house and I wondered on the off chance, whether you'd walked Buster down there. I decided to go and check. I found the gate, as well as the back door wide open, which struck me as odd, so I went upstairs ...'

'What happened next? Did you find Ruth up there?'

'Yes. When I checked the rooms, I found the last one had a locked door ... and then I heard your scream ...'

'That must've been when I fell.'

He nodded. 'I kicked the door down, which was rotten anyway, and I saw Ruth standing by the window, staring out.'

'Did she admit that she'd pushed me?'

'Not at first, but then she told me she'd done it to protect me and the children.'

'*Protect* you?' Nelle was stunned. 'From me? What on earth did she think I was going to do to you?'

'I'm just so sorry ...' His voice tailed off and he struck the bed with his fist. 'She was insanely jealous of you and our relationship. I should've read the bloody warning signs. They were there and I just didn't interpret them ...'

'Brad, it's not your fault.' Damn those bandages! All she wanted to do was to take him in her arms and she couldn't.

'It is, Nelle. I know it is.'

'Tell me what happened next.' Nelle needed to piece it all together, if it was ever going to make any sense.

'OK. Then the police arrived. Apparently, Jack had called an ambulance and the police came too because the accident was 'suspicious'.'

'Did Ruth try to make a run for it?' She wanted to picture the scene but for some reason, she couldn't even conjure up a vision of Ruth's face. It was as if she'd been obliterated from Nelle's mind after the fall.

'No, she didn't. She didn't move from that window until the police came up and arrested her. She was totally devoid of emotion.'

'I did try and tell you she was weird,' said Nelle, desperate to lighten the atmosphere.

'I know, I know, and why the hell didn't I listen to you? Why I let her stay with us after Jane's accident ...' He didn't finish.

'Did she confess to the police?'

'As good as.'

'I bet they thought she was completely mad,' remarked Nelle.

'I'm sure she is. I know that now. I only wish I'd seen it a lot sooner. I suppose they'll give her some kind of psychiatric treatment.'

'So they took her away?'

'They arrested her ... for attempted murder.'

'Oh God, Brad, this is all so appalling, and I keep on feeling guilty. None of this would've happened if I hadn't come up to Rhoslown with Jack.' She began to cry again.

'Don't cry. You're certainly not the one who should be feeling guilty. It's me who should've been more aware of her mental state. Who knows what might've sent her over the edge.'

'What happened to Jack? Did he come to the hospital?'

'No, he didn't. I wanted to come with you and he said he'd call for news and come to see you today.'

'What about Luke and Annie?' She suddenly remembered Brad's children and was concerned. 'Who's got them?'

Nelle saw a flicker of amusement cross Brad's eyes, when he told her how Jack had taken Buster and gone back to Brad's house to look after the children.

Nelle tried to laugh. 'Jack did that? Good old Uncle Jack!'

'I know. I called this morning and they were all having breakfast. It sounded like chaos.'

'Where did you tell the children you were? And what

are you going to tell them about Ruth?'

'I told them you'd had an accident and were in hospital but I couldn't say anything about what happened, of course. I said Ruth had suddenly had to go and visit a sick relative. As for long term, I don't know what I'm going to say because she's always been there for them.'

'You'll think of something.'

'I'll have to.' He took her hand gently and held it.

There was something else bothering Nelle and she just couldn't let it rest. 'I just wish I could work out why I've felt so haunted by that wretched house ever since I first set eyes on it. I've got this idea into my head that I was summoned there. That I went there with a definite purpose, but what could that have been, at night, in a torrential storm?'

'I wish I knew, and I also wish you hadn't gone. I can't tell you how much I wished that, while I was waiting for you to wake up.'

'I'm a believer in fate. If Ruth had this so-called problem with jealousy and really did want me out of the way, if something had happened another time, she might well have succeeded in bumping me off.'

'Don't even say it.' He shuddered.

'No, seriously, maybe I was lucky.'

'I don't know about lucky. I think that's a far more generous attitude than any of this ghastly mess deserves.'

'Now that I think more about it, it's coming back to me that I do remember having a really strange feeling when I got inside the house last night. I know it was dark and I couldn't see much, but it was as if everything was familiar to me. As if I'd already been there many times and I knew exactly where I would find everything ... the stairs and the rooms ... which I know is absurd, because I haven't been inside the house before. I'm sorry, I'm probably not making any sense. Maybe it's the bang on the head.'

'What, you mean something like déjà-vu?'

'I guess I must mean that. I wish I knew more about the history of the place. It might help to explain these peculiar feelings that seem to overwhelm me whenever I think of it.'

'I only know a sketchy outline of its history from bits Jane told me, if that's any use.'

'Might be. What did she say?' Nelle was interested.

'I know that her family lived in the house for several generations and I do remember she once told me a sad story about one particular distant relative.'

'What was that about?' She was intrigued to hear it.

'If I remember rightly, there was some girl who lived there with her parents, and, I think Jane said, sisters too. Anyway, the story went something like she was due to marry her childhood sweetheart and just before the wedding, he dumped her for another woman with whom he'd been having an affair and who was pregnant by him.'

'How awful,' said Nelle.

'There was a bit more too. Apparently, she never got over the heartbreak and soon afterwards, she and her father died in a sea rescue, off the coast of Rhoslown, during a violent storm.'

'What a waste of life.'

'They ... whoever they are ... say that she never rested in peace after that, and that her spirit still haunts the house in search of true love and happiness. Everyone likes to fantasize about a curse on the place, and tragedy is supposed to have befallen everyone who lived there after her, which was why Jane's family moved on. I don't know, it's probably all hugely exaggerated and dramatised to make a good story.' He played it down.

'Maybe not. Sophie told me something similar when we went riding last week, only she didn't know all the details. I still think it's a real shame it's empty and has been left to go to ruin. It could be made so nice.'

'I agree, but now about all it's fit for is being knocked down. You couldn't live in it as it is, even if you wanted to, and who would want to, with all that spooky stuff to contend with?'

'Just out of interest, Brad, do you know what the girl's name was? The one who died, I mean.'

'I'm trying to remember ...' He ran his fingers through his hair and licked his lips thoughtfully. 'I have a feeling Jane said it was something like ... Ellen. Why?'

A cold shiver shot down Nelle's spine and she turned to face the window, unable to answer him straight away. She trembled for a brief moment and then an overwhelming sensation of finally understanding what had happened spread over her, as the realisation dawned that Ellen spelt backwards became Nelle ...

The visions, the fear of boats and of cold water and even her dramatic dream, made sense to her all at once and it was an indescribable relief. To have discovered herself and who she once had been, explained so much of what had always remained inexplicable until now. At last, safe in her newly found knowledge, she could live in peace and move on with the present, burying her tormented past where it belonged once and for all.

For a while, Brad didn't push her to talk further. He thought how tired she must be, and knew only too well how totally exhausted he was too, both mentally and physically. He leant back and took a deep breath, leaving Nelle to mull over whatever it was that was going on in that pretty head of hers. Whatever it was, it struck him how calm and how serene she'd become, lying there in her hospital bed. Her face was no longer screwed up with worry and confusion, and weak from all the emotions that had passed through him in the past few days, he simply felt grateful that she was safe, that she was going to be alright and that she looked so peaceful.

'A penny for your thoughts ...' she asked, when she finally turned to face him again.

'What? Oh, nothing really ... how about you?' he replied.

'I was just trying to work out what on earth I'm going to do now, when I get out of here I mean, and what the future is going to hold for me.'

'You mustn't worry yourself too much about that. Just concentrate on getting better.'

'It's all very well for you to say that, but think about it. I'm not going to be much use at work for a while. For a start, I won't be able to walk there. Secondly, with these bandages on, I won't be able to use a computer, let alone write, and thirdly, I'm going to be pining for someone who'll be miles away up north.' She smiled weakly at him.

'Try taking one thing at a time,' he told her, moving from his chair to the edge of the bed. 'Firstly, I can make a very good case for you to come and stay with us for a bit, so we can keep an eye on you and stop you wandering into old ruined houses in the middle of the night ...'

She laughed. 'I think I've always been searching for my guardian angel. What was the second thing?'

'Secondly, as for our future, I think we'll just take it as it comes ...'

Giving her no chance to add anything, he gently scooped her into his arms and kissed her more tenderly than she'd ever been kissed in her life before.

ALSO BY : JENNY CHESHIRE

FIRE AND PASSION

A gripping story of love reaching the heights of joy and the depths of despair

TV sales executive Bronte Richardson is happily married. That is until tragedy strikes. While she is picking up the pieces of her shattered existence, a working assignment at the glamorous Cannes Television Festival leads to a fateful encounter with Hollywood heart-throb Jordan Innes which alters the course of her life.

From the bustling streets of Hong Kong, to Sydney's summer sun and the tropical paradise of the Barrier Reef, can impossible love blossom against all the odds?

And how do Jordan's unstable wife, menacing bush fires and the prying eyes of the media contribute to Bronte's painful conclusion that she is destined to be alone forever?

'A beautifully-crafted and moving love story
from an exciting new talent'
THE YORKSHIRE EVENING PRESS

421 pages
ISBN: 0-9528323-3-X
Price : £ 5.99